Village Rumours

REBECCA SHAW

An Orion paperback

First published in Great Britain in 2014
by Orion Books
This paperback edition published in 2015
by Orion Books,
an imprint of The Orion Publishing Group Ltd,
Carmelite House, 50 Victoria Embankment
London EC4Y 0DZ

An Hachette UK Company

1 3 5 7 9 10 8 6 4 2

A CIP catalogue record for this book
is available from the British Library.

ISBN 978-1-4091-4723-7

INHABITANTS OF TURNHAM MALPAS

Ford Barclay	Retired businessman
Mercedes Barclay	His wife
Willie Biggs	Retired verger
Sylvia Biggs	His wife
James (Jimbo) Charter-Plackett	Owner of the village store
Harriet Charter-Plackett	His wife
Fergus, Finlay, Flick & Fran	Their children
Katherine Charter-Plackett	Jimbo's mother
Alan Crimble	Barman at the Royal Oak
Linda Crimble	His wife
Maggie Dobbs	School caretaker
H. Craddock Fitch	Owner of Turnham House
Kate Fitch	Village school headteacher
Dottie Foskett	Cleaner
Zack Hooper	Verger
Marie Hooper	His wife
Gilbert Johns	Church choirmaster
Louise Johns	His wife
Greta Jones	A village gossip
Vince Jones	Her husband
Barry Jones	Her son and estate carpenter
Pat Jones	Barry's wife
Dean & Michelle	Barry and Pat's children
Revd Peter Harris MA (Oxon)	Rector of the parish
Dr Caroline Harris	His wife
Alex & Beth	Their children
Tom Nicholls	Assistant in the store
Evie Nicholls	His wife

Johnny Templeton	Head of the Templeton estate
Alice Templeton	His wife
Dicky & Georgie Tutt	Licensees at the Royal Oak
Bel Tutt	Assistant in the village store
Vera Wright	Retired

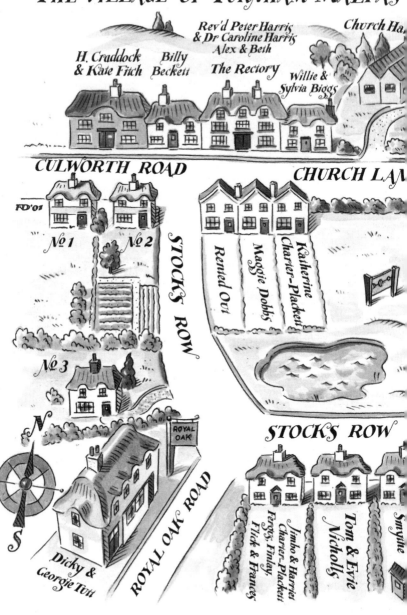

Prologue

Now that Malcolm the Milk no longer finds his round a viable way to earn a living he is not the first person to be making his presence felt at an early hour in the village of Turnham Malpas. Since Malcom's retirement it is Peter Harris who is the first to test the air, rain or shine. At six-fifteen every morning the Rectory door opens and the rector bursts out with his usual vigour to begin his three mile run. He's been rector in the village for more than twenty years and unless ill health, which is rare for him, prevents him from running, he never misses. Round the village green, down Stocks Row, straight ahead down the footpath by Hipkin Gardens onto the spare land, across Turnham Beck on the footbridge and then his run really begins.

Before Peter gets back, the person on early morning turn at the village Store is already pulling up the blinds, heaving in the newspapers left in the shop doorway and delivered at some ungodly hour during the night, and setting up the Store for the day's trading. Three people take regular turns at opening up. It is either Jimbo Charter-Plackett the owner; Fran, his daughter, who loves the retail business and refused to take the university option like her two brothers and her sister did, and Tom Nicholls who runs the Post Office counter and anything else that requires detailed scrutiny. Tom has long been something of a mystery to the rest of the villagers and is suspected of being an ex-policeman, mainly due to his ability to remove any customers attempting shop lifting or causing mayhem in the Store by the use of a very professional headlock technique which is swiftly effective and allows no time for debate. Besides, there was that time when some men from the London underworld attempted to beat up his wife and himself in revenge for, supposedly, past arrests made by Tom when he was an officer in the London drug squad, but they mistakenly raided the wrong house and beat up two well-respected members of the community instead. That had caused something of a sensation and kept the gossips in the village busy speculating for several weeks.

Then the first of the regular bus services begins at seven. The bus stop is right outside the Store so sometimes when it is pouring with rain people waiting for the bus will sneak in to the Store to keep out of the rain. Jimbo doesn't mind if they make the excuse of buying something while they wait – but if they just take the opportunity to use the Store as an extension of the bus stop then he can become very angry. It has been suggested in the past that a shelter built in front of the Store would be a good idea, but Jimbo shudders at the prospect. He is intensely proud of it and how it looks and a bus shelter immediately outside in front of his Store sounds like a major disaster to him. So when the question of building a bus shelter is brought up yet again, Jimbo smiles bravely and says he quite enjoys people sheltering in his Store and there's no need, that it would ruin the ambience of the village, and after all, they need to save the council money, etc, etc, or their rates will go up yet again.

By eight forty-five the children are arriving for the start of school. Some are able to walk to school, others come by the regular mini-buses, others again live too near to benefit from the minibuses but too far to walk by themselves so they come in their mothers' cars. This is the moment when mayhem reigns. The council has tried to put up traffic lights, create a one-way traffic system, a zebra crossing all of which ideas have been furiously rejected by the villagers, and in despair the council has had to climb down. In fact, there are members of the council and the county traffic committee who harbour seriously damaging resentment towards Turnham Malpas villagers for their intransigence and in their nightmares, in the dark hours of the night, threaten to plan traffic-control measures to be put into action so that the village wakes up to discover zebra crossings and flashing Belisha beacons have appeared overnight. But somehow they never quite dare, never quite find the courage, because they know, without a shadow of doubt, that they will be threatened by The Society for the Preservation of Ancient Villages and Buildings or some such organisation and, as almost all the houses round the village green are Grade I or II listed, the council wouldn't stand a chance, and the villagers would be hysterical with joy yet again.

One thing which does please the villagers is that there is a Templeton back in the Big House. To their horror, a demented pop star by the name of Freedom Blade decided to buy it but then mercifully changed his mind, so after years of it being a Health Club and then being owned by Craddock Fitch, who'd bribed the council to allow him to build a totally unsuitable swimming pool extension to the beautiful Tudor house and use the entire building as a training school for his construction company staff, the rightful heir came all the way from Brazil to claim his title and he has bought back the house too. Now Sir Jonathan Templeton, a man matching his ancestor Sir Ralph Templeton in his devotion to the village and its inhabitants, who is rich with a capital 'R', is proving to be a gracious and considerate Lord of the Manor and it looks as though he intends establishing a dynasty as he has married someone from the village and already has two small sons Charles and Ralph to inherit.

At the moment Sir Johnny is re-establishing the annual village events that were allowed to lapse when old Sir Ralph died so tragically in a fire which also killed his wife. Sir Johnny is also providing educational grants to enthusiastic pupils from the local secondary school who want to go to college or university to improve their chances, and he has also given grants to the village primary school to make sure they remain ahead of all other schools in the area with the most up-to-date computer technology.

3

The latest piece of news about his philanthropy is that he is to employ a teenager called Ben Braithwaite who has been housed along with his sister in the new council flats down the Culworth Road. When he has completed a college course in Horticulture, Ben is to be employed in the gardens at the Big House. Ben is virtually unemployable but Sir Johnny is to take him on, which has heartened most of the people in the village. His sister, Becky, is already making inroads into being part of village life as she has secured several house cleaning jobs and, though outspoken, is a hard-working, vigorous kind of person, welcomed by everyone. She has been befriended by Dottie Foskett, once an outcast of village society due to missing so much schooling because of her mother's 'bad nerves' which resulted in her becoming the only member in the village of that very ancient profession for women unsuited to anything other. Age, however, has caught up with her and she is now housekeeper every weekday morning at the Rectory where her diligence and exceptional housekeeping abilities are much appreciated by the rector's wife Caroline, who also values Dottie's ability to be discreet about who calls at the Rectory with the latest village news or requesting the rector's help with a personal difficulty.

In the New Year Jimbo Charter-Plackett will be enlarging his internet business. He already runs one selling jam, chutney, bottled peaches, savoury sauces and cakes, all made by outworkers in their own homes, under the combined title of Harriet's Country Cousin's Organic Produce and intends to extend this into selling meat (including veal from calves born and bred on Home Farm, a joint venture with Sir Johnny). The meat venture as a whole will be too big for the mail order office at the back of the Store so they are moving it to the back of the Old Barn, but it is still to be run by Greta Jones whose husband Vince is coming out of retirement to run the meat project. They are both intensely excited by this glorious opportunity and are looking forward to getting started.

The most frequent subject for gossip at the moment is Sir

Johnny's brother Christopher. Like his brother Johnny he is wealthy beyond belief thanks to their huge luxury hotel business back in Brazil. Chris's wealth has made him of the opinion that women are his for the taking – and why not when he is so good-looking, so charming, so attractive to women of all ages? The villagers are divided in their opinion of Chris Templeton. His flashy good looks and his obvious wealth some find very attractive but others intensely dislike his attitude to women, especially the way he treated Fran Charter-Plackett.

Chapter 1

Peter Harris has always intended to get at that mysterious trunk in the loft and this time he is determined. Once, just once, at a time when his emotions were torn to shreds and he was in no fit state to search for anything at all, he'd remembered it again, trapped as it was in the far corner where the eaves and the loft floor left no space for a twenty-first century man to squeeze in to reach it. Today, with his mind and his heart at peace, he was determined that it would no longer defeat him: he'd somehow drag it out and investigate.

Caroline laughed when he said that today was the day, mainly because he'd said it several times before and not succeeded. 'Today I *will* pull it out. I am determined, Caroline. How many years have we lived in this house? Twenty-one?'

'I think it's twenty-two years actually. More coffee?'

'No, thanks. Can I leave you to clear away?' He drained his cup, got to his feet and left the kitchen, taking with him a large rake Caroline used in the garden. It was ancient and had tough, well-made iron prongs at the business end of it that he intended to use to drag the trunk towards him until it was close enough for him to manhandle and hopefully open it up. He'd feel cheated if it was empty, but elated if it contained something.

The electric light they'd had put in when they first moved into the house didn't reach into this dark corner which is why they hadn't been aware of it for years but with the powerful beam of the big torch – normally used if he had to go visiting in the parish after dark – he could see the trunk's outline very clearly. The lid was curved, so it would be no use as a coffee table, but maybe its contents ... It appeared to have metal bands round it and a big lock. A key. He needed a key. Where had he seen a key? No, he'd worry about that when he'd got it out. Would it go down through the hatch or was it too big?

The dragging of the trunk towards him was painfully slow but with patience and a steady hand it began to move towards him. The last time they'd discovered an ancient artefact was in Turnham House and that had proved to be a treasure trove of old church silver hidden because of the threat of German invasion in 1940. Those contents had been spectacular – and the nearer the trunk got to him, the more convinced he was that this held something of value. Otherwise why hide it so carefully? Having been hidden in the Rectory it must surely be something to do with the Church? More solid silver communion vessels? More silver candlesticks? But why hadn't they been walled up with the other silver they'd found at Turnham House?

Peter was startled by a bat flying out from behind the trunk, then another and another. Bats? He didn't know they had bats in the loft. He hated bats; there was something so ghostly about their movements and he flapped his hands to make them leave him alone. He knew they were no threat to him, but they still made him shudder. It was a difficult process, dragging the trunk along the uneven floor with the prongs of the rake, first one end then the other end, and each time only a centimetre of movement but needing every bit of his energy ... finally the trunk was so close that he was able to drag it with both hands, and there it was in the light, dusty, decrepit, iron bound and ... locked.

Peter shouted downstairs, 'Caroline! Where did we put that bunch of old keys we found and had no use for? Where is it now?'

'No idea.'

'You must have! Where did you put it?'

'Can't remember. Have to think. I'm going now, OK?'

'What time will you be back?'

'About twelve, twelve-thirty, OK? I'll have a think while I'm out. Bye! Leave well alone, I say!'

'It's only an old trunk, why are you so anxious?'

'Don't know, but I am. Bye! Take care!'

Peter sat on a small stool and contemplated the trunk. Money? Letters? Clothes? Silver? How long had it been untouched in this loft? Fifty years? One hundred years? More, perhaps. It was certainly very old. He blew off some of the dust which revealed an old travel sticker, but the words had been obliterated by the passing years. Sitting quietly, recovering from his exertions Peter let his mind wander and it came to him where he might find the key. Surely it might be hanging on that old hook on the end wall of the cupboard under the stairs. They'd hung five old keys there because Peter didn't think it right to throw them away, though as Caroline had said at the time what possible use could they be for anything at all? He'd acknowledged she was right but he'd felt uncomfortable at the idea of just throwing away a piece of history.

He went downstairs immediately, opened the door of the cupboard, and, fumbling amongst the coats in the furthest corner of the cupboard, his hand touched the keys. They were quite big as keys go so maybe none of them were right for a trunk, but he'd try them anyway. He took with him a wet cloth from the kitchen, a dry cloth too and a tin of spray polish and climbed the two flights of stairs again, and there it still was – though why he should have imagined the trunk might have gone or moved itself he couldn't begin to imagine. He was bestowing on it qualities his mind knew it hadn't got but at the same time ...

Peter had also put a small can of oil in his pocket so he could oil both the lock and the key before he tried the keys and at last everything was ready for the big opening.

One of the bigger keys fitted! But was not very effective; the lock resisted with grinding noises of metal on metal but would not allow the key to turn. Peter tried more oil in the lock, more oil rubbed onto the key and suddenly the lock responded with a painful grating sound and at last it was open, except the hinges found it too painful to permit the lid to be completely opened.

A slow process of oiling and rubbing the hinges and several gentle attempts at lifting the lid eventually became effective and, protesting all the way, the lid was finally open and the contents revealed.

At the top was a very old dress, musty and crumpled, in a kind of cinnamon colour with a yellowed lace collar, Peter lifted it out and stood up so he could open it to its full length, but he needn't have bothered for the dress wasn't very long by today's standards. The waist was narrow, the sleeves a reasonable length and the only adornment was the lace round the neck and a brooch pinned to the front that appeared, to Peter's untutored eye, to be gold with a real diamond the size of a small pea in the middle. So the owner had not been a peasant. Next came a delicate wool shawl, once white but now yellow with age and that too must have once belonged to a lady. Was she the wife of a previous rector who'd died young and was long-lamented? Or the daughter of a previous rector, maybe?

After the clothes came a curious collection of treasured belongings in a small polished wooden box: a necklace, a silver bracelet, several curiously shaped pebbles, a small wooden cross intricately carved, a miniature of a teenage girl with long blonde hair wearing a soft blue dress, six shiny ribbons in a selection of colours which must have been precious to her, a scent bottle, now empty, although Peter caught a drift of sandalwood when he sniffed it, lots of dried flowers in a pretty linen bag, a tiny porcelain teacup decorated with a spray of pink roses and a miniature book with a few words written on the first page '*I shall write a book about my life and call it ...*' and nothing more.

Below the treasures lay books: a dictionary, some copies of religious tracts designed for children, barely decipherable newspaper clippings in an album, a diary which Peter slipped in to his pocket, and then, of all things, under the books, a disintegrated but complete skeleton of a bird wrapped in a piece of old cloth. Peter looked at the hooked beak and decided it must be a bird of prey. What a strange thing for a woman to keep. Letters, lots of letters, apparently from old school friends, an old broom without a handle, made from twigs that were falling to pieces, a large cross almost as long and as wide as the trunk itself, beautifully carved by a loving, skilful hand. More letters, more strange artefacts with obscure purposes that Peter couldn't fathom. Old shoes and boots, more old letters – indeed, a frenzy of letters, all written in the space of a month, and then, right at the very bottom, the last article to be brought out was a lock of hair. Well, more than a lock: it appeared to be a whole head of hair, shining blonde and neatly tied about every ten centimetres along its length with pale green ribbons made of silk.

Peter felt a powerful shudder run up his spine.

He was brought back to earth by the ringing of the front doorbell. It took a moment for him to pull himself together, then even longer to get down the two flights of stairs and down the hall to open the door. Walking away was Willie Biggs, the retired verger.

'Willie! Can I help?'

Willie stopped in his tracks, reversed and approached the Rectory door smiling. 'Good morning, Rector. Just calling to let you know that my Sylvia has taken a turn for the better this morning, from this flu thing she's had, and might get up today. I'm that relieved.'

'And so am I, Willie, that's wonderful news. Come in, please do! If you've nothing better to do, that is. I'm just about to make myself coffee so how about you join me? Mmm?'

'I'd be glad to, Rector. It's lonely with my Sylvia holed up in bed. Can't stop long though, I'm supposed to be shopping.'

Willie followed him into the kitchen which was always dear to his heart since he'd proposed to Sylvia sitting at this very kitchen table. He offered to help but Peter said no he was more than capable of making coffee for the two of them. They sat down opposite each other and after the first few sips Peter said, 'You might be the very person I need to talk to. I'm in need of some help, you see.'

Ever aware of the superiority of Peter's intellect compared to his own, Willie suggested that maybe there wasn't much he had to offer in the way of advice that a man like Peter couldn't sort out for himself.

'Well, this time I think you're wrong about that. It's like this: we had an old trunk wedged in the most inaccessible place in our attic which we never noticed for years then we did and I've kept saying I would drag it out and take a look inside it. Of course I never have, but this morning I did. Whoever put it there didn't want anyone to find it but I've found a key that fits the lock, so with a bit of help from an oil can I've got it open and there's all kinds of odd things in there to do with someone called Mary – at least, that's who the letters were addressed to, but no envelopes to give her surname. All dated in the early twenties.'

At this point Willie came alive. 'Just trying to remember who was rector at that time. My dad was born in 1919 and the rector who christened him was called ... let me think a minute ... Mr Cuttler, that's right, the Reverend Basil Cuttler. He was a widower and had just the one daughter I believe. She was Greta's mother. So what sort of things are in there?'

Peter described some of the more curious items he'd found but when he mentioned the skeleton of the bird, Willie, as quickly as he was able, leapt to his feet. 'Put it all back inside and get rid of it. A bonfire would be best and don't wait for Bonfire Night, do it now, and I mean *now*. I'm off! No! No! No! I don't want to know. Thanks for the coffee. Good morning!'

Willie hurtled out of the door as fast as his seventy-five-year-old legs would allow and didn't even pause to shut the door after him.

Peter sighed. Surely not another curious incident from the past that the whole village would take exception to. Peter began to read the diary he'd found in the trunk that began with the words, 'I shall write this diary every single day of this year.'

Peter still had a thick head of hair, with touches of silver here and there, but even so there was plenty of it. Had it been possible it would have stood on end by the time he reached the bottom of the first page for he was horrified. Other than the word 'Diary' handwritten on the front, it simply began on the first page with the words, *21st October, my 21st birthday. I am now an adult, though Papa won't think so; to him I am still a child and always will be. But I am determined to marry Silas Wilderspoon of this parish. He and I are soul mates although Papa thinks of him as a labourer fit only for digging a grave when needed, but there is much more to him than grave digging. If Papa won't marry us then we shall run away and find a clergyman who will. We shall marry before the end of the year, that is the solemn and binding promise I have made to him.*

Towards the bottom of the page Peter realised that there was far more to this diary than he could ever think possible. The word, 'coven' leapt from the page. Twice. Coven? Witchcraft? Was she a witch? Was Silas a ... what was a male witch called? Also called a witch he was sure, not a warlock.

He'd met up with curious prejudices which people in the village, especially those with ancestors who had lived in the village for generations, could rake up to match any current happening and blame it on the past like family feuds and such but witchcraft? Then he recollected the time Simone Paradise had held so called 'meetings' in Sykes Wood all those years ago and sent Rhett Wright to the edge of madness. Her meetings were about calling up the dead and such, not witchcraft, but nearly so, and where had that led? To Simone's terrifying death. Conducting her funeral service had been almost more than he could cope with, so he'd pushed the whole episode to the very back of his mind. But here he was being reminded of it in 2014. So how had the rector's daughter Mary Cuttler become involved in witchcraft?

Wilderspoon? Where had he heard that name before? Wilderspoon? No one of that name lived in the village now. Such an unusual name, not like Smith or Jones or Wright, so Wilderspoon should strike a chord immediately, and then it struck him: on a gravestone in the churchyard! Peter leapt to his feet, checked he had his key with him, and the front door slammed behind him as he left. A painstaking search of the graves and he found what he was looking for. Silas Wilderspoon. Also buried in the same grave was Mary Wilderspoon, wife of Silas, and also Mary Ann Wilderspoon, not daughter, but *grand*daughter, of the above died 1948 aged fourteen.

'That was Greta Jones's mother, that was, that Mary Ann. Died not long after Greta was born so my mum told me, and Greta doesn't like it talked about.'

Peter recognised the voice, it was Willie Biggs again. 'Them, Wilderspoons, they were a right carry on.'

'You knew them?'

'My parents knew 'em, not me. According to my dad they were into witchcraft.' He pointed at the name Mary Wilderspoon saying, 'That was the person you mentioned, Reverend Basil Cuttler's daughter, God help her.' From looking at the headstone, Willie turned to face Peter. 'Do like I said; burn that trunk and everything in it before you do another thing. You don't want no harm coming to them two children of yours and you never know with witchcraft, you just never know.' Willie's familiar brooding look came over his face and Peter realised Willie wasn't joking, he was deadly serious.

'You mean it, don't you? Honestly, Willie, it all happened years ago. What possible harm can it do if I investigate, maybe Greta might be glad if —'

Peter got no further with his persuasion because Willie was tapping him on his chest with his sharp determined forefinger. 'I'm telling you to stop it, Rector. It's dangerous and what good will it do? Certainly do Greta Jones no good, she'll be upset and not half.'

'But not all witchcraft is wicked, Willie, there are white witches you know, who do good.'

'Not them Wilderspoons. Please, sir, please have nothing to do with it. It'll be the devil's work, believe me. And you an ordained priest – you should know better. It's not right.'

Willie stormed off home to Sylvia, disapproval in every inch of his retreating back. But some stubborn disregard for old superstitions prompted Peter to get out the old records from the safe in the Church and turn to the appropriate pages.

Every single birth, marriage and burial was recorded in there and Peter sat down to an entertaining morning looking up the entries for Wilderspoon. The further back he went the more Wilderspoons there were. They confirmed what he had already worked out except there were no references to the birth nor death of Mary Ann Wilderspoon born in, he assumed, 1934, except for her having been buried in the same grave as her grandparents, Silas and Mary.

But the diary on the kitchen table drew Peter back home and, as he picked it up, he felt a thrill running through his bones. What would he learn? What should he disclose? Or should he do as Willie suggested and burn the lot, the books, the letters, the diary, the momentoes, the trunk itself and forget it ever existed? After all, there was nothing of any real value, every single thing he'd handled was worthless.

Chapter 2

Greta Jones dashed into her office on the following Monday morning, her eyes alight with pleasure, bursting to let the world know her good news. 'Jimbo! Jimbo! Are you there?'

It wasn't Jimbo but Fran who emerged from his private office. 'Dad's not here, Greta. I am though, you can tell me.'

Fran found herself being hugged to within an inch of her life.

'I can't wait to tell someone. You'll be pleased, I know you will. If I said it was fifteen years since we'd actually heard anything definite from our Terry and our Kenny you'd believe me, wouldn't you?'

Fran nodded.

'Well! We have this morning. They *did* go to Canada after all, and they're living in Toronto and they've written to ask Vince and me to go stay for three weeks next summer. Apparently they've done really well for themselves, and our Terry's married and he's sent a photo of him and his wife and their two little girls. Never thought we'd hear another word from them as the years passed but now we have. I tell a lie, we got two postcards both from our Kenny about a year after they disappeared and they told us nothing – believe me, nothing.'

'That's wonderful, Greta! What lovely news. I'm so pleased for you, so pleased. After all these years. And Kenny, what about him?'

'He's not married but he has got a live-in-woman who our Terry says is lovely but Kenny refuses to commit himself. Still, we'll have to wait and see, won't we. They've offered to pay for the air tickets so it won't cost us a penny. We couldn't go otherwise and Vince is that thrilled.'

'I'm really pleased for you, Greta. What a lovely surprise for a Monday morning.' Fran gave Greta a nudge. 'Good excuse for a whole new wardrobe!'

'How right you are, love. Must press on. We'll talk later. Toronto, here I come!' Greta almost skipped into her mail order office leaving Fran thinking how generously minded Greta must be to not have heard from the two of them properly for fifteen years and still be so delighted they'd at last got in touch. She put her head round Greta's door and asked, 'How have they made their money?'

'Furniture. Apparently Kenny got the bug when he was looking for furniture here in Turnham Malpas – you remember, when they rented that cottage of Sir Ralph's? Well, how silly of me, no, you won't, you'd be too young, but anyway they did, so now they run two businesses. Terry sells second hand furniture, and I don't mean junk, more like antique stuff, and Kenny has his own business selling new furniture. They use completely different names and the businesses are totally unconnected. Just think, haven't they turned out well when you think what they—' Greta halted abruptly and decided to say no more. After all, they had turned a new leaf now. 'Must press on, Fran, love. Bring me a coffee when you have yours, please.'

It took Greta a while to settle to her work. The breathless excitement she'd felt when she saw the letter from Canada addressed to them both that morning was still with her. Fifteen years of waiting, fifteen long years with no real news at all. Vince had always been convinced they were both clapped in irons in Canada and they had no hope of ever seeing them again while she'd tried to put money on one side over the years to build up a fund for going to Canada, but somehow it kept having to be used as the cost of living went up and up, and for repairs to the house the older it got. Tonight she and Vince would put their heads together and write a reply to those two scallywags.

As she parcelled up the mail orders, printing out the address labels as though she was totally *au fait* with computers (she wasn't, but Fran had helped her to learn by rote how to do it), she pondered the possibility that those two boys of hers must be free of any threat of imprisonment if they'd dared to get in touch with them. The six months for theft that Terry had done in his teens had almost finished him as a person and he'd never been as tough as Kenny. She'd brought up their Barry with one hand tied behind her back, he'd been so easy. Not brilliant like Jimbo's lot, but clever enough to do an apprenticeship to become a carpenter and a very skilled one too.

The mail order parcels were mounting up very nicely by the time Fran arrived with her morning coffee. 'Milk, no sugar – as usual, Greta, and I've brought you a biscuit too.'

'Thanks, Fran love. Oh! I love bourbons. Put it over there away from the orders, can't bear to have a spill.'

'I've told Dad your news and he's really pleased for you. Says it's time you had some good luck.'

'He could be right about that.'

As she worked her way through the orders Greta tried to imagine what kind of a house they lived in and what on earth she and Vince could possibly find to do during three whole weeks of leisure. Apparently our Terry and Kenny shared a house, seemed odd that but perhaps for the best – at the very least it meant Kenny could keep an eye on Terry and he needed it.

The mail order office phone rang and she saw it was Vince ringing her. 'Yes, it's me, what's up?'

'I've been thinking.'

'What now?' If he'd changed his mind about Canada she'd kill him.

'Don't you think it's too far for us to go?'

Just as she thought! 'Where?'

'To Canada, of course. All that way. Look at the time we went to Jersey, you thought you were going to die, you said. Canada's a long way, hours in fact.' She heard that nervous cough he always got when he was panicking.

'Well, this time I'm more than willing to take the risk, Vince. *I'm* going, even if you're staying at home.' Greta banged down the receiver and plunged onto her chair, trembling from head to foot. If he still refused to go she *would* kill him, be one less fare for the boys to pay for. Brimming with anger, Greta finished her coffee, grabbed her coat and, rushing out through the front of the Store, encountered Jimbo as she whizzed past the till.

'Won't be long. Got an emergency. Must go. Parcels need sending. Back after my lunch.' And whirled away like a tornado through the Store and out of the door. The doorbell protested loudly, and the single customer by the till, struggling to find a twenty pound note she knew she had somewhere in her bag, said, 'What's got into Greta this morning? That's not her usual speed. Is there a fire?'

Fran reassured her there wasn't.

Jimbo put her change into the customer's hand, saying, 'I have no doubt we'll get the whole story when she gets back.'

And he did. For she came back in tears and needed a medicinal brandy from Jimbo's emergency supply before she could tell him of her shattering disappointment.

'You see we've been all these years not really knowing what was happening to them, no address, no nothing, then we hear and obviously they've had a right turn round in their circumstances, and now Vince says he won't go. All that excitement and now he won't go, says I'll never stand the journey, but I will, I'm determined we're going.' She burst into tears all over again and Jimbo was at a loss to know what to say or do.

'Now look here, Greta, it's a good while yet before the summer – it's not even Christmas yet. There's plenty of time to change his mind. I reckon if you say you're going no matter what, he'll decide to go.

Greta raised her eyes and looked directly at Jimbo. 'There is, isn't there? Plenty of time. I'll do that, see what happens. But if in the end he won't I shall go by myself. I shall be frightened to death but go I shall. I'm determined.'

'Take my advice and don't mention Canada to Vince at all, Greta. Just leave the whole subject in abeyance; that way he'll begin by being relieved you've apparently given up on the idea, but then get curious as to what you're planning.'

Greta stopped weeping into her handkerchief and looked up at him, her eyes swollen and flooded with grief, with a hint of hope. 'You could be right. I could try it and see what happens, couldn't I?'

'Well, going on about it will only stiffen his resolve, but a chirpy, happy Greta, might just do the trick.'

'I don't know about the cheerful bit because I'm as close to murdering him as I have ever been, and if I murder him he wouldn't be stopping me going then, though, would he?'

'No, but you'll be in prison.' Jimbo patted her shoulder. 'Then you *definitely* wouldn't be going, and neither would Vince.'

'Better not murder him then?' Greta began to laugh, at first a giggle and then a wholehearted laugh that could be heard right through to the front of the shop. She gathered herself together and said to Jimbo, 'Thanks for the advice, I think that could work.'

She picked up the big plastic box full of her earlier exertions and marched out to post them with Tom's help. She'd just paid the postage to him and was carefully placing the receipt into the tin she used for the money for posting the mail order parcels – though why she had to pay the postage when the Post Office belonged to Jimbo and the profits from the mail order also belonged to him she had not yet fathomed. Unexpectedly the main door swung open with a crash and there was Vince, hot and sweaty due to the speed with which he'd hurried up Shepherd's Hill.

'Ah! Greta! There you are.'

She turned round adjusting her face so it had a welcoming smile plastered across it and said warmly, 'Hello, love. Our Barry has invited us for a meal tonight, he's coming to pick us up about six when he's finished work.'

Taken aback by this warm welcome when he'd expected to be

castigated all over again, Vince hesitated and then replied, 'Oh! That'll be nice. Right. I'll leave you to it. Right, then. Yes. Well, well. I'll be off. Yes, let you get on.'

Then he paused with his hand hovering over the door handle. 'Is there anything I could do to help?' He nodded towards the plastic box at her feet. 'You seem to be very busy today.'

'Rabbit needs cleaning out, fresh water, fresh hay in her bed and that. Try her with that new food we got, see if she likes it.'

'Right, I will. Soon as I get back. Bye, love.'

'Bye.' Greta waved a hand to him, smiling all the while.

After he'd closed the door and couldn't possibly hear what she said she muttered to Jimbo, 'He hates cleaning out the rabbit, always leaves it to me. Serve him right! Now I'll have to ring our Barry and Pat to find out if they can have us for a meal. I could be living a very interesting life these next few months.' Greta winked at Jimbo and he winked back.

Much to Greta's relief Pat agreed it would be lovely if they could find the time to come, because they hadn't been for a meal for ages and they'd chosen the right night because she wasn't working as it happened. 'Barry'll pick you up about six, OK?'

'That'll be great, Pat. Be seeing you.' Greta put down her mobile where she always kept it on top of the money tin with the picture of the beach they'd loved that time they went to Jersey, which reminded her how ill she'd felt on the flight and how she longed to land ASAP which reminded her of Canada – as if she needed reminding. But she would go, even if her plan to persuade Vince didn't work out, because this was payback time for all the money she'd had to give their Terry and Kenny to keep money in their pockets when their useless escapades hadn't worked out.

Greta warned Pat as soon as they arrived that she mustn't let on they'd invited themselves to a meal. She winked and whispered, 'Tell you why later!'

Pat gave her the thumbs up signal and they merrily reeled into

Pat's lovely kitchen keeping their faces as innocent as they possibly could.

Barry was pouring the drinks out, 'Wine tonight, Mum, choice of red or white?'

'Wine? It's usually lager.'

'I know it is but it's Johnny's birthday today and he's given everyone on his payroll a bottle of wine but we got two because of Pat's dad.'

'How's old Greenwood keeping, nowadays? We never see him.'

'Well, his arthritis restricts him a lot but, up here,' Barry tapped his temple, 'he's absolutely fine, believe me. That's him; I can hear him coming downstairs.'

The five of them spent an hilarious evening talking over old times, making arrangements about Christmas, asking Pat what it felt like being grandparents to Dean's new baby.

'Makes me feel old it does, to be honest. He's a lovely baby and his mother is doing a really good job bringing him up and Dean's thrilled to bits.'

'And what about Michelle? How's she doing nowadays? You never seem to mention her.'

'Thinking about going to live in Australia; she's even had an offer right out of the blue to go out there and work in a big new garden they're creating and the money! Oh my word, the money! I can't believe it.' Pat put down her knife and fork, found a tissue in her pocket and burst into tears. 'And ... and ... I don't want her to go!'

'You mustn't stop her going if that's what she wants. It's her life,' said Vince, 'remember that.'

Pat protested, 'I bet you didn't think like that when Kenny and Terry hopped it abroad never to come back!'

Greta held her breath waiting for Vince's reply. Would he say about the letter? But he didn't. He said calmly and purposefully, 'Different when it's a girl. Them two could survive walking to the North Pole in swimming trunks, 'cos they're men and daft with it. The trouble they caused us when they were here, if we never saw them again it wouldn't matter. The money we had to fork out for them to keep 'em solvent—'

'What money?' Greta was shocked – he'd never let on he knew.

Vince patted her hand. 'Oh, I never let on I knew what you were doing, thought it best not.'

If he knew that, thought Greta, had he worked out her scheme to persuade him to go to Canada? No, not likely, he wasn't that sensitive. Or was he? 'Oh! Right!' she said and waited to see if he would let on about Canada. But he didn't, he changed the subject completely by asking Barry if there was any more wine on offer. 'I've right taken a fancy to it.' And then he suggested they had a game of cards.

Game of cards? That wasn't like Vince, thought Greta and even Greenwood voiced his opinion that the wine must have gone straight to Vince's head.

The evening passed by in a flash, mainly because Vince suggested they played for money which added zest to the game.

'I know whist is considered old-fashioned now,' said Vince as he collected his winnings 'but it's a good game. Right, well, Greta, we'll be off shall we? Thanks for a lovely meal, Pat, and thanks for sharing the wine with us – it's made a lovely change. We'll walk home, Barry, do us both good.'

'Certainly not, I'll take you.'

'No, I insist. The exercise'll do us good. Goodnight, Greenwood. Here, Pat, let's give you a kiss. Thanks for a lovely meal, that meat pie was smashing!'

Greta wasn't all that keen on walking home – she needed time to acclimatise herself to this new husband she'd acquired. Then she remembered he'd be back to his usual self by morning, grumpy and clinging to the past as usual, and she'd still have the problem of him not wanting to see their boys. But her lips must remain sealed if she was to succeed in getting him to Canada, the old fool.

'Let's call in at the pub on the way home.'

They were halfway down the drive when he came out with this

suggestion and Greta was at a loss to understand what had come over him.

She pulled up and stared at him. 'That wine's really gone to your head.'

'So?'

'It's five minutes to ten,' she protested.

'So?'

'Well, all right then we'll go.'

'Spend our winnings.'

'Good idea.'

Vince opened the outer door for her to go through first and she stepped through the inner door to find the bar was still full of customers. Having imagined the bar would be almost empty by then, Greta was delighted. She spotted Willie and Sylvia and made a beeline for their table while Vince went to the bar. He came back with a pint of Dicky's homebrew for himself and her drink in a tall fancy glass with a paper umbrella and bits and pieces stuck out at the top.

'Oh! Vince! What is it?'

'A pina colada.'

'A pina colada? What in heaven's name is that?'

'Rum and stuff. Try it.'

Sylvia leaned across to give the drink a sniff. 'It's certainly rum, Greta. Is there something we're celebrating? I know it's not your birthday, 'cos that's in December.'

Greta, desperately puzzled but trying hard to remain cool as though pina-whatever was a usual drink for her, replied casually, 'Nothing special. We've been playing whist at our Barry's and Vince won, that's all.' Greta tentatively took a sip of her drink and loved it. She could have glugged the whole lot down in one go but decided to make it last.

'Any news?' Greta asked after another long sip of her pina-whatever.

Willie grunted, and Sylvia shook her head.

Disappointed neither of them had any news Greta said, 'Not much point in us coming in, then.'

'You've got a lovely drink, though.' Vince remarked and patted her hand.

Willie stirred himself. 'I spoke to the rector today, had coffee in their kitchen.'

'Who's a lucky boy, then?' Vince grinned.

'Not me, and I'm not best pleased. He's up to his interfering tricks again.'

'For a man who thinks the world of him that's a bit surprising coming from you. What's he done now, Willie?' asked Greta.

'The rector has a different set of values to us mere mortals. If you really want to know he's managed to drag a trunk out from where it was jammed in the eaves. Opened it up and found a load of stuff that's going to knock the hell out of some people I know.' He appeared to be singling Greta out for a special kind of threatening look.

Somewhat alarmed by Willie's expression and the deep silence that followed, Greta fortified herself with another sip of her delicious drink and asked, 'Well then, what's he found? Having got this far you might as well tell me.'

'You won't like it.'

'What on earth can there be in the Rectory loft that could possibly affect me? A pile of old sermons from a rector long gone? Mmm? Eh? Go on, tell us.'

Sylvia, instead of leaning her elbows on the table, sat bolt upright saying, 'What did we decide before we came out? We discussed it thoroughly and agreed you would not say a word about it.' Getting no reply she repeated her last sentence even more vehemently, finishing with, 'So keep your trap shut, if you please.'

When Willie did as he was told Greta said, 'That's not fair! If you've got something to say, say it. It's about me, isn't it, though what something the rector's found in an old trunk in his loft that's anything to do with me I can't imagine.'

'It's about your mother, Mary Wilderspoon and your granddad, the Reverend Basil Cuttler.'

The blood drained from Greta's face leaving her ashen with distress. 'Oh, God! Not that all over again!'

Chapter 3

Twenty-four hours later the fact that some unwelcome news about Greta Jones' past had been discovered in an ancient trunk in the Rectory loft had travelled all round Turnham Malpas, Little Derehams and Penny Fawcett, Greta had gone into hiding and Willie Biggs was in the doghouse yet again.

'You should never have said a word, you didn't need to, but oh no, Willie had to have his little say, his moment centre stage! Will you never learn? It should have gone to the grave with you because you know the rector would never have said a word, he's the epit ... epo ... you know what I mean ... of discretion, he is. Well, that's it. I shan't be able to show my face anywhere at all. Bang go all my cosy nights in the Royal Oak and yours for that matter. Telly here we come.' Sylvia had stamped off into the kitchen at the end of this speech leaving Willie crouched in gloom beside the fire. He watched the flames making short work of the logs he'd bought from Johnny Templeton and wondered if life would ever be the same again. He couldn't bear it when his Sylvia was in one of her 'huffs'. But my word, these logs were good! Snuff dry, they were, and gave out such heat like they'd never had before from this old stove. He recalled the fires they'd had in that same stove when he was a boy and remembered it had never given out as much heat as they wanted and the house had always felt cold no matter what they tried.

Willie's mind wandered about through his childhood years ... the scandal ... when was it? Must have been ... but he fell asleep and didn't wake until nearly teatime and then he wished he hadn't woken up.

'Well,' said Sylvia as she thumped the teapot down on the table, 'there's one advantage if we save the money we'd have spent in the pub, we'll be that rich by Christmas we'll be able to go away. Shall we do that? Go away? That'll be a first.'

Willie groaned inwardly.

As for Greta, she refused to show her face in the village so Jimbo, out of necessity because no one could tackle the mail order side with such dedicated methodical precision as Greta did, agreed that one of them would go down Shepherd's Hill and pick her up from home, and take her back again, as and when. Greta knew they couldn't keep that up for the rest of her working life but for now she was grateful for their kindness. But the gloom that surrounded Greta didn't dissipate one little bit and everyone who worked in the Store when she was there wished, oh! how they wished, the gloom would lift.

The only cheerful member of the staff was Fran and the reason for her cheerfulness was known only to her and she had no intention of revealing the cause, except she had told her mother and she'd told her dad and he was not best pleased. As if that blasted Chris Templeton hadn't caused her enough heartbreak in the past for him to be turning up again like some kind of bad penny! To be truthful Jimbo would have preferred him to be lost in that blasted Amazon jungle for ever, but no such luck, the beggar had been rescued, desperately ill, taken to a hospital that was world-renowned for its expertise in curing obscure tropical diseases and apparently, according to Fran, he was coming over to England to stay at the Big House for a while.

After the weeks of anxiety over him being missing when his plane came down over the jungle Fran, of course, was delighted. All Jimbo had asked for was for Chris to be missing for ever for Fran's sake. The man was too handsome, too full of bonhomie and too wealthy for his own good. All he and Harriet could do was hope the hurt Chris had caused with his casual attitude to Fran's miscarriage would have stayed with her and she would reject his overtures, because overtures there most certainly would be as he was the kind of man who fed off his popularity.

Fran, however, was in two minds. One half of her longed to be back in his arms and enjoying his caresses and his perfectly splendidly erotic kissing technique; the other half couldn't trust him ever again. If she needed someone to trust, Alex Harris was the man for that. They'd seen a lot of each other these last few months and she'd enjoyed every moment when she was with him. Agreed there wasn't the same sparkle between them that Chris gave her, but they laughed a lot, liked doing the same kind of things. Neither of them enjoyed sport, for instance. Fran remembered how cold her legs had always been when playing hockey at school and the appalling chill of the changing rooms after swimming. No, she could turn her back on sport without a moment of regret. Alex was good-looking, very good-looking in fact, just as Chris was. But Chris was a well-experienced man and, to be honest, Alex was still a boy.

It was at this moment that the two halves of her life collided.

She was taking her turn on the till because her dad was showing a couple round the Old Barn as they were thinking of getting married there and, of course, holding the reception there too. Her mother was in the kitchens, sorting out her plans for the food for an event tomorrow, Greta was in the mail order office catching up with her orders and Tom was locked in the Post Office, checking his stock of postage stamps, when in walked Alex, smiling at her as only he could. He took hold of her hands saying, 'Surprised?'

'Of course! I wasn't expecting you at all.'

'Just felt like coming home. To see you. Sometimes, still being a student, there are moments when all I want to do is come home, so that's why I'm here. Are you free tonight?'

At that very same moment the door bell rang furiously and in walked Chris Templeton.

Well, Fran knew it was Chris but this wasn't the Chris she had known for those few magical weeks last year. This Chris was gaunt and weary and she found it hard to believe that he was the same man. But maybe he wasn't ... Her entire attention was devoted to him and Alex stood back and made a space for them to meet.

'Fran!'

'Chris!'

They stood a foot apart, absorbing each other, until she reached out to touch his arm. Alex no longer existed as far as she was concerned because her mind and her heart were filled to overflowing by Chris, his almost-white hair ... white? The hand that gripped his arm could feel bone not muscle like she used to feel and the vibrant, thrusting, personality was gone.

She said softly, 'I didn't realise just how very ill you've been. First the plane crash in the jungle, then being missing for so long and then catching that terrible tropical thing – you look as though you need something to give you a boost. Go sit down and I'll make a fresh pot of coffee. I can't begin to imagine what you've gone through. It must have been terrifying.' She placed a gentle hand on his cheek and then reached up to kiss his lips. So she didn't hear the door being shut quietly behind Alex; truth to tell he'd gone completely from her mind. And he knew it.

A massive hollow feeling grew inside Alex as he walked back to the Rectory and he narrowly missed walking straight into the pond on the green because he couldn't actually see where he was going. That wonderful coming together that he'd dreamed of, which was what had drawn him home from College in the middle of term, was never going to happen. And he knew it. For certain. Knew he didn't exist for Fran, not any more; well, not at the moment. Apart from his parents he'd never witnessed someone filled with so much love as Fran had just demonstrated to Chris. And loving a man like him as much as she so obviously did she was frighteningly vulnerable.

As he stepped into the road to reach the safety of home so he could shut out the world while he recovered, his heart broke into a thousand pieces. Once home, overcome by despair, Alex fled upstairs to his room and shut the door firmly behind him, hoping his dad wouldn't come looking for him until he'd pulled himself together.

Chris had sat sipping his coffee as though his very life depended on it. When every last drop had been consumed Fran asked, 'So, Chris, feeling better? Mmm?'

Chris nodded his head. 'Much better, thanks. Just what I needed – plenty of sugar. And how's my Fran?' His low, colourless voice alarmed Fran. He was almost begging her to remember how much she'd loved him before. Reminding her of the passion they'd shared, he took hold of her hand and pressed it to his lips. Despite herself, Fran rejoiced. He still loved her, of course he did! All her distress at the way he'd completely ignored her miscarriage was forgotten; it was because, as she had thought at the time, he couldn't bear to express his sadness directly to her because it hurt him so much. And what man wouldn't find it unbearable to talk about losing his first child?

'Chris, when you feel better I'd like to hear your version of what happened, because the newspapers certainly gave it the full treatment. You turned into a hero overnight.'

'Indeed I did, according to them! Anything for a good story, eh? Just glad you weren't with me. It would have been too much for you.'

Fran wouldn't allow herself to take umbrage. 'I'm much tougher than I look, you know, Chris. Much tougher!' She grinned and clenched her fists to demonstrate her strength. 'See!?'

Neither of them had noticed Jimbo was back and when he saw how absorbed they were in each other he went to stand behind the till even though there were no customers. For something to do he off-loaded a lot of change out of the till drawer into the box they kept below.

Jimbo, longing to throw Chris out, thought up some devilish

endings in dense jungles for him, wished him in Timbuctoo or anywhere but here in Turnham Malpas, then his mobile rang and when he saw who'd dialled his number he melted away into his office to answer it. Couldn't let emotions get in the way of his business!

Finding themselves alone Fran suggested they had a meal out the next evening, a kind of coming home celebration.

'I'm not driving yet,' Chris said.

'I'll drive, usual place?'

'The Wise Man?'

'You've remembered. Yes.' Fran felt ridiculously elated that he remembered the name of their favourite watering hole. 'I'll come to pick you up; what time?'

'Make it six-thirty otherwise I shall be asleep at the table if I'm not careful.' He gave her a rueful smile as though apologising for being so feeble.

'How did you get here?'

'Johnny gave me a lift; he's picking me up from here.'

To cover her distress at his weakness she said, 'How are Johnny's boys? I haven't seen them for a while.'

'Active. *Very* active! While their eyes are open they are running about and it's absolutely exhausting. Fran, that chap who was in here when I came in, it's the rector's son, isn't it, judging by the colour of his hair and his height?'

Fran looked around and was shocked to realise she hadn't even noticed that Alex had left. 'Yes, that's right.'

Chris looked speculatively directly into her eyes and then said, 'He isn't competition is he? For me?'

She didn't answer for a moment and then said, 'No, of course not. He's still a boy ... you're a man.'

'Good.' There was a screech of brakes outside. 'Here's Johnny. So six-thirty tomorrow evening at the Big House.' He kissed her on her lips as though registering his possession of her and left.

Fran remained standing where she was when they drove away,

giving herself time to decide exactly how she felt about the two men vying for her attention. Or were they *both* vying for her attention? Was Chris, in spite of his frailty, still keen on her? She knew Alex was and knew she should not have described him as a boy, because in some ways – such as loyalty and consideration for her feelings and opinions – he was more grown-up than Chris, who loved being the centre of her world but with him in charge of it, while Alex gave her space to be herself . . .

'Fran! That's the third time I've called your name. What is the matter, child?'

'I am not a child, Dad.'

'I know, I know. Look, can you do the collection round for Greta's stock? She's running out of things for her orders, and the couple I've just shown round the Old Barn have only got as far as Culworth and have rung me having decided they're coming back to pay the deposit right now, as they don't want to lose their chance to book it. I told them I'd someone thinking about the same date and—'

'Dad! You didn't? You've no scruples!'

'It's true! I did have someone else for the same Saturday, and I did warn them it was a very popular Saturday they were wanting.'

'OK. Right. I'll snatch some lunch and then I'll go.'

Very quietly and with lots of love in his voice Jimbo said, 'Take your time with those two suitors of yours. You don't have to decide tomorrow nor today nor ever if you don't want to. As far as your mum and I are concerned you can stay at home for ever. You know that, don't you?'

'Yes. But thanks for saying it, at least I know where I stand with you.'

Jimbo slyly added, 'If I was a betting man I'd put my money on Alex. So would your mother. If they were taking part in a race Alex would be streets ahead of Chris. Younger, fitter with great prospects, all my money would be on him. He's a lovely chap. Good-looking too!'

'You'd love it if I chose Alex, I know you would, I do, but it's my life, Dad, my decision.' Fran gave her dad a wry smile. 'At least you'd get on with the in-laws!'

'Of course. Yes.'

Except right at this moment she had no idea who she would choose: Alex or Chris. They both had plusses. Alex of course was ideal, excellent family background, known him all her life, honourable, kind, reliable and absolutely lovely and he let her be herself, but ... Chris made her sparkle inside and Alex didn't. Could you live all your life married to a man whom you knew right from the start didn't make you sparkle? And never would. But he was faithful and caring and loved you to bits ... Did that make up for no sparkle? For that extra something that made your heart leap when you heard his key in the door? She recalled holding Chris's arm and finding no muscle as before, but almost entirely skin and bone, and there was that immediate something special she'd always felt when she was with him. For now, it would have to be Chris, because he needed her – sorry, Alex.

Instead of staying over the weekend as he'd planned, Alex had gone straight back to College that same evening, determined to put Fran out of his mind and instead concentrate on his degree. His MSc and then a career – he had to succeed in something. In his room Alex dug out of his wallet the photograph of Fran he'd taken during the summer, when he had her to himself because Chris was still in hospital in Brazil. She was wearing a big floppy straw sunhat and sandals with light blue shorts and a matching top, looking perfectly splendid sitting on a big rock beside the sea the day he'd done as she asked and had driven a long way to a lonely beach that he loved. He'd put together a picnic for them and his mum had found a bottle of wine to go with it, and even though it was summer they were alone in the cove. Such a wonderful atmosphere, peaceful, together, with no intrusions of any kind, and they'd talked seriously about what they wanted out of life.

With Chris out of the picture, Alex had asked if she'd had any thoughts on changing her life, maybe going to university.

Fran had declared she definitely wasn't going to university because working in the Store was what she wanted; she didn't work there as some kind of easy option, she'd said, or to please her dad; it was what she actually *wanted* to do. Alex had felt closer to her that day than ever before and he convinced himself they were truly meant for each other. For life ... and he'd rejoiced at the thought. Now there wasn't much point in mooning over the photograph any longer; might as well face the fact, here and now, that she obviously belonged to Chris. Instead of returning it to his wallet he slipped the photo into his bedside drawer beneath the personal jumble he always kept there. It felt like the end of a chapter.

Chapter 4

The following morning Fran popped down Shepherd's Hill to pick up Greta and decided, as she turned round before pulling up outside Greta's, that she would suggest very gently that it was time Greta showed her face in the village.

Greta slipped into the front passenger seat saying as she slammed the door, 'Thanks, Fran, thanks very much.'

Before she started off up the hill, Fran decided it was now or never. She switched off the engine and said, 'There's not been a single word of gossip about you and whatever it is in the trunk in the Rectory loft and I reckon it's time to pack it in and behave as normal. What do you think?'

It came as a shock to Greta and it took a minute for her to reply. 'Not a word?'

'Well, Dad gets all the gossip and he's not heard a word, so how about it, Greta, you can't hide for ever. Can you?'

'I don't know ...'

'Aren't you bored? I would be. Drive me crackers not going out.'

'To be honest, it's driving me crackers too. Vince always comes back with the wrong things from the market and I'm getting thoroughly fed up with him.' She gazed out of the window for a moment. 'But ...'

'I think you should. How long have we been driving you back and forth? Three weeks is it?'

'Three weeks and three days. You're right.' Greta took a deep breath. 'I'm being ridiculous, aren't I? I'll go home by myself tonight.'

Very carefully, not wanting to make Greta go back on her promise Fran asked what on earth was it that Greta didn't want everyone to know?

The moment the words were out of her mouth Fran regretted her forthrightness, because Greta's face went a funny grey colour and she began hyperventilating. Fran immediately put the car in gear and hurtled up Shepherd's Hill as though the devil himself was right behind her.

'Keep calm, Greta! I didn't mean anything at all and I don't know a thing. Right. Breathe steadily, deep breaths, steadily. We're nearly there.' She pulled up outside the Store and ran round the car to open Greta's door. Greta was still breathing rapidly but not quite so fast as she had been.

Fran rushed Greta into the Store calling out, 'Glass of water, Bel, please. Sit down here Greta, no, I know you don't want a coffee, just *sit down*, Bel's gone for a drink of water for you. Breathe steadily, Greta, that's better. Here's the water, don't gulp it, just steady sips.'

By the time she'd drunk half of the water Greta was almost restored to normal, but there was still fear in her eyes. 'Thank you, love, I'm better now. Better get on, or I shall get behind and I hate that. Thank you, Fran.'

'I've got to press on too. Both of us have to. I should never have said anything, Greta, I'm sorry.'

'Yes, you should have spoken out. I needed a prod. One day perhaps I'll tell you the whole story.'

'Right. Thanks. OK then.' Fran squeezed Greta's shoulder to reassure her. 'And if you do, I won't tell anyone at all.'

'I know you won't. Right, must press on. Like I said, I'm taking myself home tonight. OK? I'm letting it get to me far too much. Got to pull myself together. '

But that very afternoon a smidgen of the gossip about Greta let itself be known in the village Store.

It was a woman from Little Derehams who mentioned it to Jimbo. 'This latest bit of gossip that's going round,' she said, 'it's her that does your mail order, isn't it? In that back office.'

Instantly excited because he loved gossip, Jimbo's ears went on red alert. Then he remembered the sacrifices they'd been making on behalf of Greta these last few weeks and that she worked for him. 'Sorry, haven't heard anything at all. There's your change. Oh! That sounds like my phone, excuse me. Sorry.'

After his phone call, he returned to the front of the Store thinking the woman would have disappeared by now having no one to talk to, but she hadn't. She was just bringing a birthday card to the till. 'Oh! There you are. Forgot to choose a card, it's my granny's ninety-fifth birthday this weekend. It's amazing how they keep hanging on nowadays, I mean, ninety-five and skin and bone she is. She can't half eat though, mention food and she's at the table in a jiffy. As I was saying ...' and Jimbo couldn't stop her, 'This news about Greta is ...' she drew in a great breath 'that her mother was only fourteen when she was born, Greta that is, and she was brought up by her grandmother, so Greta's illegitimate.' Then the customer ended her news by saying, 'And this is her with an opinion on just about everything, real self-righteous she can be when all the time—'

'Considering the number of children being born nowadays and their parents aren't married and not likely to be, I can't imagine why this so-called news qualifies for being spread about with such glee. It's not Greta's fault anyway, and it must have been a tragedy for her family at the time. That card costs one pound ninety-nine pence, please.'

'What's up with you?' she said indignantly. 'You always relish gossip. Many's the time I've been in here and—'

'Well, I've changed. Like I said that card's one pound ninety—'

Spitefully the customer replied, 'It's too expensive, I won't take it.'

'In that case then drive into Culworth or catch the bus and then see how much your Granny's card will have cost you, driving all that way. You won't find a card of that quality for that price anywhere in the whole of Culworth.' Jimbo folded his arms and waited.

'You're right there. OK then, I'll take it.' She paid her money and stalked out, vowing never to come in the Store ever again, but knowing full well she would because his food was so good and so tempting and it was so convenient. Funny him changing his mind about gossip, though, but then Greta did work for him. Mind you, he hadn't given her a chance to tell him the rest of the gossip about Greta which she felt was much more explosive, so with a triumphant smile on her face she leapt in her car. He'd missed out on that, with him being whiter than white nowadays. Serve him right.

Fran was barely conscious of what she did the day after her splendid evening with Chris at The Wise Man. She'd never expected that she would enjoy herself so much but she did. Despite his frailty he'd made a great effort to be his usual self but by half past nine his lively effort began to flag and she realised she'd have to make an excuse to leave.

'I think I shall have to go home,' she said. 'I'm on early start tomorrow morning and if I'm not careful I shall be sleeping in by mistake. How about you, are you ready to leave?'

'I'm ready if you are. You don't want another drink? Another pudding?'

'No, thanks, Chris, I'm too full. We'll go then.' Fran began to open her bag to get out her credit card.

But Chris forestalled her. 'Put that away, you may have asked me to come but I'm paying.'

'Thank you, Chris! It's lovely having you back again, I've really enjoyed myself tonight. Thank you so much.'

'It's been a pleasure. I'm getting better every day, stronger, you know. Been a terrible shock to my system.' Something of his former energy flashed on his face but only for a moment. Fran thought, he's got a long way to go yet before he's back to normal. She drove him back to the big house and though he suggested she went in for a while she declined.

'Off you go, Chris, straight to bed. Goodnight and thanks, I've really enjoyed your company. Night. Night.' Chris kissed her, but with none of the fervour she remembered from before lingering in the kiss.

She watched him walk to the door and disappear inside. She'd enjoyed herself, but somehow the magic simply wasn't there. Not at the moment anyway. As she drove home Fran rather supposed that she would have been dead if she'd had to face months lost in the Amazon rain forest and then been seriously ill with some obscure tropical disease all those weeks. Poor Chris! Then, as she parked on the Store car park for a great big think before she went in home, Alex sprang to mind. She really shouldn't have just ignored him once Chris came in, she should have made both of them coffee or perhaps even taken them home, together, and given herself the chance to compare the two of them.

Age-wise Alex was right, Chris *was* too old. On the charm front, for different reasons, they were equal. Sex-wise she didn't know about Alex because he'd never even come near to suggesting it, which made a girl feel impossibly ancient and unattractive. But maybe that was for the best: at least one didn't run the risk of getting pregnant in the heat of the moment. What she should have done all those months ago was gone to the doctors and got contraceptive pills, instead of relying on Chris taking precautions. All the sadness of losing their baby came crashing back into her heart and she found herself with tears on her cheeks.

There was a rapid knocking on her driver's side window and there stood Tom Nicholls with his dog Tatty going out for their pre-bedtime walk.

Fran opened the window. 'Hello, Tom!'

'Hello, Fran. Can't find your way home?' Jokingly he pointed the way to their house. 'It's the last house before Royal Oak Road. Mind how you go!' Tom gave Tatty's lead a pull and they left. Fran felt a fool, because he'd obviously seen her tears and even more obviously had felt embarrassed by them, because he couldn't get away quickly enough whereas normally he would have stayed for a chat.

What a fool she was, an absolute fool. No, she wasn't, there would have been a baby due to be born very shortly if she hadn't had the miscarriage. She thanked her lucky stars she hadn't deliberately ensured it aborted, because she would have felt so guilty right now.

Did Chris ever give the baby a thought? she wondered. Clear as day her answer arrived in her head unbidden.

No, he didn't. And she couldn't decide what she thought about that. Did it make him strong being able to put unhappy things out of his mind so completely? Or did it make him a thoughtless, inconsiderate, cruel man? Fran turned the key in the ignition, put the car into gear and paused for a moment while she reassessed her feelings, remembered the wonderful times in bed with him before his plane went down and brought such a heap of troubles on his head, and decided that in future she would be more in control; she'd allowed Chris to dictate the nature of their relationship far too much.

Would she say the same thing about Alex? No. Because they made joint decisions about their relationship. She'd ring him tomorrow to find out if she could see him before he went back to College, she decided, but she changed her mind and rang him that same night only to find he'd already gone the previous day. She felt surprisingly deserted and absolutely miserable. Driving home all that way and going back on the same day, it was ridiculous! What was he thinking of? Her, presumably, and she recalled the lingering kiss she'd given Chris right there in front of Alex. No wonder he'd gone back, he must have presumed she was in love with Chris. But was she? Perhaps Alex knew her better than she knew herself.

Next morning as it was Fran's early turn day she checked the emails on the computer belonging to the Store and found one from Craddock Fitch's daughter-in-law, a doctor like her husband, with a long list of groceries required for delivery at Nightingale Farm asap that morning as they were moving in immediately. The list was well structured with dairy products in one quarter, fresh vegetables and fruit in another, household cleaners etc., in another and meat and fish in the fourth. She reckoned in her head that the order was worth well over three hundred pounds, if not more. Wow! But five children! What a family.

Just what the village needed. When she knew for certain that her dad would be up, Fran rang home to let him know his presence was needed as soon as possible and his response was a loud cheer. Within twenty minutes he was in the Store searching for cardboard boxes and starting to organise things. It was the biggest order they had ever had to deal with and Jimbo's spirits reached their highest point for a long time. He frequently had days when he emphatically decided on closing the Store and relying on the private events he organised for the Old Barn instead. But today he'd changed his mind: if he could look forward to big orders like this coming in every week he'd be a fool to close it.

By folding down the back seats he got all the groceries in his car and leapt into the driving seat to take them to Nightingale Farm. The previous owners had had a big family too but had shopped in the supermarket to cut down, as they thought, on their costs. When Jimbo arrived at the farm he wondered for a moment if he should wait until things had calmed down because he could hear a man's voice raising the roof in temper and children laughing with a rather worrying disregard.

He remembered Craddock Fitch being intensely proud of the

fact that he and Kate had had all the family for a meal and how impressed Kate was about their behaviour. The noise he could hear did not seem impressive, rather the opposite.

The front door burst open and five children of varying sizes shot out as though fired from a gun. They raced in a cluster down the field in front of the house and disappeared. As their Red Indian screeches faded into the distance, Jimbo emerged from the driving seat and, after taking care to lock the car door, he approached the front door of the farmhouse.

Two blasts on the doorbell brought a charming, composed forty-year-old woman to the door. 'Good morning. I'm Jimbo Charter-Plackett bringing your order. From the Turnham Malpas Store ... you emailed us.'

'Wonderful!' she exclaimed. 'Thank you so much. I'll prop the door open and give you a hand. It's most kind of you.'

'Not at all. It's a pleasure. It really is.'

Between them they heaved all the boxes of food inside and Jimbo waited for payment. 'I'll take cash or cheque or credit or debit card if you prefer.'

He stood looking round the tired kitchen and wondered just how much money they would have to spend on the entire house which wasn't exactly small. She was a long time finding her hand-bag, but then they had only just moved in and moving house wasn't exactly the easiest of activities. No matter how organised you were there was always something slipped through the net.

She reappeared. 'I'm Anita, by the way. I can't find my bag so will it be OK if one of us comes down to the Store later today? It is here somewhere and I remember putting it down, but not exactly where.'

She smiled beautifully at him, showing a row of beautiful even teeth and putting all her charm into the smile.

Reassured, Jimbo accepted her reasons for not paying. 'That's absolutely fine, one day soon you'll be organised and wondering why on earth today seemed so hard. See you later today, then.

Hope you settle in OK. We're a nice lot once you get to know us. We close at seven, by the way.'

Jimbo smiled at her and she smiled again and he waved himself away in a friendly fashion and left confident one or other of them would be in before seven.

He purposely stayed in the Store until closing time but neither of them appeared to pay up before he went home.

'Harriet! I'm home! Where are you? Mmm?'

'In the kitchen. Don't stand in front of the oven. I'm just going to take a look in there,' Harriet said when he went in. 'Move over.'

She paused for a moment to look at Jimbo's face. 'What's the matter?'

Jimbo said, 'Funny thing. The younger Fitches ordered over three hundred pounds worth of groceries, give or take a little, and promise to come back in and pay before we closed, but they haven't. It's just a mite worrying.'

'You mean Craddock's crowd?'

'Yes.'

'Darling! Have a heart – five children and they moved in only late last night? I mean!' Harriet thumped a casserole dish on the worktop and stood, hands on hips, waiting for his reply.

'Of course, I'm being ridiculous, aren't I?'

'Yes. They won't even know what time it is, let alone dashing round here to pay. Probably can't even remember where their cards are right at this moment.'

'Of course, and she seems so honest.'

'Ready to eat?'

'Yes, I'm really hungry. I didn't even get my pork pie today because there weren't any left.'

'Don't you ever get bored with pork pies?'

'Yes, but I'm too lazy to bother with anything else. Shall I call Fran?'

'She's out.' Harriet pulled a face. 'With the gorgeous Chris. I'm serving right now so don't disappear.'

'Why on earth did he have to come to recuperate here,' Jimbo grumbled. 'He used to say he hated the English winters, but here he is.'

'Sit down, just put the knives and forks out and we'll eat in here.'

The two of them settled down after they'd eaten, Harriet to writing letters to friends that should have been done weeks ago, and Jimbo to working on the month end accounts for the Old Barn. About eleven they heard the front door open and went out to the hall both rejoicing that Fran was safely home.

'Hello! darling, good time?' Harriet needn't have bothered asking because she could hear Fran breathing heavily before she saw her. 'What's happened? Fran?'

But Fran had raced upstairs and slammed her bedroom door so hard the whole house shuddered. Jimbo and Harriet faced each other. Eyebrows raised, Jimbo whispered, 'Go up, see what's the matter.'

'I might.'

'Please, darling, she sounds in a bad way.'

Desperate to know what had happened Harriet raced up the stairs and tapped on Fran's door but got no response, which was hardly surprising seeing as she was still crying loudly. Harriet debated what to do and decided to ask because now the tears had changed to racking sobs. What the so-and-so had done to cause this she couldn't imagine. Little Bonnie, who had rapidly learned how to climb the stairs, was scratching at Fran's door, trying to get in. So Harriet opened the door for her and followed her in.

Bonnie was clinging to the bed valance endeavouring to clamber up onto the bed but couldn't quite make it. Fran was lying on the bed, still weeping.

'Fran! Fran! He isn't worth it! I'm putting Bonnie on the bed, which I know isn't allowed but she's desperate. Now, pull yourself together and tell your mother what's happened.'

Fran sat up, scrubbed her eyes free of tears, picked up Bonnie and kissed her, and then took a deep breath and said, 'You're right, he *isn't* worth it. Do you know what he's done?'

'No, I don't. Tell me.' Harriet made herself comfortable on the end of the bed and waited.

'A woman friend of his from Brazil has turned up unexpectedly so there was nothing he could do about that, he said. One minute she was in Brazil ringing him up and the next she'd arrived. He didn't warn me that when we met tonight we'd be a party of three. She's spent the entire evening dropping big hints about how close she and him are and he *encouraged* her, looking in admiring mode into her eyes and squeezing her hand when she put it within reach. Apparently she's been helping to nurse him, visiting him in hospital and then at home. She's called Annunciata or something highly improbable and she's the same age as Chris, has known him for years. She found me very amusing, treated me condescendingly as a kind of innocent little sister. At one stage they were holding hands and I got the distinct impression that she was there to illustrate something, but I'm not sure what. Oh! Mum!'

'Fran, that's your phone.'

Fran dug in her bag and pulled it out. 'It's him! I'm not answering.'

'Well, I am.' Harriet snatched the phone from Fran and said. 'Hi! This is Fran's phone, but it's her mother answering because she isn't around at the moment. How can I help?'

There was a short silence and then Chris said, 'I'm sure. Would you be so kind as to tell her that we'll be round to pick her up tomorrow, about eleven?'

'Does she know about it?'

'Oh yes, we've been talking about it tonight. Just wanted to confirm it.'

'Fine, I'll tell her. Goodnight, Chris. You sound to be feeling much improved after your dreadful ordeal; we were all so worried about you.'

'I am beginning to perk up now, thanks.'

'You're coping well with the English winter then?' she said coldly. 'You've always said how much you hate it.'

Chris laughed. 'Well, you can cope with a lot if you have good company to while away the hours.'

'Of course, of course. I'll say goodnight, then. See you tomorrow, perhaps.'

If she never saw him again it would be too soon! Harriet gave Fran her phone back and decided to speak her mind. 'You heard what he said? Where are you going?'

Fran appeared puzzled for a moment and then said, 'I was supposed to be picking him up, so what's he talking about? Oh! That blessed Annunciata must be coming with him and she'll be driving his car!'

'You're going to have to get your mind very clear about that young man, I'm sorry, Fran, but you are. It's no good looking like that at me, all defiant. It's true what I say, thought you'd decided he was a waste of space before he came back and you didn't feel for him like you used to?'

'I don't feel about him like I used to, but there's something about him ... he's just so irresistible.'

'When we came back from our walk the other night, you were so happy playing with Bonnie and Alex ...'

Fran replied disdainfully, 'That's something kids do and for a few minutes that's what we were, a couple of kids, but with Chris ... grown-ups like Chris don't play with kittens. In fact, he shudders at the *thought* of touching her.'

'Not everyone likes animals, I suppose. But I'm afraid he's a cheat, Fran. You're best getting rid of him.'

'I know.' And she burst into tears again. So the two of them sat together on the bed and hugged each other. Harriet broke off from hugging and pressed on with her strategy advice.

'I know it will hurt terribly being final about it, and telling him it straight from the shoulder, but, in the end, you'll feel all the better for doing it, believe me. There are many more fish in the sea than want-it-all-with-no-commitment Chris Templeton. Honestly, Fran I know I'm right. Was she a nice person? This Annunciata or whatever she's called?'

'I don't know. She appeared to be, but there was something about her I couldn't put my finger on. I'm tired, must get to bed. Thanks for listening, Mum. You're right, I know but ...'

'Fran, next time he rings to ask you out, say no.'

'OK. OK I hear what you say. Goodnight.' Fran dragged herself off into her bathroom without a backward glance.

Harriet captured Bonnie and carried her downstairs, cursing Chris's charm and wishing he'd go back to Brazil. Surely to goodness Fran would not go with them tomorrow? Harriet really wanted to meet this woman, though, assess her for herself, not through the eyes of a lovesick twenty-one-year old. What had happened to the independent, strong-minded daughter she used to have? If Chris whistled she went running to him like a well-trained dog. She'd fallen deeply and irretrievably in love, that's what.

Chapter 5

Despite the fact that everyone knew about the trunk Peter had finally rescued from that exceptionally awkward corner in the Rectory loft, and that an extremely elderly lady in the nursing home where Vera still worked had, in one of her many protracted ramblings, revealed the reasons for Greta's distress, it could be said that whereas gossip usually flew round the three villages within twenty-four hours, Greta's huge family secret appeared to be known to very few, and now after several weeks, Greta had become convinced that she had escaped the wrath of the village gossips. Occasionally she had a bad night when she awoke about three in the morning with the whole story pounding about her brain and the shame of it would get the better of her, but by lunchtime the following day she'd be over it and all she longed for was bedtime and the chance to catch up on her sleep.

If Peter had examined the papers in the trunk it wouldn't take much speculation on his part, with his sharp mind, to understand the bare bones. But maybe there was more than just the bare bones of the events described in it. And did the revelations in the trunk make her so evil that she shouldn't mix with decent people, Greta asked herself? She'd worry about that, but then she and Jimbo would have one of their humorous exchanges and she'd feel convinced her secret was safe, because if anyone knew about it Jimbo, with his love of gossip, would be sure to know and he never ever mentioned it.

More than anything Greta dreaded her boys knowing about it and with the time growing ever nearer when she and Vince would be off to Canada on her much-longed for trip ... she was so deep in thought that when the door of her mail order office unexpectedly burst open late one afternoon she almost jumped out of her skin.

There stood Peter with his face creased by that wonderful compassionate smile of his and his bright blue eyes shining with love. Greta flushed bright red because of the ridiculous trembling she felt in her knees. He always had this effect on her and she should have been used to it by now, but she never would be. 'Sir! What a nice surprise!'

'How many times must I say it, my name is Peter, after all these years!'

'It's disrespectful to your calling for someone like me to call you Peter.' Greta fidgeted with a corner of her apron, a nervous habit she could never cure herself of.

'Everyone else does and I don't see why you shouldn't. However, if you feel better calling me "sir" then I shall have to put up with it.' He smiled again and then added, 'Greta, I haven't seen you for weeks, where have you been hiding yourself?'

'Not been too well.'

Peter closed the door to the mail order office and said, 'I thought you might have gone to Canada to see your boys.'

'That's a while away yet, not until the summer.'

'So you're still going, then?'

'Try and stop me! I can't wait.'

'And Vince – how does he feel about it? I heard he didn't want to go.'

'He didn't, but he is going. I told him if he didn't *I* was, all by myself. He said I daren't do that and I said I would because nothing and nobody was going to stop me and when he realised I was definitely going on my own, he grumbled that he'd have to go with me as I wasn't fit to go all that way by myself. The big fibber! It was just his excuse. He's just as keen as me to go, but most of the time he doesn't admit it.' Greta grinned at Peter and added, 'There's more than one way of skinning a cat.'

'Good, good. I'm glad you're both going.' Peter turned to check the door was still safely closed and then faced Greta again. 'You know about the trunk I found in the loft, of course?' He knew she did but had found it difficult to mention without some kind of preamble. He had finished reading Mary Cuttler's diary and had been saddened and horrified by what he'd learned. 'You know I will not divulge anything I found out by reading what I did. It must be hard for you, Greta. Have you always known about the black magic and what had happened?'

'My mother told me years ago, on one of her bad days when she hated me more than she usually did. I'd annoyed her ... dropped a bowl and it smashed and the custard and the bits of the bowl spattered out all over the kitchen floor. She told me then. Oh, sir, I couldn't leave home fast enough. Got a live-in job at a house over Little Derehams way and never spoke to her again until two days before she died. Vince said I had to make my peace with her before it was too late. So I did. But truth to tell I didn't mean it. Well, I meant it when I said it because no one should have to die such a tortured death as she did, but when she was dead I knew I hadn't wanted to make my peace with her, not really. It should have been her doing it, after all the years of my life she'd ruined with her hate.'

'I'm glad you did say what you said before she died, it was the right thing to do. After all it was she who'd suffered in the first place, and afterwards she'd never forget what had happened. Never feel guilty about it, Greta, because it wasn't your fault. There's no burden of guilt to be laid at your door.'

Greta began fidgeting with the hem of her apron again and not daring to look Peter in the face she muttered softly, 'Makes you feel ... d-dirty.'

'Don't let it. It's not you that's to blame like I've said, *you* are the innocent one, never forget that.' He raised his right hand and made the sign of the cross on Greta's forehead. 'God loves you and always will, so be at peace.' Peter opened the mail order office door, and before he left he asked her, 'When do you move to your new premises, by the way?'

'In the New Year, sir. Both me and Vince are looking forward to it.'

Greta stood absolutely still for about five minutes after Peter left, running over in her mind how much she appreciated what he'd said and how very genuine were his words. He could find the right words, whereas others wouldn't if they ever found out. One thing for certain, he'd never tell, she could rely completely on that fact. The day he came here was the best thing that had ever happened to this village, she thought. That poor old Rev. Furbank, him that was before Peter, if *he'd* ever found out her secret he'd have told the whole wide world and then been amazed when she, Greta Jones, had committed suicide because of it. And she'd been close to it time and again in her teens. It was the shame— Her reverie was broken by a commotion in the Store. Greta glanced at her clock, nine-forty, it was no good, she'd have to go help because there was only Fran and Bel in there this morning. What on earth was going on? She slammed and locked her office door, stuffed the key in her apron pocket and marched purposefully into the front shop.

Mayhem reigned. It was them Fitch kids again, behaving like hooligans. They'd done it only last week, but this time it was more vicious. All of them had lost control of themselves; two customers who'd been innocently choosing their shopping were clinging to each other by the coffee machine, Bel was trying to safeguard the till, but Ross's little fingers were scooping the small change out and he was pushing his booty into his trouser pockets as fast as he could, Max had a Turnham Malpas Store carrier bag in his hand and was filling it with chocolate bars while Judd and Gemma were throwing handfuls of sweets at each other. Fran was shouting to no avail and Greta knew she had to strike. Immediately. She reached across and turned off the main light switch. Instantly they were in total darkness. Ross began to scream as he was afraid of the dark,

Gemma and Judd couldn't throw sweets and because the village had no street lighting and it was now half past four and black as night outside, there was no light inside whatsoever.

Greta was livid. 'You stupid children! What do you think yer doing? Wait till I tell your dad what you've been up to. I'm not turning the lights on until you've all said "Sorry." Right? Sorry and meaning it. I'm waiting. I haven't heard anything yet. None of you move. Do you hear me. Do not move. I'm still waiting for an apology. When you've all said "Sorry" I'll put the lights back on. You're hooligans, do you know that? Hooligans. I thought the lot of you would behave better than this. Wait till I tell Mr Fitch, your granddad. He'll be so disappointed in you. Ross! Keep still and stop screaming. *Now.*'

His small voice said sorry, followed slowly by three more voices each saying sorry.

'That's more like it. When I turn the lights back on you've to put everything back. Do you hear me? *Everything.* Sweets, chocolate, money so that when Mr Charter-Plackett comes back, in about five minutes he can look round and not know what you've been up to. Mr Charter-Plackett is not a pretty sight when he's cross, believe me. He'd frighten the devil himself, he would. I know. Right, I'm putting the lights on. Everything back, remember. OK?'

To her utter surprise, once their eyes had adjusted to the brightness of the lights they quietly did as she told them. Bel and Fran and Greta helped a little but left them with enough to do in order to drive the lesson well and truly home.

'Thank you. Oops! You've missed those two sweets just by the leg of the freezer, look Max. Ross, shake your pockets please.' Greta held her hand close to her ear looking as though she was listening really hard for the sound of jingling coins and she heard them all right. 'You've missed those. Get them out and give them to Bel.' Ross looked reluctant so Greta rapidly dived towards him and Ross, scared out of his wits, hurriedly got them out and then jumped up and down and no one could hear the sound of coins clinking.

'Thank you, Ross. Now,' said Greta firmly, 'how are you going to get home?'

Gemma, being the eldest there, turned her big dark eyes towards Greta and said in the most civilised and reasonable manner but with a hint of vulnerability in it, 'We shall have to walk home in the dark. And we're scared of the dark in the country ...'

Greta was contemplating the next step in teaching them a lesson, desperately hoping Jimbo would walk in. And miraculously he did just that. Knowing nothing about the mayhem they had just caused all he saw was four of those Fitch children with all four pairs of eyes, mutely intent on Greta Jones. Such well-behaved children, he thought, and such nice parents – Stella had arrived at the Store first thing in the morning, the day after he'd delivered her shopping, full of apologies for not getting down the night before.

'Oh! Good evening, Mr Charter-Plackett, you've come just in time,' Greta said. 'These children are needing a lift home because with it being dark we can't ask them to walk all that way by themselves, now can we, and they claim they are not quite sure how to get there anyway with being new to Turnham Malpas. No moon you see.' There was something significant about her raised eyebrows and the solemn manner of her speech and Jimbo guessed his next job was taking these children home.

Jimbo gracefully invited them to get into his car and drove them home. Not a word was spoken all the way there and each one as they piled out, said, 'Thank you, Mr Charter-Plackett.' And disappeared into the house. What delightful children, thought Jimbo. So well mannered.

He heard the whole story from Fran when he got home and he was rather less kindly disposed then. 'I can't believe it. They were so well behaved in my car. Stealing from the till? Pinching chocolate bars? Throwing sweets about? I don't believe it!'

Fran agreed with him. 'Neither do we, Dad, but it's true. Greta was brilliant. Bel and I tried to stop them but we had no effect at all. It was Greta who calmed them down and took charge. She turned the lights off, you see, with the master switch and they couldn't see a thing.'

'They'll be in school tomorrow,' he saide decisively. 'I'll go up to Nightingale Farm and spill the beans. They're like people with two personalities those children, like a kind of Jekyll and Hyde. I wonder what they're like in school?'

'Apparently they are extremely difficult, even little Ross in the nursery, Kate's seriously worried about them,' Harriet told him.

'Must be very worrying for her, her being their surrogate grand-mother so to speak. '

The first words Jimbo said when he got back from Nightingale Farm the next day were, 'Graham and Anita are out of their minds with worry.'

Fran answered, 'So would I be if I were their mother. Someone whose little boy comes on the school bus with them every day told me how dreadful they are and if she hadn't got newborn twins at home she'd take her son to school herself rather than take the risk. Apparently they are out of control.'

'I wonder if old Fitch knows?'

'Dad! Of course he must, remember Kate? The headmistress is Kate Fitch, his wife.'

'Of course, yes. I must be going crackers. Of course I knew, just didn't put it together.'

'First sign of old age, Dad? Confusion? Mmm?' Fran grinned at him. 'Did they apologise?'

'Profusely.'

'Well, that's something I suppose. Must be murder living with them.'

'Apparently they've changed out of all recognition. Where they lived before, in Leeds, they were renowned for their good behaviour, in school and out of school. Here four of them are absolute scallywags. Sarah, the eldest, is fine. She's at secondary school in Culworth, being twelve, and is loving it. No problems at all.'

'Maybe they just don't like the countryside. I mean there're no shops, nothing going on, no handy cinema etc., etc., and, to boot, relaxed happy-go-lucky farming children for companions. Let's face it, the children at the school here are not exactly the sharpest knives in the drawer, are they?' Fran shrugged her shoulders. 'Most of them would rather be catching tadpoles or doing a butterfly survey or riding their ponies or something, or feeding the chickens.'

'But all of the Charter-Placketts were all right there, Fran, happy as a pig in muck you all were, weren't you?'

'Thanks for the reference, Dad. Pig in muck indeed!' Inspired by what Jimbo had just said, she expanded on her theory. 'Maybe that's just what they need, though, some animals to look after – and I don't just mean a couple of guinea pigs. Something big and with a need to be cared for. I know... a neglected donkey. They've got the stables, haven't they? And they've kept two fields nearest the house for themselves. Do we know a donkey in need of a home?'

'I haven't met one just recently. Sorry. But it *is* a thought. You could ring that vet you took Bonnie to for her injections, he might know of someone.'

'Excellent idea, Dad. I'll do that right now.'

'No, no you won't! What you will do is speak to Graham or Anita first – they might think it's the worst idea since Hitler decided to take over Russia.'

'You have a point there, yes, I'll do that. Which comes first, though, the permission or the donkey? No point in asking either of them if there are no donkeys. On the other hand no point in raising anyone's hopes that they've got the possibility of a home for a donkey they can no longer look after.'

Jimbo clutched his head in desperation. 'Stop. Stop! I can't puzzle about it any more, I've got to get on right now. *You* sort it.' He fled to his office and shut the door firmly behind him.

He'd had enough problems when they were all growing up, what with Finlay and his nervous tic, Fergus with his bedwetting, Flick with her wilful determination to do as she liked right from day one and Fran, well, there was nothing in particular about Fran except this current problem of that dratted Chris Templeton and her miscarriage. But why should he worry about those problem grandchildren of old Fitch, they weren't his responsibility after all, though if he'd any more trouble with them they'd be banned from the Store for life. He'd have a word with Greta, she seemed to have frightened the life out of them.

He opened his office door and bellowed, 'Greta! Got a minute? In my office.'

There was a short delay – no doubt he'd cut right across her concentration – and she finally arrived looking anxious. 'Yes, what's up?'

'Nothing's up. I just wanted to say thank you for stopping the Fitch grandchildren from destroying my beloved Store. You did a good job there, so if they come in again and start trouble I shall send for you.'

'Mmm! Well, I'm not too sure about that, it might just have been a fluke, but by hell! They don't half need some discipline, the little devils.'

'Their parents are at their wits end,' he said. 'I've just been to tell them about yesterday. They were horrified. Moving has upset the children no end. Apparently Kate is having problems with them all at school, even that little heartbreaker, Ross, in the nursery.'

'He *looks* angelic, he does. Mind you, five children; it's an awful lot o' kids. Glad I didn't have five. You'll have to ban 'em if they cause trouble again. By the way, if the reverend comes in I've got his hat; he left it by mistake, but if he doesn't come back for it I'll take it over to the Rectory when I leave.'

Greta turned to go.

'Was he wanting to see me?'

'No. Me.'

'You! Oh! Right,' Jimbo raised an eyebrow, inviting Greta to enlighten him. But she didn't and he was disappointed. He'd hoped for a bit of gossip to cheer his day but obviously he wasn't going to get it from Greta. 'Must press on.'

'By the way, that order for twelve jars of the new runner bean chutney, the credit card isn't valid so I'm not posting the order. I've tried three times to make contact and there's no joy. It's wrapped, ready to go though, if and when ...'

'Thanks, Greta. Where we'd be without your organisation I do not know. Give Fran a talking to about pitfalls, she'll be in charge while you're in Canada next year.'

'She'll do a good job, you can always rely on her.'

'I know, but your experience counts for a lot. I shall miss our little talks when you move to the Old Barn.'

'So will I! But I shall be glad of more space – that's the problem now we've expanded so much. I used to do about twelve orders a day on a good day, now it's more like fifty or sixty a day on a normal day that is, not at Easter or Christmas and with the meat and that, when Vince starts on that, well ... heaven alone knows how much will be going out. But by Jove I love it!! The more orders the better, that's what I say. But you've never decided on how he'll get his orders off, have you? There's no room in that little cage of a Post Office Tom has for huge sides of beef to wait and be collected.'

'I like your confidence about how busy we shall be, Greta!' Jimbo laughed. 'And don't worry, Vince and I will have a talk about it.'

'OK then, I'll leave it to you.' Greta turned to leave but Jimbo had other ideas.

'Everything all right with you? Not still upset are you?'

'Me? Upset? No. Just glad to be busy.'

Greta hastened away from him. Before she knew where she was he'd have it all out of her and she wasn't having that. The longer she could keep her secret the better it would be for her and Vince.

Chapter 6

Fran, just back from going round the villages collecting the home-made produce they sold in the Store and on the internet, heard her dad talking to someone in the front of the Store and immediately recognised who it was. Oh, no! Not Chris. Not when she'd made up her mind that she wanted nothing more to do with him. As far as she was concerned it was the end of Chris for her. But this determination was fine only so long as she didn't speak to him. Then it was easy to keep her word, but she only had to hear his voice or see him smile at her and her iron will would immediately disintegrate and she was back remembering ... remembering the pressure of his lips on hers and what it did to her heartbeat, the wonderful aroma of his exceedingly expensive aftershave, the feel of his hand on the small of her back – and just recently she'd realised that his muscles were no longer wasted as they had been when he'd first come back from Brazil which reminded her of his passion in earlier times. Damn it!

Blasted Brazil, why couldn't he just have stayed there for ever? One thing for sure, though, she couldn't hide in the kitchen pretending to be busy any longer. So, today she simply wouldn't give in to that rush of excitement that came out of nowhere, today she'd be polite but detached. Friendly but not emotional. Considerate but abrupt. Well, as much detached as she could be with her heartbeat accelerating when she'd told it not to.

She walked into the front of the Store as though she didn't know he was around.

'Dad! Have you finished ... oh! Hello, Chris! Haven't seen you for a while, thought you must have gone back home to Brazil.'

'No, still here. Annunciata's gone back but not me. Been trying to build up my strength so I've got a physio coming three times a week, can't spend the rest of my life a weakling, can I now? Got to get back into shape and test my muscles – you know how I was when I first came back. How are you, sweetheart? Working hard?'

'Dad's a hard taskmaster, believe me.'

She wasn't going to touch him but he'd held out his right arm and braced his muscles for her to test, drat him! His eyes were sparkling but she wasn't going to let him know how reluctant she was. So she stretched out her hand and squeezed his forearm as hard as she could. Oh yes! There was a big improvement. But she said, 'Not fully up to strength yet, though.'

She could see he was disappointed she hadn't been completely amazed by the change. Honestly, a grown man almost begging for her approval!

'I was wondering when it was your day off? Perhaps you could show me a walk I could tackle to improve my leg muscles. The physio is brilliant, but I really need to exercise every single day.'

Here we go she thought. 'I would have imagined Johnny would be able to help you with that; after all he owns most of the land around here. Ask him.' Fran briefly turned away to ask Bel a question about whether or not there was enough change in the till for the two part-timers who came in to work the last two opening hours, a perfectly pointless one because she knew the answer anyway, but it served to snub Chris.

'Must press on, Chris. Glad you're feeling better. I'm just about ready for off, Dad. OK?'

Chris stood perfectly still resembling a spare part never to be required again. 'What about a meal tonight at The Wise Man? Johnny and Alice have a baby sitter in while they snatch an hour or two out on their own. Take pity on a lonely bachelor?'

Fran deliberately took a moment or two to think about her

answer. Yes, she would, she would test herself. 'The friend I was going out with has rung to say they've got a ghastly bug and can't leave the house, so shall I, Dad?'

'Up to you, Fran,' Jimbo said after a moment, hoping that this would give her an opportunity to sort Chris out once and for all.

'Then that would be lovely, thanks Chris,' she said, turning to face Chris. Test or not, she cursed herself for letting him win because her heart began pumping furiously and she knew she'd agreed because that was what she wanted. All that thinking about finishing with him and the harsh words she used when she thought about him and his neglect of her, when she'd lost the ... no, it was fifty per cent her fault and fifty per cent his so ... Chris, feeling he'd healed the breach between them, took hold of the hand that was nearest to him and pressed it to his lips. 'We'll meet there shall we?'

'You're driving then, now?'

'Just around and about, not long distances. See you then.'

Jimbo tried to catch her eye when Chris was safely out of the way but Fran wouldn't even look at him.

'I'll be off then.' And Fran left without another word, leaving Jimbo livid with disappointment.

Would she never learn he thought? Chris had only come to see her because he was at a loose end now Annunci-whatsit had gone back to Brazil. He'd a good mind to go to The Wise Man tonight with Harriet and sit it out, glaring at the two of them. Even though he acknowledged it was Fran's life and she had a right to live it as she wished, he would love to do it.

Decision made, he picked up the phone and rang Harriet.

Under the illusion that Fran was going out with a school friend of hers, Harriet, late home, showered to make sure she didn't smell of cooking which she'd been working hard at all day, flung fresh clothes on and hastened out after Jimbo who was impatiently waiting outside in the car.

'If we're only going to The Wise Man I can't see why we have to rush out at this speed,' she protested. 'They never are full on weekdays. It's only really at the weekends they're terribly busy.'

'I'm hungry. Missed my pork pie at lunchtime again. Are you in? Belt fastened?'

'Yes.'

And Jimbo hurtled off. However, realising he was making Harriet suspicious with his haste he slowed down. 'Of course you're absolutely right, Harriet, they won't be busy – they never are on Tuesdays. You've had a busy day?'

'Yes. Very busy. I'm thinking of taking on a trainee, by the way, straight from college. I can't keep up the pace.'

Jimbo reached across and patted her knee. 'Of course, why not? You deserve more help.'

Rather surprised at Jimbo's immediate agreement Harriet replied, 'Good. I'll get onto that first thing before you look at the figures and change your mind.' She laughed and Jimbo did too, glad she was in a happy mood because very shortly she wouldn't be. He began to feel a complete cheat for the trick he was playing on his nearest and dearest.

But Chris and Fran weren't in the dining room so maybe they had changed their minds. Jimbo felt thoroughly deflated by the thought of missing his big moment, because he'd hyped himself up to give that Chris an absolute roasting in front of a full dining room.

He and Harriet chose a table and had a glass of wine each while they decided on what they wanted to eat. They both chose steak, with a jacket potato for Jimbo and French fries for Harriet as she didn't need to lose weight, and a selection of vegetables.

'You know, it's so nice to come out and let someone else do the cooking,' Harriet said, smiling. 'In fact, it's not just nice, it's wonderful! Such a pleasure. And see, I told you it wouldn't be very busy tonight and I was right. I'm glad you chose the wine, Jimbo. I never have got on with that business of saying things like, "there's an underlying flavour of thyme over laid by Turkish delight" or some such rot. To me wine is wine and tastes like it does and if I don't like it I don't pretend I do just because it's cost a hundred pounds a bottle or it's come from some obscure vineyard which is "beginning to make a name for itself". Load of old rubbish it all is.'

'That's my Harriet, no pretence. I love you for your honesty. I really do,' he said, meaning every word.

'How else should one be but honest, when the alternative is being a liar?'

'I agree.' Jimbo began to feel hot under the collar.

'That's the trouble with Chris Templeton – it's hard to know when he's being honest. I always feel he's being nice only to get his own way, manipulative you know. I mean, he didn't really love Fran when he did what he did, did he?'

Jimbo began to feel even worse and wished he'd never come up with this idea. 'Maybe he did, just at that moment.'

Harriet jeered at Jimbo's reply. 'And then again maybe he didn't! I understand Annunci-Whatever-she's-called has gone back to Brazil so I expect he'll be sniffing round Fran again. Damn the man!' She shook her head then toasted Jimbo and then sipped her wine. 'This is rather good. Yes, you've made a good choice and I am absolutely starving. Where's my steak, I say, where's my steak?' She took a moment to look around the dining room, 'Oh look! There's that dreadful woman I met in Culworth a couple of weeks ago in the loo at the Abbey. I couldn't get away because she talked endlessly. Oh help! She's recognised me and now she's waving.' Harriet raised her glass to the woman and toasted her in acknowledgement. 'My word I'm glad I'm not married to that man she's with – always supposing they are married. He looks a complete out-and-out rotter. *He* wouldn't know the truth if it jumped up and hit him.'

Jimbo grinned. 'I hope you'll be more like yourself when you've eaten, because you're being very critical tonight, Harriet.'

'Tired, that's what I am. Tired.'

As they began eating, Jimbo, who was facing the stairs leading to the bedrooms they'd renovated for the new B&B side of the business, caught sight of Chris and Fran coming down the stairs, hand-in-hand. He'd never been anywhere near to a heart attack in all his life but at this moment in time he felt almighty close to one. What was Fran thinking about? They'd obviously been making use of one of the bedrooms if they'd been upstairs though they both looked a bit tense.

'Harriet! Darling. Guess who's here.'

Harriet, eager to devour her food, didn't take a blind bit of notice of the tremor in his voice.

'Someone we know here, then?'

'Oh! Yes. Definitely.' Jimbo raised a wary hand to Fran and Chris, 'Hi! Didn't know you were coming here. Surprise, surprise!'

Alerted by the pretend amazement in his voice Harriet looked up. By now Chris and Fran were level with their own table, but whereas Jimbo, half prepared for the chance of seeing them, had a rigid smile on his face, Harriet leapt to her feet saying loudly, 'What *do* you think you're doing, Fran? Have you gone mad?'

One of the diners, who, like Jimbo, had seen them coming down the stairs from the bedrooms, snorted his amusement and then added, 'Whatever they've been doing he looks to have had a great time!'

'Fran!? Chris!?' Knowing immediately she was making a fool not only of herself but also of Chris and Fran, Harriet picked up the napkin she'd dropped, sat herself down again and said, in a very controlled voice, 'How lovely seeing you here, just sorry we're on a table for two otherwise you could have joined us.' She followed her last sentence with a synthetically sweet smile.

Chris, unabashed, leaned forward to shake Jimbo's hand and then Harriet's saying, 'Lovely to see you both,' in the most pleasing tone, then taking hold of Fran's elbow added, 'We'll sit over there, leave you to it. Your steak looks like a good choice.'

Fran, speechless and intensely aware that tonight she'd made the biggest mistake of her life to date, allowed Chris to guide her to a table as far away as possible from her parents. He thought it rather amusing to have been caught out, but he knew from Fran's face that she was deeply upset.

When he'd got her settled Chris said softly, 'You are an adult, you know, and free to do as you choose. Look here's the menu, what do you fancy? Your parents' steaks looked good. We'll both have steak then, shall we?'

'There you go again, telling me what to eat now. You won't allow me to do as I choose – in anything.'

Puzzled, Chris looked up saying, 'What do you mean? Didn't I do exactly what you said you wanted upstairs?'

'Only because I got angry and wouldn't sleep with you! I didn't come here tonight thinking about bedrooms, Chris, it was the last option of all as far as I was concerned. But the bedroom was already booked and Chris Templeton was heading straight for it without so much as a by-your-leave.'

'I thought that would be what you wanted, it's been a while since we—' The waiter was there asking if they had chosen what they wanted to eat, and would they like a drink first.

Fran slapped her copy of the menu down on the table, and said, 'I honestly couldn't eat a thing I am so angry. And don't attempt to persuade me, Chris, because if I try to eat I shall be sick. My parents sitting over there must be convinced I've gone completely mad seeing me come down from the bedrooms with you!'

'Their opinion doesn't matter one bit. They're another generation and their standards just don't count. Not now, not in this day and age. You live your life like you want to, there's no need to judge what you do by their old-fashioned outdated ideas. You're as free as air – you are, Fran. Come on! Cheer up! You'll feel better when you've eaten. Darling! Please!'

But Fran stood up and said more loudly than she realised, 'This, Chris, is the last time you'll have the opportunity to persuade me to do anything at all. I don't want to see you ever again. The only reason you wanted to see me tonight was because Annunciata has gone back to Brazil and is no longer here willing to ...' Every person dining in that room waited with bated breath for her next sentence. 'Devote herself to your well-being. Well, that's a polite way of putting it! Neither am I willing to, not any more. So goodnight, Chris, thank you for all the fun we've had in the past. You are good company, I'll say that for you, but I'm just glad we came in our own cars tonight. Goodbye. Enjoy your meal.'

Jimbo's skin shivered as he saw the bravery shining forth from Fran's face when she marched away from that creep of a Chris Templeton. He half rose from his chair, intending to catch up with Fran to give her a great big well-deserved hug, but Harriet shook her head.

'Leave her, she's making a brilliant exit and it serves him right. Let us give thanks that she has finally seen the light. God! he looks furious!'

Chris sat there until he'd absorbed what Fran had said and he had then come to the conclusion that she was completely wrong. She was quite simply incapable of recognising what a thoroughly worthwhile chap he was. Look at what she would be missing out on – all his money for a start, his charm, his sparkling conversation, his intuitive understanding of what a woman looks for in a man, and his good looks. There wasn't a woman living who wouldn't acknowledge they'd be proud to be seen out with him. The thing was, he could very easily have proposed tonight. Well, it was her loss. Plenty of other fish in the sea. He went back to studying the menu, but couldn't see a single meal he fancied.

He'd go back to Turnham House, get the sitter-in to make him a sandwich and then plan how to go about getting Fran back on side.

At home Jimbo and Harriet, anxious about her welfare, were brought up short by the notice taped to Fran's bedroom door. It read:

Do not disturb. I'm sorry you witnessed the scene we created in The Wise Man. I feel better for what I said. I need to change my life completely. Goodnight. Love Fran.

They crept away and retired to their bedroom for a conference.

Harriet flung herself down on the bed saying, 'What a night! As for that nice quiet meal we'd looked forward to ... I think she's going to leave home don't you? That's what she means by *Change my life completely.*'

Jimbo shook his head. 'No. Not Fran. She loves working in the Store, she won't do that. Not her.'

'You wait and see, Jimbo! Oh, I could kill that man. Picking her up like that just because there's no Anni-whatsit! He must think of her as a ... a tart.'

'Exactly! I'm wondering if I should go up there and see him and ...'

'... and what, Jimbo? And what? She's grown-up, she's not a child. She told him in no uncertain terms exactly where she stands so leave it be. I'm going to bed; I shan't sleep I don't suppose, but that's the price we pay for having children.'

Jimbo nodded. 'She gave a magnificent performance, didn't she? I was so proud of her.'

'So was I. And tomorrow the Store will be buzzing with it, so prepare yourself.' Harriet put her bedside light on. 'There's bound to have been someone there from around here who knows us and gleefully enjoyed the entertainment they provided. But Jimbo, I got the feeling you didn't seem all that surprised when you saw them.'

'Me?'

'Yes, you.'

'I was surprised. I was.' He felt ashamed of his deception and wished he'd never thought of it, let alone carried it out. Should he confess? No, it would only make matters even more complicated than they already were so he said, 'Maybe we did her a good turn being there. Made her recognise where her roots really are, not with some fly-by-night who picks her up and puts her down as and when he feels like it. I could kill him for it, treating her like a tart. Maybe I should go up there to Turnham House and do the dirty deed – one of your big carving knives straight through his heart, mmm? Right now I'm capable of it. What do you think?'

'Certainly not! I won't allow it, Jimbo, not even just to talk. You keep right out of telling Johnny what a so-and-so his brother is. Our concern is Fran.' Harriet sighed. 'You know he has had a tremendous attraction for her, but now she's told him to his face in public what she thinks of him, so leave it be.'

'I still think a carving knife is the best solution. It's what he deserves. Too much money, too much sexual attraction, too much charm, and absolutely no understanding of other people and what makes them tick. I've decided that I *am* going to have a private word with Johnny. Surely he must have enough influence to make him go home, don't you think?'

Getting no response he turned to look at Harriet and found he'd been talking to himself. Perhaps as well thought Jimbo, this is a man's job and the man in this house will do that very thing tomorrow without asking anyone for their opinion.

Which he did first thing the next morning on the pretence of going to the Old Barn to check that Pat Jones had the right number of staff organised for the high-flying lunch Harriet had been cooking for all the previous day.

Chapter 7

Despite the freezing weather, this particular day had turned out to be almost the best of the winter so far. The Old Barn when Jimbo called in there was a hive of activity and his spirits lifted enormously as he saw Pat Jones in her smart black suit hurtling about keeping everyone busy laying tables, organising the flowers, checking cutlery, sorting tablecloths.

'Pat. Good morning! Thought I'd call in to check you were coping OK. You found the extra staff you needed, I see.'

'Morning, Jimbo. Yes, I did.' She surveyed the hectic but organised activity with delight, remembering how once she was the humble school caretaker and now she was in charge of all this. Who would believe it? 'We're well ahead with our plans, no need to worry.'

'I never do worry when you're in charge. Tell me: Greta, your dear mother-in-law, is she all right now?'

'My mother-in-law is fine, thanks. Why?'

'I meant about that scare she had over the trunk and what Peter found. I honestly thought she would be stopping working over it.'

Pat gave Jimbo a long hard stare. 'Has she told you about it then? You know what the problem is?'

'Not a word.'

'Because my Barry, even though he's her eldest son and the most reliable of the three, even he doesn't know. It's obviously something very difficult about Greta herself and we might be able to help if only she would tell us what's up. I don't think Vince knows, but then again, he's good at secrets is Vince, under torture he wouldn't give anything away.'

Jimbo laughed along with Pat and the two of them agreed they didn't know and most likely wouldn't ever know.

'Must press on Jimbo. Leave everything with me.' Pat turned away leaving Jimbo admiring the well-organised bustle that would bring hundreds of pounds into his coffers. Then he recollected the urgent business he had to attend to with Sir Johnny Templeton, lord of this Village's manor.

Turnham House was looking superb this morning in the bright sunlight, with the slight hint of frost touching the roof tiles and whitening the brickwork enhancing its attraction. What a responsibility to own a property like this! Grade Two listed and all that entails. Jimbo really rather felt it would be a project even he couldn't undertake. Such a big improvement, though, taking down the swimming pool extension old Fitch had bribed the council to let him build; pulling it down had transformed the house into something exquisitely beautiful.

Johnny and Alice were standing outside the front door with their two little boys, obviously ready for a walk as they were all well wrapped in overcoats and fleeces and woolly hats and scarves.

Jimbo swung his car round, parked, switched off the engine and called out cheerfully as he opened his car door, 'Good morning, one and all! Charles! My word you are growing fast, and Ralph, you're walking! Wonderful. What a clever boy. Came for a word with you Johnny but ...'

'That's OK. It's Alice who's going out and me who's just back from the farm. So if it's me you need to see ...?'

'Yes, it is. Not to say I would be glad to see you too, Alice.'

Johnny kissed Alice, patted the boys on their heads and, opening the front door, invited Jimbo inside. They settled down in what had been Craddock Fitch's office, with Johnny behind the desk and Jimbo sitting opposite him.

Neither of them spoke and then they both broke the silence at the same moment.

Johnny said, 'I've an idea I know what this is about. My farm manager celebrated his wedding anniversary at The Wise Man last night.'

Jimbo said at the same time, 'It's Chris, I've ...'

'You first, Jimbo.'

'Ah! Right.' He cleared his throat, crossed his legs and leaned back in his chair. 'I haven't spoken to Fran today yet, because it's her day off so she'll still in bed. However, you know what happened?'

'No, I don't, because Alistair said if anyone should tell me what happened last night it should be my brother, not one of my employees, and then he shut up and went into an in-depth discussion about mating the lamas – which I thought was rather appropriate in the circumstances if Chris was involved.'

Jimbo leaned forward to emphasise his point. 'Well, Johnny, I think "irate father" might be a good description of me at the moment. I am so angry about the way your brother is treating my daughter that I've half a mind to come up here and stab him clean through the heart! I asked Harriet if she'd lend me one of her carving knives from the Old Barn kitchens but she didn't think that was a very good idea. By the way, I haven't told her I was coming here this morning, and I don't want her to know.'

Jimbo told Johnny of the events that had taken place in the pub dining room the night before, remembering word for word Fran's memorable speech, unwittingly spoken so loudly that everyone present heard and understood every word she said. 'He only took her out for a meal and, without her knowledge, booked the bedroom because that Brazilian woman had gone back home and he had no one to ... well ... anyway, I don't need to explain that to you. I want him back in Brazil. It seems to me that's the best place for him.' Jimbo sat back in his chair again and waited for a response.

'I can't just order him about,' Johnny protested.

'Why not? He's reached the point where he is detrimental to the way in which you want your relationship with the village to go. He besmirches you and your reputation every time he puts his nose out of your door. I want him gone, Johnny. Tomorrow wouldn't be soon enough. It occurs to me to question how many other girls round here besides our Fran he has got involved with? The most enormous scandal could be brewing up right now – are you going to let him live here until it erupts? Best upstage him and get rid of him before it does because it could do untold damage to you and Alice.'

'I hear what you say and I too am appalled by the things he gets up to, Jimbo, but he's been like that all his adult life and no matter what my father said to him when he was alive, Chris didn't change. My mother thinks the sun shines out of him and he can do no wrong. Just a boy, she says, not a man yet, he'll learn. But it's taking him an almighty long time to grow up.'

Jimbo shook his head angrily. 'But he *is* an adult and has been for some time and I do not take kindly to my daughter being treated like dirt! You understand me, Johnny, something has to be done about him and I reckon Brazil is the best place for him. Remember what I've said: he's a danger to everyone he comes in contact with, and that includes you and Alice.'

Jimbo got to his feet and left. But he was almost shaking with temper at the fact that Johnny had portrayed himself as someone incapable of insisting his brother was no longer welcome to stay in his house. Whatever kind of man was he to allow this rotten-to-the-core brother of his to remain in the village?

He arrived home to find Harriet and Fran together in the kitchen talking, but they stopped abruptly as he walked in.

'I'd like a coffee too, please, if I may.' He decided to continue being outspoken this morning. 'Now Fran, what have you got to say for yourself? After last night's episode?'

'That I never want to see Chris ever again. Just like I said last night, as far as I am concerned he can go to hell.'

'Do you mean it, though?'

'I do, never more certain of anything in the whole of my life. But, as I've just been saying to Mum, I've decided I'm going to university. Which one and what for I do not know, but going I am. I've got top grades in A levels despite Grandmama's derision at my not having benefited from private education like the others. Too late to apply this year, but I will apply for October next year. I think I need a broader experience of life than I get here in the village, then perhaps I shall be more astute in my relationships than I am now. You can manage without me for three years, can't you, Dad? I'll have lots of time to help you when I'm home from university, won't I?'

Appalled by her decision, Jimbo managed to sound as though he welcomed her leaving. 'I shall miss you, darling Fran, but if you feel that's what you want to do, then so be it. Go for it, I say.'

'Thanks, Dad, for supporting me. And from now on if that Chris comes in the Store asking to see me, tell him I am not available. *Definitely* not available. Oh, I have been such an idiot! But he has so much charm and he feels so vital — one touch of his hand, or his arm round my shoulders and that's it, I'm hooked all over again. If I could trust him I would marry him and go to Brazil with him tomorrow, but he's proved himself to be untrustworthy and that's no basis for a lifetime commitment is it, Dad? Not one like you and Mum have.'

Jimbo took time to finish his coffee before he replied, because he felt guilty not informing Harriet about going to see Johnny and telling him exactly what he thought about his errant brother, especially when she'd specifically asked him not to interfere. But someone had to make a move, someone who, like himself, felt entirely justified in what he said.

Chris Templeton had come downstairs for his breakfast only minutes after Jimbo had left the house. The kitchen was deserted, and Chris couldn't find anyone anywhere who would take pity on him and assemble his breakfast for him. He was disinclined to ask Becky, Alice's part-time domestic help, because she refused to have anything at all to do with him on the basis that he didn't treat her with the respect she knew she deserved. Like Alice, Becky Braithwaite had understood what made him tick from the very first moment she clapped eyes on him and his over-the-top charm certainly hadn't succeeded in winning her over.

'Frankly, Lady Templeton,' she'd said, 'I might be a lowly domestic without much brain but I will not put up with his patronising ways! I understand he's wealthy beyond belief, but that doesn't mean he can treat me like dirt, so please, don't ask me to do anything for him, because if you do it'll be a resignation job and the last thing I want to do is lose this place. Sir Johnny treats me right, so why can't his brother do the same?'

Alice, not wishing to intentionally allow this dream of a helper to leave her house never to return, accepted what Becky said, so, much against Alice's standards as a hostess, that meant that Chris got into his bed just as he left it each morning, and Alice changed the bed linen only on laundry days.

Johnny found Chris in the kitchen, struggling with the coffee machine. 'Here, let me do it.'

Once Chris's breakfast was sorted out Johnny and he sat at the table in the kitchen, Chris with his breakfast and Johnny with a very welcome mug of coffee. Johnny opened their conversation with the following sentence. 'I've had a complaint about you from an irate father.'

Chris almost choked on the first sip of his coffee, only recovering after a multitude of coughs, and said gruffly. 'No prizes for guessing who that might be. James Charter-Plackett, no doubt.'

'Indeed. The very man.'

'To hell with him, why can't he leave his daughter to fight her own battles? She's old enough.'

'Alistair, my farm manager was there and heard every word, apparently.'

'Told his beloved Lord of the Manor everything that was said, did he?'

'No, he refused to spill the beans, said it was so bad I ought to hear it from my brother himself.'

Chris stirred two spoonfuls of sugar into his coffee and didn't reply.

Johnny offered him the one remaining slice of toast. 'More toast? No? So tell me. I do know the entire dining room heard every word Fran said. It'll be all round the county by now.'

'She told me where I could go with my money and my good looks and my charm and she never wanted to see me again. She resented Annunciata deeply, you see.'

'You sound surprised. Chris, is there any wonder she resents her? You ignore Fran, carry on with Annunciata and think you can go back to Fran when Annunciata realises, at last, that she'll never get you down the aisle and goes back to Brazil and you then expect Fran to welcome you back? You are beyond belief, Chris, you really are, and I'm disgusted with you! No wonder Jimbo is angry.'

'You are a sanctimonious, self-righteous man, Johnny! You're welcome to your colourless Alice with her music and her pesky little boys. How many more of them is she going to have for you?'

Johnny leapt to his feet his face flushed with anger. 'It is absolutely none of your business how many children Alice and I have and I will not tolerate you speaking of her so disrespectfully.'

'You've enough to say about the women I go with but I can't say anything about your amours?'

'I only have *one* amour and that is Alice and she is the mother of my children and my *wife*. As of now, you are no longer welcome in this house. I want you to pack your bags, Chris, get on a plane and never darken my door again until you've learned better manners.'

'Oh! Right, I'll go, then. First thing tomorrow. I'll leave you to it – I've got a plane seat to book.' Chris stormed out of the kitchen and bounded away upstairs to his bedroom. He snatched up his phone from the beside table and began making his plans for leaving. If that was how Johnny wanted it, well, it was fine by him. It was supremely boring in Turnham Malpas anyway. In fact, at the moment, he couldn't conjure up a single place more boring.

Brazil, where there was plenty of sunshine and where the women all adored him, that was the place to be. No killjoys in Brazil: to a man they envied his lifestyle, but here it was pure jealousy that motivated everyone. Disapproval registered on every face. They were all small-minded, mean, envious and dull. Getting away was the very best action he could take. And he would. He'd not even eat with those two miseries tonight, he'd eat with ... Chris sat on his unmade bed wondering who there was who would make him welcome for a meal. He could think of no one at all, he'd made enemies of everyone.

But what the hell! It didn't matter – one more night and he'd be gone. He could even perhaps spend tonight in a hotel in London. The Ritz, the Dorchester, the Savoy ... after all, he could afford it. He'd leave most of his clothes here; that would give them something to do, imagining he intended coming back. Which he didn't. Wouldn't. Couldn't. Not when the Turnham Malpas 'bore' factor dulled his mind more than usual. It was the silence that irked him the most. Nothing going on except the rustle of leaves in the wind, the occasional car passing by, the birds chirruping with such enthusiasm – and what was there for a bird to sing about, heavens above? – nothing! All they did was sing and chirrup to annoy Christopher Templeton; endless happy birds letting the world know how fantastic they found this ancient village.

He'd buy new clothes when he got back home to his mother, who adored him no matter what he did to annoy her. All his life he'd always been her favourite, even when he was at his most disruptive. He smiled at his memories of his childhood and the trouble he'd caused playing one brother off against the other, depending on the mood he was in, It had all been such *fun*. He could still get plenty of mileage out of annoying the two of them even now.

Chris went to stand at his bedroom window, looking down at the four cars parked by the front door. His was the most vivid, most outstanding of the four. The battered old navy blue Saab belonged to Alice. He'd only spoken the truth about Alice; he honestly didn't know what Johnny saw in her. What he did know was that Alice saw clean through him, knew his every move before he made it, thus rendering it impossible to dominate her. Johnny's car was the big ancient Land Rover he'd bought from that Craddock Fitch as part of the estate. And the fourth car belonged to that foul Becky Braithwaite. She was another one who'd weighed him up immediately and found him lacking every likeable quality.

Unexpectedly, Becky came out of the front door and went to her car, opened it up, leapt into it and drove away. Chris glanced at his watch. Only just after eleven, far too early for her to leave. Funny that. Where on earth was she going? He found himself as interested and as curious as someone from the village would be and he grew angry with himself. He'd been here far too long ... and why? All because of the attraction he felt to Fran. In his mind he recalled the gentle female strength of her, and remembered how he'd valued her response to his overtures: she caught any mood he happened to be in, any whim, any sexual approach and spun it back to him in droves. As soon as he was told of her pregnancy he'd panicked, seriously panicked. He felt trapped, no longer an individual, no longer free as air and Chris Templeton needed to be free as air if he was to lead the kind of life he loved. The relief when he realised she was not pregnant but had already miscarried was overwhelming. He'd come far too close to fatherhood and marriage than he liked and was so filled with gratitude that she was no longer pregnant he could have skipped with joy all the way down the drive right to the gates, and back. Two miles of skipping! Wow! Miscarried! Thank God!

There came a brisk knock at his bedroom door. Before he could answer, the door was flung wide open and there stood Alice, breathing heavily and with a face like thunder, struggling to control her voice.

'Johnny's told me what happened last night at The Wise Man. Have you no respect for anyone except yourself? Fran Charter-Plackett of all people! There couldn't be a nicer girl in the county and you make her give the performance of her life in a crowded pub. I imagined you'd done enough damage there, but how wrong I was. There won't be a single person in the whole of the three villages who won't know what's happened!'

Chris slowly got to his feet and, facing her, he said gently (after all seeing as he was leaving it wouldn't do any harm for Alice to think he regretted what he'd done). 'I didn't *make* her say what she said. She just came out with it and no one was more surprised than me.'

'You are a creep, Chris! From head to toe, that is what you are. Best thing you can do is go back to your ever-loving, all-adoring mother and stay there! You are not getting another meal in this house. I don't expect Johnny will tell you to go – you trained him too well over the years – but *I'm* not afraid of upsetting you. I want you out, immediately. Pack and go. Just go and don't turn up here ever again because you'll find the front door slammed in your face!' There was a pause and then Alice added, 'By *me* and don't persuade yourself that I shall take pity on you, because I shan't. Book your plane ticket and just go, you're no longer wanted here.'

In less than ten minutes Chris had left Turnham House in his flashy hire car, racing down the drive as though the devil himself was behind the steering wheel. Glad to be gone.

Chapter 8

Becky Braithwaite had rushed out to the village Store to pick up a few necessary items for Charles' and Ralph's lunch. They were driving Alice crazy at the moment as they had both decided that they would only eat what they wanted to eat and anything else was spat out or totally refused by them shaking their heads and clamping their lips tightly together. Even Alice's sweet persuasion was wilfully resisted.

When she entered the Store she found it empty apart from Tom in the Post Office cage and Bel who was energetically returning the greengrocery displays to Jimbo's impeccable standard.

'Good morning, Bel. Tom.' Becky was well liked since the first day she had taken up residence in the new council flats down the Culworth Road. They all had sympathy for her because of her brother, Ben who, though grown-up in years but not in his head, required constant devotion and care. Occasionally he braced himself and made the effort to come in the Store on his own and spend a jolly half an hour drinking all of the supply of coffee from Jimbo's machine, having been taught by Fran how to work it. When he'd exhausted the coffee supply he would bring his purse out of a voluminous coat pocket and, carefully taking out a pound coin, he would examine the chocolate display and choose some things which added up to a pound. Occasionally his calculations went awry and he went home with more than one pound's worth of chocolate in his pocket but the staff in the shop never pointed this out, not wishing to upset him.

Bel and Becky were having an enjoyable chat about the latest news going the rounds in the village when Bel broke off their conversation to open the door for Judd and Max, two of the Fitch grandchildren, who rushed in, thoroughly agitated and incapable of speaking plainly. No one could make sense of what they were saying and they all realised that the two boys were in shock.

Bel said comfortingly, 'The two of you sit down in the coffee corner and I'll get you a drink with sugar in; you're in a right state the two of you, what's happened?'

Bel engineered the coffee machine to make two very milky coffees into which she put sugar to help combat whatever shock they'd had. They'd just begun sipping it when the doorbell jingled and in rushed Greta, back from the dentist's, clutching her chest as though her heart was about to burst out of it. She said breathlessly, 'Oh! Thank God! You're both all right!' and plunged down onto the coffee corner seat between the two boys.

'My God! Did you see? He could have killed them!' Greta gasped.

Becky, whose affection for children knew no bounds, went a strange shade of grey and, grabbing hold of the greetings card display shelving for support, she asked, 'What do you mean, "could have killed them"? You mean the two of them nearly got run over?'

Greta nodded emphatically. 'Yes. They were just crossing from the Green to come here and that blankety-blank fool of a Chris Templeton missed them by barely an inch. Driving like a madman he was. My, you were quick on your feet, never seen you boys move as fast! That Chris didn't even pull up to apologise or anything, drove on as though nothing had happened. Jam sandwich, I thought the two of you were.' Greta comfortingly patted Max's arm while with her other hand she wafted herself with the end of her scarf. 'Near thing it was, you have to look both ways when you're crossing the road, you know. Remember next time.'

'Where's Sarah, your big sister? Or your mum or your dad? Mmm?' asked Becky.

Judd replied reluctantly, 'Mum and Dad have gone to work and Sarah's at school.'

'And Gemma, where's she?'

'Said she didn't want to come 'cos, she's sick of looking after us.'

'What about Ross, who's looking after him?'

Becky waited for an answer, finally Judd volunteered that Ross had fallen asleep in Mummy's bed so Gemma was keeping an eye on him.

'Why aren't you at school today?'

'Training day for teachers.'

'Hmm,' Becky said. 'Right, I'm taking them both home before I take this shopping back to the Big House. I'm really upset, they could have been ki ... anyway, it's not their fault, is it? That blasted Chris is to blame. He only cares for himself, so it's not surprising he didn't stop. Wish to goodness he'd disappear off to Brazil. They're welcome to him!'

Becky paid for her shopping, collected the two boys and left Bel and Tom to their shelf stacking and eventually got back to Turnham House full of apologies about the time it had taken her to buy lunch for Ralph and Charles and explained her reasons. 'I'm so sorry. I just couldn't help it, I had to see they were all right.'

Alice asked her who almost ran the two little Fitch grandchildren down and, reluctantly, Becky admitted it was Chris. 'I'm afraid it was your brother-in-law.'

'Oh no! Well, he's left for good and won't be back if I have anything to do with it. No, no, don't keep apologising, Becky, I'm just glad those two boys are safe. How about lunch today? I know you don't normally stay.'

'Well, when I leave here I am going back to Nightingale Farm to look after those children, thanks all the same. They seem such good parents – doctors, both of them, too – and so caring, you know, but then they allow this to happen. Four children and no adult anywhere in sight, it's not good enough. They need reporting to the social. Gemma's sweet, but as she is only ten, they can hardly describe her as someone old enough to be in charge of herself and three younger children, one of them only two, can they?'

'No, I wouldn't have thought so.'

Alice, having got rid of Chris at last, decided after her lunch that while the two boys were safely tucked up in their cots for their regular sleep and Becky had gone to keep an eye on the Fitch grandchildren, she would open up the grand piano Johnny had bought her for her thirty-fifth birthday and sit down to play. She loved playing the piano, more so when the house was quiet, the boys asleep, Johnny busy with the estate, housework done. This was surely the best time of all. With Chris gone too, she could almost feel the restlessness of his presence melting away into peace and the house settling back into its usual calmness, so she was able to indulge herself. She really didn't get enough of playing her piano, not like in the old days before the boys were born; then she could play for hours at a time. She'd have to get back to teaching piano again, even though Johnny said there was no need.

Her fingers trailed to a stop on the keys while she thought about Chris. In some ways she'd miss him, because on a good day he could be a very charming and interesting conversationalist with his tales of his worldwide travels and the people he met and the fun he had. But ... there was always a but ... Thank heavens he hadn't run those two children down! Alice trembled at the thought of her Charles and Ralph in such danger, and also, to be honest, why did he think he had the right to treat Fran as he had? She didn't deserve his treatment of her. Alice could easily understand the attraction that drew her to him but would he ever meet a woman with whom he longed to spend the rest of his life or, for that matter, one who would put up with his twenty-four/seven total interest in his own needs. From upstairs came the sound of two small boys waking up, so Alice closed the lid of her piano and went up to see to her sons.

At the same time in Nightingale Farmhouse Becky was getting Ross up. He had a bad cold and a cough, was grumpy and thoroughly uncooperative but eventually he decided to cheer up.

'I think young man that you need a drink,' Becky said. 'Let's go downstairs and get you one. What would you like? Water, orange juice or something hot?'

Ross, his face buried in Becky's shoulder, agreed he wanted orange juice to drink. As they passed Gemma's bedroom she was busy at her desk using the computer, so he called out to her, 'Gemma! Becky's here.'

'I know. I'm coming down, Becky. Won't be a minute.'

'Right! I'm making a cup of tea for everyone, OK?'

'Lovely!' Gemma called out eagerly.

It didn't take long for the four children to be seated at the kitchen table along with Becky, with mugs of tea plus slices of cake that Becky had brought with her. Ross had changed his mind and decided on tea like the others because he said he was big now and wasn't a baby any more. Becky chose his grown-up moment to get him to blow his nose. They lingered for a while after they'd finished their cake and tea as though wanting to extend the pleasure they found in Becky's company, and a nasty feeling came over her that it wasn't the first time they'd been left with no adult in the house.

'Let's get a game out,' Becky suggested because she didn't feel comfortable to be leaving them with no one in charge. What if one of them had an accident after she left? She'd never forgive herself. So they settled down to hilarious games of cards and then board games.

At a quarter to five Sarah came home from her Culworth school and still neither Anita nor Graham had returned. It was half past five when their father walked in.

'Hello! You look to be having a good time! Hi, Becky!'

'Hi, Dr Fitch! Had a good day? Cup of tea?'

'Yes, please. Anita not back yet?'

'No.' She gave him a quizzical look which made him follow her into the kitchen.

'I wasn't expecting you here today,' he said.

Becky switched on the kettle then leaned with her back against the worktop saying, 'Your boys, Judd and Max nearly got run over this morning. I thought you ought to know.'

Graham asked, 'Where?' He looked as though he was endeavouring to look calm but felt anything like calm inside.

So Becky gave him the details of their adventure with Graham prompting her occasionally.

'I don't mind telling you I was scared to death,' she finished, 'so I've been here taking care of the four of them all afternoon. I'm afraid it's not right, them being on their own. Not even Sarah is old enough, in my opinion, to be minding four children when she's still only twelve – still less Gemma. Did you know?'

Graham muttered something, sprang his mobile out of his pocket and dialled, then decided to disappear. He came back into the kitchen just as Becky was pouring his tea.

'Anita's five minutes from home.' Graham picked up the tea and went to sit with the children while Becky excused herself and left the house with Graham's shout of 'Thank you!' ringing in her ears.

Thank you, indeed! She was furious. Those children were getting neglected; the pile of washing waiting to go in the machine in the back kitchen, the dishevelled, disorganised look of the house, the children left to their own devices. Something needed doing – and when she and Ben came for her regular evening sitting in, or better still the afternoon she came to clean, she'd have something to say and not half. It couldn't go on like this.

Graham, multitasking as he did most of his days, sat talking to the children, drinking his tea, and contemplating what he could do to resolve this trap he was in. Judd and Max began a tempestuous quarrel and Ross burst into despairing tears as he couldn't bear it when they quarrelled. Gemma cried, 'I've had enough!' leapt to her feet and disappeared upstairs. Which was just what Graham wished he could do, abandon the lot of them and melt away into his study, closing the door firmly behind him.

Since their first day in Turnham Malpas there had been nothing but trouble. A happy family had become a group nightmare overnight. For the first time since they'd arrived Graham began to wonder if they'd done the right thing, moving to the country. But there was no going back, what with their old house sold and every last penny committed to making this house habitable, they were stymied.

He lifted Max onto one knee and Ross onto the other and jogged them up and down as though they were both on galloping horses. They began to laugh and so did he and the upset melted away. What they really needed was Anita at home, caring for them all. Hang this blessed obsession she had with holding down a career and caring for a large family! If they only had Sarah and Gemma then, yes, they could cope, but not *five* children and a career. The image of Judd and Max almost getting run over suddenly chilled his heart.

He hastily pushed the image of the two of them crushed under the car, put the two boys on their feet and declared he was about to make their evening meal.

Judd said, 'The easiest for you, Dad, would be those pizzas we have in the freezer. I'll have the ham and pineapple one and we could use up those fancy ice creams, those like ready made cornets, love those.'

'Yes, yes, I say yes, please!' Ross shouted.

'But I thought I'd make—'

Judd hurriedly interrupted his dad. 'Don't worry about *making* anything, Dad, they'll do and at least Ross will eat those.' As an afterthought he added, 'And they're quick. I'll lay the table.' He stood at the bottom of the stairs and shouted, 'Gemma! Come and lay the table, Dad's making pizzas. Hurry up!'

Having neatly rid himself of the job of laying the table, Judd, along with Ross and Max, switched on the TV and settled down to wait for their food.

Aware Anita would be incensed by their diet, Graham shrugged his shoulders and took the easiest way out just as Judd had suggested; after all it wasn't his fault she still hadn't got home.

Little Ross was the first to hear her car pulling up by the front door. 'Mum's home!' he shouted. The pizzas were finished and Sarah was giving out the fancy ice cream cornets just as their mother walked in.

The emotion she felt was not anger at what they were about to consume but tremendous relief that she didn't have a meal to prepare. Graham, clearing plates into the dishwasher, turned to greet her and saw immediately the extreme exhaustion in her face and the relief that they were all being fed.

Sarah poured her a cup of tea from the big pot they used when they were all at home, placed it on the table in front of her mother, and gave her a kiss. 'You look tired, Mum. Busy day? Which pizza do you want? We've got one ham and pineapple left and one choriza and cheese.'

Anita sipped her tea gratefully before Sarah got her answer. 'Choriza, please. And thanks for the tea. Just what I needed. Sorry I'm so late, been so busy. Car accident on the bypass.'

'It's always on the bypass, why is it always on the bypass?' asked Max.

'Don't know.'

Judd remembered. '*We* nearly had a car crash, Max and me. This morning, not on the bypass though, in the village.'

Graham knew that Anita was more than simply tired; she was completely exhausted because her reaction to what Judd had told her was almost non-existent. 'Oh! Well, I'm glad you didn't get hurt.' She rubbed her eyes and said, 'I'll have another cup of tea, please, Sarah. Is my pizza ready? I'm so hungry! I didn't have time for lunch.'

'Mrs Jones saw us and she nearly fainted,' Judd went on. 'She had to go in the Store and have a coffee with us. That coffee machine is wizard, and free too. You should try it, Mum. She's nice is Mrs Jones. Very kind.'

'I see ...'

Anita didn't appear to notice how disappointed Judd was by her vague reaction to the big, important happening of his day. To keep her attention on him he gave her more information. 'Becky brought us home and we played cards. She's really good at Snap, is Becky, and she knows that Newmarket card game we like.'

'Becky? It isn't Wednesday, is it? She stayed, did she?'

'Yes, she did. Till Dad got home.'

After Anita had eaten what passed for a meal she leaned back in her chair and before she knew it her eyes had closed and she was enjoying what Graham called a 'power nap'. He and Sarah cleared up the kitchen, and then Graham set about putting Ross to bed which required diplomacy above and beyond what an international crisis situation would have demanded. By the time he switched off Ross's bedside light Graham had serious reservations about being a doctor; maybe he should have joined the Diplomatic Service, he certainly had the skills.

Finally the four younger children were all in bed, leaving Sarah finishing her homework, Anita still asleep and Graham glad to sink into a chair and switch on the TV, thinking he couldn't go on like this a moment longer. Everything was falling apart; the children were thoroughly upset, even the two girls, Anita was exhausted twenty-four/seven, and while he realised that a family the size of theirs couldn't expect to live tranquil lives all day and every day, when it reaches the point when someone from the village takes charge of their children out of the kindness of their heart then ... And they'd twice been asked up to the village school because Max and Judd were being disruptive which was so unlike them. At this critical moment in his deliberations Anita appeared in the sitting room doorway, rubbing her eyes and apologising.

'I've not done the washing. Very soon none of us will be able to go out as there'll be nothing clean to put on to go out in, but I'm so tired I'll have to go to bed. Where is everybody?'

'Except for Sarah, they're all in bed.'

'Is it that late?' She glanced at the clock. 'Half past eight. I'd no idea. I've got early shift tomorrow. You'll have to see them off to school.'

'No.' Graham turned the TV off. 'I can't.'

'There's no "can't" about it. You must!'

'No. It's Wednesday and it's my turn for this new scheme we've started.'

'What new scheme?'

'If you weren't so busy you would have remembered. The one where first appointments begin at eight-thirty and it's my turn, so I shall have to leave home by eight at the latest to make sure I'm in Culworth on time.'

'It's all very inconvenient. They won't mind if you arrive a bit late, will they? Patients are very good at tut-tutting when doctors are running late; in fact, I think they quite enjoy it.'

'Sorry. I can't do it, Anita. I thought your shift was nine till one?'

'Well, it was but I've agreed to do longer. We really do need the money, Graham. This house is going to cost a lot more to put just the basics right than I ever expected and we really need an en-suite for the two girls.'

'They don't actually *need* an en-suite, Anita.'

'Wait till they're in their teens! Believe me, we shall be glad they have one. You included.'

'Anita, right now what our children need is to see more of *you*. You're their mother and they are crying out for you, but you don't hear them. It didn't even register with you that Judd and Max very nearly got run over today.' Graham waited for her reaction, and when it came he knew things were very wrong.

'I told them not to leave the house!' she said angrily. 'What were they doing in the village?'

'Anita, we could have been identifying them in the mortuary today – just thank God we didn't have to!'

'You're being ridiculous! Exaggerating just to make your point.'

'They were taken into the Store and given hot drinks of some kind and Greta Jones, who witnessed what happened, also went in there in shock. Becky was there and brought the boys home. She stayed with the children all afternoon till I got home. It won't do, Anita, it won't do.'

'I owe her for that, then. Who was it? Driving the car I mean.'

'Chris Templeton. He never even stopped to check they were all right.'

'Mmm. Brazil's the best place for him, then.'

'It still hasn't registered, has it? They could have been *killed*.'

'They weren't, though, were they? So stop going on about it. I've too much on my mind to worry about something that didn't happen.'

Graham stood up and, placing his hands on the arms of the chair she was sitting in, said in a slow, deliberate manner, 'Remember how you felt when Ross was born? You said to me "he may be yet another boy but I shall love him just as much if not more than the others". You used to love them *all* like that, boy or girl. But not any more. You should have been hugging Judd and Max, grateful they were still alive, but this new Anita is too tired to *feel*. Now, go to bed, I'll stay up and get some washing in the machines. The children are nothing but trouble since we moved here, except Sarah, so any extra hours for you are out. Absolutely out. I insist.'

'I know!' she exclaimed. 'Your dad could look after them till school starts. He's only got to walk down the village street and pop them through the school gate, or Kate could take them when she goes. Ask him. Go on, ring him, now, this minute. He reckons to be so proud of them, well, he can do his bit. It's not much to ask.'

'It is far too much to ask and I won't. He's not used to children at all. You promised me ...'

'How many times have you broken promises to me over

working long hours? Dozens of times, times when I had a houseful of children, none of them old enough to give me a hand and where was their dad? I'll tell you where he was, working all hours. You didn't listen to me then, and it's me not listening to you now, and you don't like a dose of your own medicine. *I'll* ring your dad, he'll be only too glad to have something to do.'

Except Craddock Fitch had arranged to play golf first thing the following morning but, glad to feel needed by someone, he agreed to do as she asked. However, after his experiences that first morning he rather hoped she wouldn't call upon him for granddad duties again, because he found it totally disorientating and irritating, and the children difficult because he kept calling them by the wrong name, which the three boys found hilarious, and he missed that second cup of coffee he always had after Kate had left for school. As for reading *The Times*, he didn't even manage to read one whole paragraph never mind the article about the forthcoming mini budget and it took him until almost noon before his nerves settled. They were a blinking lively lot, but imagine caring for them twenty-four/seven. Maybe he loved the idea of grandchildren but not the actuality of it.

Chapter 9

At the moment Greta Jones' biggest worry is opening the post. Normally she loves opening any letters, even the ones she knows are bills, but no longer, because she's begun getting anonymous letters, sometimes at home, but sometimes at work. It is as though someone, somewhere, knows her movements as well as she does, or even better than she does, because letters never come to work when it's her day off. If they're delivered on her day off they arrive at home. Stamped and ominous; smart white envelope, the flap always well secured with a neat strip of sticky tape, though they don't need the sticky tape because the flap is always well stuck down without it ...

The third letter she received was so vicious she decided that if any more came she'd keep them unopened, and hide them in the bottom drawer of her wardrobe under her summer tights to use as evidence if ever she had to bring the police in. So she put the next three unopened under her tights, but then not knowing became much worse than knowing what they said, so she began opening the letters again. Poison pen letters, they were, that's what they were called in detective novels. Poison pen letters, and poison they were, in just three or four vitriolic sentences.

She'd found that word 'vitriolic' in a crime novel she'd read that Vince once borrowed from the Library Van. It came to the village once a fortnight on Tuesday mornings at 10.30 outside the Store, and if Vince was free to visit it, he always brought home a pile of crime novels. She wished he didn't, because if she had nothing to read she would borrow one of his books and the stories seemed to cramp her brains as the tortuous tales wound themselves around her brain till she believed they were happening in Turnham Malpas and she had to stop herself suspecting everyone she met of being a murderer or a thief. But now, horror of horrors, there was a real, live crime novel happening in the village and she was the victim.

Whoever it was writing the letters to her knew the terrible story of her family; well, *her* terrible story. Not word for word, she thought, but enough to terrify her. If she went to the police they would have to read them and nowadays how could you know if you could trust the police? They might sell her secret to a newspaper, like they did sometimes now, or, worse still, demand money from her for their silence. They wouldn't care about a year in prison if they got well paid in cash and hid the money.

Greta was sitting in the bath thinking about the letters and what action to take, and suddenly she began to laugh at herself for the fanciful thoughts she was having, then the water felt really chilly and she turned the hot tap on to warm it up. But no matter how painful some of her thoughts, the letters were very real.

Eventually, when she finally got downstairs wearing her cosy winter nightie and that lovely plush dressing gown Barry and Pat had bought her last Christmas, the first words Vince said were, 'You've been a long time. It's long past my hot chocolate moment.'

Still upset about the poison pen letters she snapped angrily at him, 'It isn't beyond the bounds of possibility to make a mug for yourself, you know. It's not some kind of miracle of modern science known only to me, making hot chocolate.'

Vince looked startled, 'What's up? Is it something I've done?' As an afterthought he added, 'Or not done?'

For a split second she decided to tell him, then Greta knew she mustn't. Not Vince. Because he'd never known and never would whilst ever she had breath in her body. And what about her boys finding out? That thought made her tremble from head to toe. She'd never really faced up to that, knowing two of them were far away and couldn't find out by accident. She'd do murder before she'd allow that to happen.

'Sorry, Vince. I'm tired and I stayed in the bath far too long and I've got really cold.'

He knew she was fibbing because her voice didn't ring true. 'Never mind, I'll make it tonight, love, it's just that yours always tastes so... tasty. You have the knack, you see. You sit by the fire and get warm. Biscuit?' He patted her hand as he passed in front of her and noted it was as warm as toast.

Vince set about making the hot chocolate. Greta always bought the kind that had to be made with milk, not that pathetic stuff that only needed hot water (not boiling, it always said on the instructions). It was a filling, sleep-inducing drink, was Greta's hot chocolate, made you sleep real deep. He didn't care if he put weight on with all them decibels or whatever.

Vince went into the sitting room where Greta had the fire roaring as though they were six feet deep in snow. There'd been years, when the boys were in their teens, when he could have run away for ever because life, married to Greta, combined with the two younger boys, Kenny and our Terry, was sheer hell, but somehow, over the years since then, he'd mellowed and so had she and he was looking forward to a pleasant old age, especially now they both had a job thanks to Jimbo so money was more freely available than when they'd had those three great boys eating them out of house and home and causing all that trouble with the police.

'Here we are; I've tried to do it right.'

'Thanks, Vince.'

'You're not yourself tonight. What's up?'

Greta didn't answer immediately. It took three sips of her hot chocolate before he got his reply.

'There's nothing wrong with me.' Greta Jones, you're starting to lie and getting good at it thought Greta. 'Except – have you finally made up your mind about going to Canada to see Kenny and our

Terry? Last week you said you definitely weren't going, that wild horses wouldn't drag you there, so are you *still* not going?'

'Still not going, but ... there's a chance I might. Well, can't let you go all that way on your own; it's not right a woman travelling alone.'

She laughed. 'I don't know what you think you could do if someone tried to run off with me! In any case, who'd want to run off with someone my age and not even good-looking?'

'I think you're good-looking, always have. And your hair is your crowning glory like they say in books. It's red but not that brassy red that drains the colour from your skin. There must have been red hair somewhere back in your family 'cos your dad and your mum both had jet black hair didn't they? Not a bit of red at all.'

When had he ever complimented her on her red hair? Well, she called it auburn because that sounded more smart, and now he chooses this moment, just when her whole family history could be public knowledge any minute. 'Shut up, Vince, I'm off to bed.'

'You've not finished your hot chocolate yet. Stay here talking for a while longer.'

'No. Watch the football, it'll be on now. I'm off.'

When Greta looked in the mirror the next morning she appeared to have shrunk; she was thinner, almost gaunt. That was what worry did to you, drained you of your vitality. She'd better buck up her ideas because Jimbo always noticed when his staff appeared to be on the frail side, fearing they were going to be off ill.

Just as she thought, his first words were, 'Greta! Good morning. You're not looking too bright this morning, had a bad night?'

'No, I've had a good one, as a matter of fact. Remember your advice about ignoring Vince not wanting to go to Canada? Well, it appears to have worked, because last night he sounded much more positive about going with me. Some fat-headed excuse that it wasn't right for a woman to be travelling on her own in case she got accosted. Enough to make a cat laugh, that is. As if anyone would want to accost me!!'

Jimbo laughed too but in the kindliest way. 'Oh, I don't know about that! I think it's because he cares about you, and that's important, isn't it? It's the only excuse he can come up with to justify changing his mind.'

'Well, whatever's made him change his mind, I'm glad. I just hope he sticks to it this time!'

'So do I. And I've been meaning to say, Vince seems to have enjoyed that diploma course I sent him on about butchering and food hygiene.'

Greta grinned. 'He certainly did, first course he's been on ever in his life. Only drawback was he was the oldest by at least twenty-five years! We've had some laughs about that.'

Jimbo, cheered by the improvement in Greta's mood, patted her shoulder saying, 'Must press on. Any time you have problems for heaven's sake speak to me, be only too glad to help in any way I can. OK? Oh, and you've a pile of post waiting.'

Greta's spirits sank immediately but she turned away so Jimbo couldn't see her face. She recognised the handwriting on the envelope now, so she never opened one by mistake. If there was another one this morning she'd tuck it in her apron pocket as usual and hide it away when she got home.

And there was.

It looked like all the other envelopes that came, as though it was a customer's order coming through the post enclosing the cheque to pay for what they wanted. For some pig-headed reason this morning she decided to open it. Same notepaper; she fingered the paper and wondered who'd touched it before she had. Someone possessed by the devil, no doubt, someone who relished what they wrote, who enjoyed the thrill of frightening her, someone filled to the brim with hate.

Greta unfolded the letter and read:

Your hour has come. Your secret is to be revealed. I know it all.

She gripped the back of her chair to stop herself from screaming. This was the most threatening letter yet – the earlier ones were trivial compared to this. And what she could never understand was how had they found out? There was no one alive who knew the full horror, absolutely no one, yet still her mind raced through the possibilities. Friends of hers from the village school? People she'd worked with in the intervening years? No, how could any of them know? Unless someone who had been a part of Silas Wilderspoon's wicked group had told one of their children. That could be it. So was it someone who worked with her now in the Store? Bel? Tom? Fran? Jimbo? It was impossible for it to be one of them. Wasn't it? And it certainly wasn't the reverend, no way. He knew *everything* but she *knew* that he always kept his word and would not have divulged a single iota of what he'd found in that blasted trunk, especially the black magic stuff.

Funny about that; it seemed as though black magic lingered on in the very air of the village from one generation to the other. She thought about Simone and her terrible death in the flames, about the police sergeant's wife going crackers, to say nothing of that poor lad Rhett Wright on the verge of madness at the thought that their black magic goings-on had actually brought that old dog Sykes back to life when in fact they hadn't. Though it had seemed a strange coincidence at the time.

Greta was still holding the letter, fingering it, challenging her memory. Had she seen this notepaper before? It had to have been bought somewhere. But where? In the market in Culworth? In the smart stationers in the High Street where it cost a small fortune to buy even the smallest greetings card?

Then it hit her and she thought she'd explode – it was for sale in the Store! Of course it was! No matter how conspicuous it made her she immediately went into the front of the Store to look along the stationery shelves. When she saw a stack of it in the most prominent place in the display Greta stifled her terror as best she could and hurtled back into her mail order room, slamming the door shut with no care for the noise it made. Whoever it was who was writing these poisonous letters, they had more than likely bought the paper here in the Store. She'd possibly even spoken to them, gone into the front of the Store for a jar of something or other she was short of and passed the time of day with them. They were brazen! But who were they? Who knew her family history?

It couldn't be a man or a woman her own age. It must be someone much older than her, someone with a very long memory who had perhaps been a part of Basil Wilderspoon's wicked group.

The question nagged at her all day long. Every parcel she taped up, every credit card she checked, every postal address and email address she made a note of for her records were imprinted on her brain and checked and rechecked and none of them matched up to anyone who could possibly know her dreadful secret. Deep in her heart Greta knew that one day well before it drove her to the brink of madness she'd have to tell Vince. She paused for a moment and recollected what Vince had said about her red hair. Sometimes in the past he'd made a comment that recalled their courting days and at the time she'd want to tell him and then didn't. If only she had told him what this vicious writer knew she wouldn't be in this predicament right now.

Chapter 10

Johnny Templeton hadn't heard from his brother Chris since he raced out of the Big House the morning he'd lost his temper and been told to leave by Johnny and by Alice. They had blithely assumed he'd gone straight home but when, two weeks after he'd left, their mother rang from Rio asking to speak to Chris, Johnny found he hadn't.

'Sorry, Mum, isn't he with you? He left us here ... let me see ... almost two weeks ago.'

There was a rapid drawing in of breath on his mother's part and then she managed to say, 'He did admit he'd had a row with you about his behaviour and that Alice had also told him to leave. She's never liked him, you know. Never. I knew that when we met her at your wedding. Too self-opinionated, that's her trouble. You should never have married her. I did tell you at the time.'

Johnny restrained himself from snapping at her and muttered between tight lips that he told his brother to leave too, so it wasn't just Alice. 'He has been behaving in a manner not suited to an English village and thus bringing our name into disrepute.'

'You're being ridiculous! What on earth could my Chris do to bring about such a situation? "Your name into disrepute", of all things – you've lived too long with those stuffy English.'

'He's been doing what he usually does, Mother, sleeping with anyone willing to perform their duties according to Chris Templeton's rules and it won't do here. Frankly, I'm glad he's not here.'

'So you don't know where he is?'

'Like I've said, I thought he was at home with you! He booked a seat on the plane, I overheard him doing it.'

'He booked a seat! So he intended coming back then.'

'Presumably.'

'He could be anywhere. He's got off the plane and ... the silly boy.'

'Mother, you've never said a truer word. He *is* a silly boy. When do you suppose he'll grow up?'

'Johnny, I'm beginning to really worry now. I just thought he was busy at your place enjoying life as only Chris can and forgotten us all here. I'll ring round some of his friends, see if they've heard from him. It's serious, you know, Johnny, and it's not like him. Normally the first thing he does when he gets home is make a bee-line for old Nan; she hugs him, he tells her how much he's missed her, which we all know isn't true, but she believes him, and then he dumps his washing on her. She has so little to do nowadays she's delighted to be useful. This really is seriously worrying, Johnny. As soon as you hear from him let me know, won't you?'

'Of course, but don't worry too much – you know what he's like, Mother.'

'How can I not worry?' She switched off her phone abruptly and left Johnny almost as worried as she was. It was odd. Very odd. Chris might be a pain in the proverbial but in the past they had at least known where he was, except that time when his plane came down in the Amazon.

Johnny went to stand in the huge bay window from which he adored looking out at his favourite view. The leaves had all fallen from the trees that lined each side of the drive so he could see the Old Barn, just as old as the house itself, right where the drive bent round to the left and then went in a straight line to the gates. He'd watched Chris driving away that morning and been terribly aware how angry he was. He'd witnessed Chris being angry many times, but after his rejection by Fran in The Wise Man and both himself and Alice telling him to go the next morning he ...

But Alice, when he told her about his mother's phone call, straightaway ever practical, checked the wardrobes in the bedroom Chris had slept in and found the majority of his clothes still hanging there. 'He's not gone far,' she reported. 'His clothes are here. And his suitcases too, so he's intending coming back. We'd better enjoy ourselves while he's away, Johnny, because he's sure to be back to pick up all this lot. I wonder if Fran has gone with him, I do hope not.'

Johnny stopped worrying, but that same day he did deliberately go into the Store so he could ask about Fran and, if she was there, ask her if she had heard from Chris. 'Not seen Fran for a while, Jimbo, is she away?'

'Only today. She's heard of someone who does a good line in shortbread and, as our usual supplier has gone to the eternal shortbread factory in the sky and is therefore no longer available, she's hoping theirs will be as good as our clients are accustomed to. Shortbread is one of our most popular lines.'

'Do you have a few minutes?' Johnny nodded his head in the direction of Jimbo's private office.

'As it happens I do.'

Jimbo closed the door firmly behind him. 'How can I help?'

'About two weeks ago my brother Chris left our house in his hire car and of course we naturally assumed he was going home to Rio. But neither Alice and I, nor our mother, have heard from him. So I wondered if Fran had or if she has any idea where he might have gone?'

Privately Jimbo gave three cheers, but with a dead straight face he answered Johnny with a firm 'No. She hasn't heard a word from him and doesn't want to. Sorry. That must have been the day he almost ran two of Craddock Fitch's grandsons over right outside here. Apparently it was a close-run thing.'

Appalled, Johnny ignored the hostility in Jimbo's voice and said, 'You see, I know he booked a plane ticket over the phone because

I overheard him giving his details and asking availability etc., so are you sure she hasn't heard from him because at the moment he seems to have disappeared. My mother is frantic now she knows he's not here and I have to admit *I'm* getting worried. He doesn't answer his mobile phone, either.'

'He is a grown man, Johnny – well, I suppose that's debatable – but I'm definitely not going to lose any sleep over him being missing. The damage he has done to our Fran ... anyway, enough's enough. Sorry I can't help.'

Johnny stood, statue-like, looking out of the office window not saying a word, so Jimbo squeezed past him, sat down at his desk and woke up his computer. He'd deleted three junk emails before Johnny stirred. 'You see,' he said, 'all his life he's been an individual; he never conformed to anyone's rules but his own, not that he had many, and he was the most difficult of the three of us. He got more leeway than Nicholas and I and I realise now that he manipulated the two of us shamelessly so that we always got the blame for everything he did wrong, because he could persuade grownups that black was white with immense charm, and Nicholas and I were feeble compared to him.'

Jimbo could see from where he sat that Johnny had clenched his fists and, being an only child himself and always longing for brothers, or even a sister, so he had someone to play with, instantly suspected that maybe he'd been lucky; better to be lonely than constantly angered by a brother who accepted no rules but his own.

'Johnny, someone as resourceful as Chris won't come to much harm. He'll turn up when he's ready, so tell your mother not to worry. After all, he's not like that twelve-year-old boy in the paper the other day, ran away from home after a serious row with his mother and then was found dead three days later, buried in the local woods after getting absorbed into a boys' gang from his estate. Chris is in his thirties and streetwise to boot. I expect Fran discarding him and then you and Alice telling him to go he thinks he'll give you all a fright. Has he taken all his clothes with him?'

Johnny turned to look at Jimbo, and the grin on his face told everything. 'He's left almost all of his clothes in the wardrobe. First thing Alice checked.'

'There you are, you see, he's giving you a fright to pay you back. Tell your mother, it'll put her mind at rest. So he's not grown-up after all, still playing you off against each other like he did as a boy.'

Ruefully Johnny agreed. 'Maybe you're right but if—'

The office door was flung open and there stood Fran, her face alight with joy. 'I told you I'd get a spectacular shortbread before I was done, didn't I? Well, here it is! Try a slice. I've not promised anything at all, just said the boss would have to OK it, but it *is* fantastic and a very reasonable price. Here, Johnny, try a piece. Dad. Here you are. Well?'

Both Jimbo and Johnny tasted the shortbread immediately and had to give Fran the thumbs up.

Simultaneously they both said, 'Brilliant!'

Jimbo hugged her whilst taking another bite and Johnny agreed wholeheartedly that she was a genius. 'This is wonderful, Fran, it really is and not even made in Scotland, home of the shortbread. Sometimes shortbread can be very dry but this, well, it's almost moist but still biscuity. Well done.'

'I'm going to give Tom and Bel a piece, see what they think.'

By the time Fran had confirmed that everyone – even the customers in the Store who begged a piece to try when she gave Tom and Bel their taste of her miracle shortbread – thought it was very special. 'Hopefully it will be on sale here in Turnham Malpas by the end of next week,' she said and hurried back into Jimbo's office to tell him how everyone who tasted it loved it, and then coming down from cloud nine, she addressed Johnny.

'Have you come to see me?'

'Well, I did, but I don't need to now. I came in to ask if you'd heard from Chris, but your dad says you haven't. He doesn't seem to have gone back to Brazil and he hasn't contacted us here, so I just wondered if you'd heard.'

'No, I haven't, and I don't specially want to. Charming, captivating man that he is, he has no scruples – he's all about what *he* wants from everyone he meets. He's a taker not a giver. I'm sorry to be so frank but that's the truth, Johnny, I'm afraid, and one day, perhaps, he'll get his comeuppance. Right, I need a cup of tea and something to eat – in the excitement I forgot to have lunch. Bye Dad, bye Johnny. I'll take this home to Mum, she'll be so jealous.' Fran laughed. 'So very jealous, won't she, Dad?'

But as she walked home from the Store, the brightness went from her face and she almost wept. Would she never be free from that blessed man? She might sound unconcerned about Chris in front of Johnny but inside the same old yearning came back the moment his name entered her mind. No! Today she would put a stop to it, she had to let him go. Missing? Well, so what? He'd be holed up somewhere with another female who allowed him to control her just as he always had her.

Well, he'd better not turn up at the Charter-Plackett residence. She opened the front door shouting, 'Mum! Put the kettle on. I've brought you a pressy.'

The two of them, mother and daughter, sat at the kitchen table, drinking tea and tasting the shortbread. Fran had guessed right; her mother loved the shortbread and was envious of the makers' skill. 'This is fantastic! Can they meet the volume we will need, though? Will they have to change the packaging, and can they do different pack sizes, you know the sort of thing? Perhaps special tins for Christmas and plastic packaging other times. No, not plastic, that wouldn't be right, and what if ...'

They spent a happy time discussing a name change for the shortbread, new packaging, new design until Fran declared herself exhausted and went to lie down on the sofa in the sitting room to play with Bonnie, hoping to put herself to rights in the peace and quiet. Bonnie began plaguing her by standing on her chest and playfully nipping her nose and enthusiastically licking the flavour of the shortbread from around Fran's mouth. Fran pushed her away and Bonnie fell off the sofa and ran off, offended, but Fran didn't care, because right out of the blue she was worrying about Chris being missing, and loading herself with guilt for rejecting him that night. She should never have done it so publicly, that was her big mistake. No wonder he'd left Turnham Malpas after an exhibition like that.

She'd not given a toss about his feelings, had she? But did she care? No! He deserved every word she'd said because it was the truth. This, then, was the end of her fine romance.

Fran wasn't the only one feeling guilty because Johnny felt like she did too and blamed himself entirely for Chris disappearing like he did. All his life Chris had been unable to cope with facing the truth and in less than twenty-four hours he had been rejected by his brother, his sister-in-law, and, in no uncertain terms, by his girlfriend. Johnny went home hoping to get Alice to somehow relieve him of his guilt, but he found her in the middle of cleaning Ralph from head to toe because Charles had been incredibly sick all over him during a rough and tumble they'd organised, so the two boys were both crying and Alice was at the end of her tether.

Feelings of guilt about Chris melted away as he helped Alice to cope with the two of them. Fortunately Ralph cheered up by the time he was clean and in fresh clothes and Charles went to lie down on the hearthrug, white as a sheet and looking as though being sick again was about to happen very, very soon.

Now, equipped with a bucket and a new roll of paper towels, Johnny was in charge of the boys while Alice put the washing machine to work on Ralph's revolting clothes and washed her hands. So for the moment it was only Chris's mother who fretted about her son's disappearance, and the only practical action she could take was to leave a message on his phone insisting that he ring her immediately. She got no response from him.

Chapter 11

The sudden disappearance of Chris Templeton became the main topic of conversation throughout the three villages but more so in Turnham Malpas. Having imagined that he was safely back in Rio with his mother only to find he was missing, a carefully constructed list of his last moments in the village was put together by the group of villagers who usually sat on the old settle alongside the ancient table that easily seated six in the Royal Oak hostelry.

'Well, Greta, you were one of the ones who saw him last, after he'd nearly run the two Fitch grandsons down outside the Store. Which way did he go after that?' asked Willie Biggs.

'One thing for certain, I didn't see him pause for a single minute after; he just put his foot on the accelerator and disappeared. In any case, seeing as I thought I was heading for a heart attack I never noticed which way he went. You have no idea how fast my heart was beating, terrible it was. Them two Fitch boys were shaking and I was positively rattling with my nerves. I can't bear to think of it. What a shock I 'ad,' Greta replied, fanning herself with a beer mat.

'You know, after that he might have been involved in a traffic accident, going at that speed. Perhaps he's unconscious in Culworth Hospital and nobody knows who he is,' Vera Wright mused.

Willie scoffed at Vera's imagination. 'Sometimes, Vera, you get carried away. He was supposed to be driving to the airport, wasn't he? He'd have all his identification with him, surely. Passport and that.'

Vera wagged her finger at Willie to emphasise the rightness of her solution. 'Ah! But was he? He might have *said* he was going home to Rio but was off to another of one of his women.'

Marie Hooper decided to join in the speculation at this point because Willie was struck dumb by this new idea. She took a single sip of her wine and said softly, leaning forward so they could hear without the people on the next table also hearing what she had to say, 'Don't think he was only seeing Fran, because I know different.'

Sylvia, amazed by this information, whispered, 'Really? We know he had that fancy piece Anunny or whatever she was called; you mean there was someone else too?'

Marie nodded. 'Opposite us, that tall thin girl with the very short blonde hair who's married to a soldier in Afghanistan and waiting for married quarters; he did keep calling there.'

Greta couldn't bear the injustice of that piece of news. 'You'd think with him risking his life day after day in Afghanistan she'd stay faithful to him, wouldn't you? That's disgraceful. The poor chap,' said Greta. 'But maybe he just went to keep her company. It must be lonely for her, with no kids to look after.'

'And leaving at two in the morning?' said Marie, confident she was right.

'Awful thing, loneliness,' muttered Sylvia. 'I know all about loneliness, I do.'

They all glanced at Willie and wondered what on earth Sylvia was talking about. Hunched over his glass of home-brew, had he died while they all sat there talking and only Sylvia had noticed?

Finally Greta asked, 'But what about Willie? You've got him. You're not a widow. Look! He's sitting next to you. We can all see him and ... and he's just moved his hand. Look!'

Sylvia looked at them each in turn then said, 'If I get five words out of him before twelve noon I'm lucky. Between noon and bedtime unless we come in here he never speaks. Gawps all the time at Sky Sport on the telly. I've had to buy a little portable TV otherwise I'd never see a single programme except if there's a film on with sport in it, like *Bend It Like Beckham* which is on tonight. Biggest cause of divorce is TV sport – I read that somewhere. He'll watch anything so long as there's a ball moving across the screen, whatever shape or size it is.'

Inspired, Vera said, 'You'll be all right then when it's darts, there's no ball involved.' They all sniggered at Vera's sense of humour.

'No such luck! He switches channels and watches football or something when it's two teams from absolutely anywhere and sometimes he doesn't even know which team is which and still he watches it. I've got myself a comfy chair and a little TV in the kitchen and I switch on the heater and it's roaring away keeping me cosy and I'm watching exactly what I like.'

They all sat round in glum silence, absorbing the horror of Sylvia's predicament.

'Think of the electric bill, Sylvia, it must be colossal.' said Marie.

Sylvia agreed. 'It is. He's always complaining about the size of the bill, but I've told him good and proper that it's entirely his fault.'

'Good thing Chris Templeton didn't take to calling, otherwise you might have been tempted – but at least you wouldn't have needed the heater on,' suggested Zack. Whereupon all of them dissolved into hysterical laughter excepting Willie who sat bewildered, wondering what all the laughing was about.

At that moment Becky Braithwaite came in and she made a beeline for their table.

'Good evening one and all! Is there anyone without a drink? You've finished yours, Willie, how about another? Home-brew? Right, it's my shout.' Becky put her bag on her chair seat and taking her purse went off to the bar. 'Good evening, Georgie, busy in here tonight. All good for trade though!'

Georgie agreed with her. 'Indeed, indeed. Your usual?'

'Yes, please and whatever Willie is drinking. Home-brew isn't it?'

'That's right. He's been drinking our home-brew since the very first batch my Dicky made. You'd think he'd get bored with it, wouldn't you, after all those years? Your brother, Ben? Keeping well is he?'

'He's got a bit of a cold today so he's staying in watching the TV.'

'I think it's lovely the way you look after him, Becky,' said Georgie.

'Of course I look after him, he's my brother, for heaven's sake.'

Picking up on the hint of indignation in Becky's voice Georgie said, 'I know, even so it must be hard work. I admire you for what you do.'

'It's a pleasure, actually. A real pleasure caring for him. There's the money, Georgie. Thanks.'

Becky headed for her chair, handed Willie his home-brew, put her purse away in her bag and sat down. 'Your good health, everyone.' They all toasted her in return and waited for her to speak.

'You'll have heard, then?' Becky said.

'Heard what?'

'That no one knows where the sexiest man in Turnham Malpas is? Well, the sexiest apart from the rector, that is; he's the very sexiest.'

Greta, considering what she owed the rector at the moment, was horrified. 'Becky! Honestly, what a thing to say. We hold the rector in the greatest esteem.'

Vera and Sylvia giggled their appreciation of what she had said. Becky might not have been long in the village but she said things that most of them would have said had they ever dared.

Because Peter Harris was gorgeous and even though he was years older than when he'd first come, he could still make one's knees turn to jelly with one look of those splendid all-seeing, startling blue eyes of his and if he added a smile ... well, they were all his slaves. As though he knew they were talking about him he walked in at that very minute, and right behind him was Ben Braithwaite.

'Good evening, Becky! Everyone. Ben said you were here.

Ben's fancying having a drink with you, Becky. He knocked on the Rectory door, so I've brought him round.'

Ben beamed at them all, so despite their embarrassment they squeezed another chair in for him next to Becky while she sorted out what he would like to drink. 'Fizzy elderflower, Ben? Mmm?'

He shook his head.

'Orange?'

He shook his head.

'Lemon?'

He shook his head.

'Fizzy orange?'

Ben nodded.

'Fizzy orange it is then. I'll go get it.'

None of them ever knew what to say to Ben and in the past had found it best to remain silent, but Ben wanted to talk. He mumbled some long sentence of which they could only catch the odd word, so they all left it to Peter to take pity on him.

'Ben? Does Becky know you watch that programme?' Peter asked.

Ben shifted uneasily in his chair and then, with a wicked grin on his face, he put a finger to his lips to signal to Peter not to say a word. The moment his fizzy orange was put in front of him Ben picked it up and drank the whole glass full in one great big gulping attack. Becky, as always prepared for emergencies when Ben was with her, dug in her bag and brought out a huge man's tissue and dried his mouth and chin for him. 'Now we're going home.'

Vera protested in a kindly tone, 'Oh! Becky! You've nowhere near finished your drink. Sit down for a bit and finish it. We don't mind Ben being with you.'

The withering look Becky gave Vera made sure they all knew that they shouldn't mind Ben being there, after all he was a human being. 'No, thanks, we won't stay. Ben was told to stay at home and he's disobeyed me and that spells danger for someone like him. He's not safe out on his own except going to the Store now and again, when he's having a good day. Come on, Benjamin Braithwaite. Home.'

Peter, realising Ben was about to make a scene, said so softly they could barely hear him, 'I'll walk home with you, Ben, if that's all right with you. You can show me where you live, can't you?'

Immediately Ben struggled out of his chair and went to stand beside Peter, ready to go with him.

Becky went with them and the others felt so embarrassed at what had happened they didn't speak for a while after the three of them had left. It was Willie who broke the silence. 'You look at that splendid figure of a man called Peter Harris and then you look at Ben, and you wonder why they should be so different. One, years older than the other, but still fit, good-looking, vigorous, a blessing for us all him being so wise, and then you look at Ben who'll never, ever, make anything of his life. Always need protecting, always need caring for. It's not right.'

Very thoughtfully Sylvia said, 'And does anyone think about Becky? That burden to carry all her life. This world isn't very fair, is it? Who'll want to marry Becky when Ben is part of the bargain? I don't know how old she is but I bet she isn't thirty yet. We should count our blessings we should. Come on, Willie, we're going home, we've a film we'll both enjoy to watch and we don't want to miss the start.' The two of them wandered off leaving Greta, Vince, Vera, Marie and Zack to talk.

Fortunately for them it was Dicky's night for doing one of his comic turns; or, more truthfully, he declared it was in view of the cloud of depression that appeared to have settled in the bar. Within minutes they were smiling and then, before they knew it, every single customer was hooting with laughter. Where *did* he get his jokes from? Ten minutes of laughing and the whole atmosphere changed. He was a good chap, was Dicky. He might be on the small side for a grown man but he did know how to make people laugh.

Just as Dicky's ten minutes of laughter came to a close,

Grandmama Charter-Plackett arrived, bursting in through the door as though she was being pursued. In one swift glance round the saloon bar she spotted Vera on the settle with Vince and Greta facing her and Zack and Marie sitting at either end. She picked up her double whisky and water from the bar and drifted over to join them. 'May I?' But she'd sat down beside Vera before they had a chance to give their permission.

They didn't mind, though. She was always good fun was Katherine Charter-Plackett ... when she was having a good day that is. 'Cold tonight, isn't it? Where's everyone else?'

'Gone home.'

'Gone home?' Grandmama glanced at her watch. 'Bit early isn't it?'

'Well,' said Greta, 'Willie and Sylvia have a film to watch on the telly, Becky came in and then the reverend with Ben who'd been left at home with a bad cold but he'd decided to go out to find Becky and landed up at the Rectory, so Peter brought him in because Ben said Becky was here. Anyway we are glad for your company so long as you've something interesting to impart.'

Grandmama took a sip of her whisky before leaning across the table confidentially and saying, 'Well, you know Chris Templeton has disappeared?' They all nodded. 'But did you know he's not only been seeing my Fran but he's also been calling, weekends only, occasionally, on that Bohemian-looking girl halfway down the Culworth Road, right hand side, the red brick house with the fancy chimneys?'

'No!' they all exclaimed.

'I only found out two nights before he disappeared. If I'd known earlier I would have gone round to the Big House and given him a piece of my mind, double-timing a granddaughter of mine. Disgraceful!'

Marie, with no daughters to keep her eye on, said, 'It doesn't matter now like it did. All that virgin business, keeping yourself pure. That's all been thrown in the bin. They march down the aisle in full white wedding regalia, even the royals, with nothing virgin about 'em.'

Greta added her pennyworth by saying, 'I bet there isn't a single virgin bride going down any aisle anywhere nowadays.'

'Oh no!' declared Vera dismissively, 'he doesn't go there for *that* ... yer know what I mean? She's a superior fashion seamstress who designs and that somewhere in the West End, I think, and when she comes home at the weekends she sometimes brings things he's been having made by the company she works for up in London. They specialise in casual clothing, but high-fashion stuff, not supermarket stuff, real high-class stuff. Costs a bomb it does. She brings it home with her and he collects it from there rather than risking the post. She told me herself. She works twelve hours four days a week and then comes home to the village for three days over the weekend.'

'Are you sure?' asked Grandmama in shocked relief.

'I am. She says about Chris ...' they all leaned forward to catch every word Vera had to say, '... she wouldn't touch him, Chris that is, with a bargepole, because he has too many women in tow for her liking. Her grandmother lives at the nursing home where I used to work. Lovely old lady, that's why the granddaughter has a house here. She's definitely gone off the boil though, has the granny; can't remember a thing unless it happened seventy years ago. Used to live in Little Derehams as a girl, did the granny.'

Grandmama sat back, sipping her whisky. 'She looks a nice girl.'

'She is very nice. Her name's Fleur, French for flower she told me.'

Grandmama decided that with such a distinguished name Fleur wouldn't want to be associated with a man like Chris and she decided that she'd have a stern word with Fran because she shouldn't be associating with him either, if a nice girl like Fleur didn't want to be. Mind made up, she took action. She downed the last of her whisky, grabbed her bag said, 'Goodnight, everyone,' and disappeared off into the night. However, there was no one in at the

Charter-Placketts' so her dressing down of Fran would have to wait till the morning and it really aggravated her that, just when she needed a word, they were all out. And what was worse, they'd not told her where they'd gone, and that always annoyed her.

She was aware that Jimbo found it amusing when she wanted to be informed about their comings and goings and sometimes he was deliberately secretive, but Katherine Charter-Plackett had had enough of deception with Jimbo's father, who'd managed to keep a so-called wife and three sons secret for several years before she found out. But she'd loved him deeply despite his waywardness and was grateful when he came home to her to die. His courage in the face of death had impressed her enormously and the day he died she'd decided that that was how she would face death when the time came, with dignity. But on the day of his funeral when the last of the mourners had said goodbye, she declared to herself she wouldn't bother with the dying bit, she'd just keep on living. For ever. Life was far too interesting to miss out on.

Chapter 12

Fran had done nothing about her bright idea of finding a needy donkey for the Fitch children to look after so, feeling badly neglected by both Chris (where on earth was he?) and, let's face it, Alex Harris, she decided she would start on that project immediately. Instead of ringing the vet she decided to visit the veterinary clinic the very next time she was in Culworth, and on her next day off she made the clinic her first port of call. The waiting room was full and the reception staff very occupied so she had a few minutes to stand watching the scene while she waited for someone to come free to speak to her.

'Hi! How may I help?' said this bright young thing in an emerald green and white tabard.

'Good morning. My name's Frances Charter-Plackett and I'm a client of yours because my cat Bonnie is one of your patients – but I've not come about my cat.'

'Right.'

'I've come to see if you know of anyone who has a donkey or two they can't look after any more and who would be grateful to pass them on to someone who has stables and two fields that might be useful.'

'That's you, is it?'

'No, it's a neighbour of ours.'

'Is that what they want, two donkeys to look after?'

'Well ... actually, they don't know anything about the idea, but I think that's what they need for their family. Five children aged from twelve down to two.'

The receptionist hesitated. 'Five children? Donkeys are not cheap to keep, you know. Have they the money?'

'Oh, I'm sure the money wouldn't be a problem.'

The receptionist began to look full of doubt. 'If they need donkeys why haven't they come to talk to us about it?'

'Both doctors, too busy.'

'Look, write your name and address and telephone number or email down and leave it with me, I'll ask the vets here and see if they come up with something.'

So Fran, who'd imagined she'd solve the whole matter of donkeys for the Fitches immediately, because she was like that, came out of the clinic despondent. Then she realised how naive she'd been. Would *she* want two donkeys to look after? No, she wouldn't. First, they had no room for two in their garden, and second, they wouldn't be allowed. The half dozen chickens they had were only just acceptable to the council so donkeys certainly wouldn't be. And of course it was incredibly important that the children's parents were willing, although even more so that the children would be interested might be even higher on the agenda.

Never one to let the grass grow under her feet Fran decided to go immediately to Nightingale Farm because, it being Saturday, there was a good chance someone would be at home. She drove the long winding road to the Farm full of anticipation. She knew she was right. Donkeys would be the answer and the two younger boys would still be small enough to ride them. In fact, perhaps only Sarah would be considered too big. Could you ride donkeys, any donkey, or would they need to be trained? Why on earth had she thought up this daft idea? But there was no going back because Sarah was sitting on the fence beside the road watching her driving up.

Fran pulled up opposite her. 'Hi! Sarah! All right?'

'Just waiting.'

'What for?'

'Mum coming home. What time is it?'

Fran glanced at her dashboard clock. 'Half past eleven.'

Sarah shrugged her thin shoulders.

'Can I give you a lift up home?'

'No, thanks. I'll wait.'

'Dad in?'

Sarah shook her head.

'In that case, then, I'll turn round in the field gateway just here and go home.'

'OK.'

'Is Becky here?'

Sarah shook her head again. 'No. It's Saturday, so Ben doesn't go to that College place, only Monday to Friday.'

'Oh! Right!'

Sarah slipped down from the top of the fence and, leaning into the driver's window, said, 'Were you a maths person at school?'

'I was.'

'Good. I've got some paper here and a pen – can I sit in your car and talk?'

'Yes, if I can help.'

Sarah was round the front of the car and sitting in the passenger seat before Fran had switched off the engine.

'Right. Now this is the problem. Algebra. OK?'

'Oops, it's a while since I did any, but I'll try.'

They spent the next ten minutes sorting out Sarah's problem and to Fran's relief she was able to work it out by dragging fragments of algebra from the very back of her mind and arriving at the answer.

Sarah's relief was almost tangible. 'So that's how you do it! That's wonderful, I knew there was something I hadn't quite understood, that's just great. Thanks.' She leaned her head against the back of the seat and stared out of the windscreen, silently enjoying the thrill of having solved the algebra question.

Fran sat quietly, waiting for her to speak, sensing that the girl needed to talk.

A rabbit ran across the lane in front of the car and a few moments later there was a loud fluttering sound as a pheasant launched itself over the fence and disappeared into the field.

Fran laughed. 'It's busy round here this morning, isn't it?'

Sarah said grimly, 'If that's what you call busy ...'

'Not liking it round here, then?'

'None of us do.'

'Why not?'

'Nothing to do. Nothing happening. No one to talk to. The boys are driving me mad. Is there anyone sillier than a boy under eight years old? The only one with any sense is Gemma, but she's content with loads of homework and reading everything in sight.'

'So moving to the country is a dead loss for you?'

'Definitely. Where we lived before my friends were all round about, there was a cinema nearby, a park with tennis courts, swings – you name it the place was alive.' Sarah shouted the word 'alive' as though shouting it would make the dratted countryside come to its senses.

'What would make it better for you?'

'Bikes for Gemma and me for a start. But most of all, Mum at home. I know it's costing a lot of money making the house right and Mum wants Gemma and me to have a bathroom of our own which would be lovely because the boys are dreadful to share with, you walk in and there's wet towels dropped everywhere, wet footprints all over the tiles, toothpaste with the top missing and toothpaste oozing out of the tube. Have you got brothers?'

'Two. When they're home the bathrooms are just the same as yours. A complete mess.'

'Kindred spirits we are, then.' She smiled for the first time and made Fran glad she'd found time to spend with her.

'Your mum and dad thought the countryside would be good for you all.'

'They were wrong.'

'Perhaps if you did countryside things like—'

'What?'

'Riding? Do you do riding?'

'Frightened to death by horses, I am. Too big for me. That's that then.' Sarah paused for a minute and then added, 'I'll be gone.'

'I shall give this some thought,' Fran said.

'Thanks. It's Fran, isn't it, from the Store? What did you come for?'

'Actually to see why you were all unhappy. You children, I mean, and if there was anything I could do about it.'

Sarah picked up her pen which had dropped into the well in front of her seat, and as she sat up again she said very softly, 'Mum and Dad aren't happy either. Bye! Thanks for the algebra.' Sarah left, running up the lane back to the house as fast as she could in case there was a question from Fran hanging in the wind.

So what they really needed was something happening, exactly as Fran had thought, so the first thing she did when she got back was to look along the brochure racks that Jimbo always kept well up-to-date where anyone with anything going on always made sure he had a plentiful supply.

Someone advertising riding stables on the Culworth side of Turnham Malpas, Evie from the Embroidery Group advertising tuition, someone with a dog that needed a home – now that might be an idea – and, well, nothing else of any use in her scheme to help the Fitch grandchildren. Why she felt personally responsible to improve their lives she didn't know, but she did.

Fran went home to talk to her mother about it.

'Darling Fran, it's not your responsibility, you know. They have got parents, believe it or not.'

'But their parents always seem to be absent. It's just not fair on them especially the younger ones. Well, no, the older ones too,' and she followed on by relating the incident with Sarah. 'Her mum and dad aren't happy either, she said, but then she rushed off as though she didn't want to talk about them at all and it had slipped out by mistake.'

'I'm sure it's illegal to leave children of that age unsupervised. Look Caroline would know; go to the Rectory and ask her.'

'I expect it could be. Shall I? She'll think me an old busybody and there's plenty of those in this village without me being one at the tender age of twenty-one.'

Once they ceased laughing at the idea of Fran being a busybody Harriet said, 'I know for certain I would never have left Fergus nor Finlay in charge of you all at Sarah's age. They weren't fit to be left in charge of a tadpole never mind three children.'

'You wouldn't? Right. In that case I am going to see Mr Fitch and Kate and tell them what's going on.'

'Right now?'

'Right now.' Fran left the house immediately.

While walking round the green to the Fitch household Fran decided that Kate would be the person who would understand what she was worried about, she guessed, old Fitch not having had much to do with children, but it was he who answered the door.

'She's not in, gone for some retail therapy in Culworth and I've the lunch to make for one o'clock, she said.' He glanced at the hall clock to make sure he wasn't running late. 'Can I help in any way or do you want to leave a message?' He opened the door wider, as though inviting her in.

Fran decided he might not offer much help but at least she would have enlightened him to the dangers his grandchildren were in. 'I could tell you,' she said.

'Come in, then. Do you drink coffee? I've just this minute made a pot and there's far too much for just me.' At her nod he took her into the kitchen and poured a cup. 'Sugar?'

'No, thanks. But I will have some milk.'

'It's cream.'

'That's lovely, it won't harm just this once.'

Mr Fitch smiled at her and then encouraged her to sit with him by the fire in the sitting room.

'Might as well enjoy ourselves to the full. Follow me.'

The fire was roaring up the chimney and the room felt like a furnace.

'Fran, you sit there; there's nothing like a wood fire to spread warmth, and not just to your toes.' He smiled benignly at her and she thought how much he'd changed; maybe he was more congenial than he used to be now he was retired. So she began her story. At first he didn't appear very alarmed at what she told him but as the story progressed Fran could sense he *wanted* to hear more.

When she'd finished her story with the algebra incident he said, 'Obviously I knew they were trouble at school because of my Kate, but she said don't worry, they'll settle down in a while. I hadn't heard about the mayhem in your dad's store. One morning I did have them here before school and then I walked them round to the school gates – it's always so hectic at that time you know, what with the school minibuses and the parents who have to bring their children in their own cars, I couldn't let them go without me – and they were hard work. But I didn't realise things had got so bad for them. You say they need things to get interested in? Is it that they are just bored?'

He noticed her hesitation and encouraged her with a wave of his hand to continue so she did and came out with what amounted to the neglect that the children were suffering. When she paused for breath he didn't speak, just sat there, sipping his coffee with the flames from the roaring fire illuminating his face giving the impression he was about to ignite.

Mr Fitch very carefully put his empty coffee mug on the hearth, stood up, and said, 'I'm going up there right now. Yes this very minute. I didn't get a chance to bring up my two boys but the least I can do is see my grandchildren get taken proper care of. Thank you for telling me, Fran, and thank you for being so concerned. I really didn't know things were so bad. Do you mind?' He rattled his car keys at her and she took the hint.

'Should we put a fireguard round this fire, Mr Fitch? I'd hate you to come back to find your house ablaze.'

'Ah! Yes. Good thinking. And I'll just leave a note for Kate to tell her to eat on her own.'

Fireguard safely in position, the two of them went out, Mr Fitch heading for his car. Before he got in she said, 'Mr Fitch, I hope they won't think of me as a sneak, telling tales out of school, kind of? It's just that I felt so sorry for them.'

'My dear Fran, all I can say is thank you for your kindness. I'll be in touch.'

On his way to Nightingale Farm Craddock Fitch repeatedly ran through in his head the names of the children. He couldn't afford, on such an important day, to make foolish old-man mistakes with their names. If he did, he'd lose all credibility and he couldn't afford to do that. Quiet, calm authority was needed because he had to have the children on his side. If neither of their parents were there he would organise food then they'd clear up and he'd take them all out in his car. He'd leave a written message for Graham and Anita so they'd know where the children were when eventually they got home and he'd see to the parents when they all got back. All got back? All got back from where? Where did you take children nowadays? Then he remembered there was a fair in Culworth this week, on the common land known to everyone as The Billing. They'd go there. Yes, they'd like that. All children loved rides on fairgrounds.

The lunch went down well; they raided the freezer and consumed what he felt were absolutely dreadful beefburgers and frozen chips followed by wolfing down an entire box of fancy ice cream with a pint of fresh cream they found in the fridge that was only just within its sell-by date.

Some memory of his own two boys before they disappeared with their mother made him insist that everyone went to the lavatory before they left. He lined them up to assure himself they were looking passably clean and had warm coats on and gloves but the biggest problem for him at the fair was not losing any of them. They spent two dramatic hours there despite the cold, and when he declared he was going home not one of them said no because they were all so tired. Little Ross even asked if he'd bring them again tomorrow. On the way home the younger ones dozed, leaving the two girls to talk through the entire events of the afternoon as though it had been the highlight of their lives.

Both Anita and Graham were home when they arrived, but Craddock Fitch said nothing that might spoil one of the best afternoons he'd ever had. He rang Kate and she drove up to the farm and had supper with them all. The children went to bed and it was only then Craddock said what he had to say.

He drew in a huge breath and said, 'Through no fault of my own I never had the pleasure of bringing up my boys, but I am dammed if I'm going to stand by and watch my grandchildren being neglected. Kate is having one hell of a bad time with all four of the ones at the village school, and that includes Ross of course; there's been mayhem in the Store, stealing money and sweets, and the children, worst of all, are being left with no responsible adult in charge for several hours. It is my opinion that, in the likelihood of someone in the village reporting you to the social, I for one would applaud. They would be completely justified. I might report it myself.' Having said his piece as crisply as he could he sat back in his chair and waited.

The response from Kate was shock that he had dared to say what he'd said, because as head teacher of the village school she'd striven to keep the worst of their sins to herself.

Anita was steaming with anger and about to boil over any moment.

As for Graham, he appeared to be cast in stone. Horror, agreement, anger flooded his face in turn.

As no one replied Craddock added, 'Today Fran Charter-Plackett, who was driving up to the farm to see you both, sat with Sarah in her car helping her with her alejedbara. It's just not right.'

Then he got his reply. From Anita.

'How dare you? How dare you? You didn't care a toss all these years about Graham and Michael – they could have starved to death as far as you were concerned, and now you feel justified, *justified*, I say, to be free to say what you have just said. Go home and mind your own damn business! Go on! Out!' She got to her feet and opened the sitting-room door. 'Well!'

Craddock Fitch didn't move a single inch, but sat there waiting for her to admit the guilt she so clearly bore. Anita spluttered out in her defence that she didn't move here because she wanted to, she moved because Graham wanted to. 'But now you are complaining. Report us to the social what for?'

Craddock got to his feet. 'For leaving your children without proper responsible adult care. You are both educated to a level of which I know nothing, having left school at the tender age of fourteen, but I do know that leaving children, the eldest only twelve, on their own, is not responsible and for two pins if it wasn't a Saturday I would be in Culworth telling them at the social what is happening here. It is totally irresponsible! Sarah is only twelve. If some major incident occurred while she was in charge of these four children, the guilt of it would dog her all her life. She is not old enough.'

Anita fumed. 'In that case, then why don't you come up and look after them for us? Mmm? Why not? Oh! Of course, *you'd* be too old, too much for an old man like you. Ha!' Anita, beginning to feel a fool holding the door open for him to leave when he wouldn't, moved away from the door and stood, arms akimbo, in front of the fire, waiting for someone other than her to speak up in her defence.

Graham went to stand beside her. 'Major incident? What kind of major incident would that be?'

Now Kate spoke up. 'One of the children getting scalded trying to make a hot drink. One of them getting burned trying to cook a meal, or a wholesale fire; it does happen. Old Lady Templeton died because she had become incapable of cooking due to senility and she set the house on fire and being thatched, like this farmhouse is, it went up in a horrifyingly short space of time. You may want to remind Craddock of his neglect, Anita, but he couldn't find his two boys, she'd changed their names and her own so the police couldn't trace them. But whatever has happened in the past has nothing whatsoever to do with the danger and the boredom – and believe me, extreme boredom can drive children to ridiculous extremes! Please, listen and take steps to make sure they are well looked after. It's all too late when something dreadful happens and you're left saying "but we didn't realise" or "well, you see I had to work late". Neither of you are idiots. Just pause and give your-selves time to reflect. Your children are a delight, highly intelligent and a pleasure to teach. It's you who moved them into what is for them a completely alien environment, so just do something about it, please. Now we're going. Thank you for the meal – you've a wonderful family and there are hundreds of people who would be so grateful to have them because they have none. And remember, too, no one made you give birth to five children, it was entirely your choice, and you have a responsibility to make sure they are safe and well cared for ...'

Kate stood up, put her arms around Graham and kissed him heartily, embraced Anita kissing her on both cheeks, and said cheerily, 'Goodnight both of you, our love to the children. So glad Craddock found you and you came to live nearby. We haven't fallen out, have we?'

Anita, who had been thinking while Kate spoke, answered, 'Absolutely not. Thank you for taking the children out this after-noon, Craddock, they obviously enjoyed themselves.'

After the door closed behind Craddock and Kate, Anita turned to face Graham. 'Well?' she said.

'Well?' asked Graham. 'What have I been saying to you for months now?'

'It's all very well for you to be self-righteous about it all but (a) we need the money, (b) it's not you being asked to stay on because of a major incident and they are short-handed in Emergency and (c) I love my work. So?'

Graham went to sit down while he had a think. She was right on all counts but ... 'It's our very own children we are talking about, Anita. Not some mythical children in a social worker's files, but they soon damn well will be if we're not careful, and I will not allow our children to be put under the microscope of Culworth Social Services – they could even take them away from us. We would not be starving to death if only I worked. Some families would be if only one parent worked because they can't earn enough, but I do. Don't you see?'

Anita vigorously shook her head.

'Darling, just think of the improvement in your life if you didn't work so much. You don't have a life at the moment because you are continuously playing catch-up with everything: the food shopping, the washing, the cleaning, everything, and I'm sick to death of our entire lives being in a huge great muddle. With your qualifications, in a few years you'll be able to indulge yourself with a fine job and do it without your entire world falling apart every single day. You are exhausted, doing all these extra hours, and whilst ever you are willing they will put on you and leave you to live a miserable life without batting an eyelid. Remember how you looked forward to having time in the house on your own once Ross went to nursery? Time in the house to assemble your brain and get a perspective on life? Becky coming one half day helps a little but not enough. You might even read a novel, perhaps?'

Anita, who'd been sitting with her head in her hands, refusing to acknowledge what he was saying, looked up and recollected that moment of looking forward to having time to spare and briefly toyed with the idea of having the house to herself so she could think what she was doing.

'But what the blazes would I do with myself if I did have time? You've not won this particular battle, so don't imagine for one moment that you have, Graham. It's all very well your father stepping in and having his say—'

'Every word he and Kate said about the children's safety was correct, Anita. Be generous and admit that.'

'I suppose so ... about their safety perhaps he is.' Anita paused for a moment. 'Do you know, I can't remember how long it is since I read a book? People buy me them for presents, remembering how much I used to read before Ross came, and now I never get round to reading them. Maybe a fifth child is what broke the camel's back.'

Graham smiled at her; he could feel she was beginning to see his point of view. He did his best to help in the house and with the children, but he worked long hours himself and he knew how difficult it was to be reasonable and patient with five children at the end of a long day.

'Think about it? OK? It's your welfare I'm thinking of, darling. It would be good if Becky could come more often but she's far too busy, isn't she?'

Anita nodded her agreement. 'She is. Five different jobs she has and then Ben to look after. Look, I'm going to bed – I can't do anything more tonight. I'll think about what you said about the hospital putting pressure on me.'

Chapter 13

Becky Braithwaite couldn't put in any more hours than the three she already did every Friday morning up at Nightingale Farm. She wished she could do more for them, but there simply were not enough hours in her busy week for her to do so. Since the Fitches had moved in a transformation had begun that must have cost a fortune — but the result so far was a breath-taking kitchen. She looked around her own while she waited for the kettle to boil and wished ... oh, it wasn't that it needed decorating or needed new units, they were all new when she moved in, but they were so plain! So plain that even though they'd only been in use three months they were already on the verge of looking slightly shabby. But they'd have to wait. She still had the bedrooms to furnish properly, especially her own, but that would all come in time.

Becky counted herself lucky that she and Ben had been allocated this flat by the council. To live in such a beautiful place was something neither of them had ever imagined was possible. They had lived in the rough end of Culworth all their lives but when her father died the council agreed to re-home her and Ben in these new flats in Turnham Malpas and there was nothing more certain than the fact that here in the village he didn't get tormented like he had been in Culworth. There had been endless stories of him being surrounded by bullies with nothing better to do than think up punishments for him, or they'd steal his money or his sweets.

He loved his sweets, did Ben. Ben, with a bag of sweets in his hand, was the happiest man on earth. Well, not man, boy, really, because he'd never be a man. Becky poured the hot water into the teapot, calling out, 'Ben! Want a biscuit?'

This was their ritual, as soon as he came home from the College. Four-thirty prompt the taxi always drew up outside the house, he would have tea and two biscuits then he'd sit and watch children's TV until his evening meal was ready, then he watched the soaps and then he went to bed and what was left of the evening was hers. Saturdays, no College, so they went to the market in Culworth, had lunch in the chippy, went for a walk in Sykes Wood during the afternoon if it was fine, had something a bit special for their evening meal it being Saturday, then Sunday she went to church if she could persuade Ben into going too, but sometimes he was too stubborn and couldn't or wouldn't be persuaded.

But Becky never complained about caring for him; for one thing, he was the only living relative she had that she knew of and so he was precious. She'd faced up to not marrying whilst ever he was alive and the day she'd accepted that, really acknowledged the fact deep down inside her, she had learned to live with it and, better still, amazing really because she'd never felt love for him before, she'd discovered at the same time she loved him too which gave her life real purpose.

Ben joined her at the kitchen table, which he didn't usually, because he didn't like to miss his programmes but today he did. 'Had a good day? Mmm?' Becky asked.

Ben didn't answer her.

'I asked if you'd had a good day. Ben? At College.'

'No. Gardening, all day.'

'Well, of course, that's the course you're on. That's what you go to learn. You always love it.'

'I don't now, not now. Nasty, that's what.'

'Why? Has someone upset you?'

'New teacher. He's nasty, nasty, nasty!'

Under her breath Becky said, 'Hell's bells.' She dreaded the unexpected with him. If she could anticipate problems she'd have

time to work out how to approach them, but unexpected ones ...
Out loud she asked, 'Why?'

'What's that I can't do?'

Becky guessed. 'Swear?'

Ben nodded as he was drinking his tea and it splashed down his sweater. Having sorted out the mess Becky said, 'Well, he shouldn't. You know better than to swear, don't you?'

Ben nodded. 'I know lots of things.'

'I know you do, because you listen properly when I tell you things. You should always listen when Becky tells you things, because I love you, don't I?'

Ben grinned at her. 'Sometimes I listen.'

'Sometimes? Only sometimes? But you *always* listen. You're good at that.'

'Not that night I went in the pub. It was fun in the pub, all that talking. Fun. Yes, fun.'

'Well, that's the only time.' Becky laughed. 'Only once. You were sensible and went to Peter for help.'

But then Ben's left knee began dithering so hard his left heel was beating a tattoo on the tiled floor. His knee dithered rapidly up and down time after time and she knew what that meant: he had a secret. That giveaway signal had begun when he was ten. He'd stolen someone's sweets at his school and ate them coming home in the taxi till he was sick all over the lavatory floor when he got home.

Becky remembered how angry her mother was, and it happened again within the week. This second time that rapidly dithering knee gave him away. He wasn't sick the second time, Becky remembered, but he couldn't eat his supper being so full of stolen sweets, and was sent straight to bed. They never did find out where he got the sweets from and her mother never told the school.

Now she was faced with the dithering knee and she didn't know what to do. The beat of his shoe heel on the floor felt like she was being stabbed straight through her heart each time she heard it.

Becky asked him twice to stop dithering his knee but it appeared he couldn't hear her voice, so she stood behind his chair, put her arms around his shoulders and hugged him tightly. 'There, there, you can tell your Becky. I won't tell anyone, Ben.'

At that moment the doorbell rang loudly three times. This was the wrong moment, so she ignored it. 'Tell Becky, then.'

The doorbell rang again and again. She had to answer it! Becky opened the door, a welcoming smile on her face because, being new to the village, the doorbell did not ring very often.

'I'm Dottie,' said the woman on the doormat, 'Dottie Foskett. I'm collecting the envelope for the Salvation Army Appeal; I left it on Monday.' Dottie displayed her authorisation badge and waited.

For a moment Becky was at a loss and then she remembered the envelope she'd put behind the kitchen clock. 'Please, come in. I'll get my purse.'

Dottie spoke to Ben: 'I've heard about you, you must be Ben. My name's Dottie.'

That irritating dithering knee was still working hard. Ben turned round to face Dottie, because he liked the sound of her voice. He saw she was a funny round little person with a big smile and big happy eyes. He liked her so he spoke to her while Becky dug into her purse. 'Yes, I'm Ben. I'm learning to be a gardener and then Sir Johnny's giving me a job. He's got a big garden and I'm going to dig it.'

'Well, Ben, that sounds like a good idea. As I said, you'll do well at that. My name's Dottie. If you see me in the village next time you're out, remember to have a word with me.'

'Can I come for the envelopes with you?'

Dottie wasn't quite sure what he meant but guessed he wanted to help collect the envelopes. 'Only if Becky says yes,' she said.

'Right.'

'Just round the village green and then back home again. That's all, then I've finished. That's if Becky says yes.'

'No, absolutely no. You can't, Ben.' Becky winked meaningfully at Dottie, conveying that she understood Dottie didn't really want Ben to go with her.

'He can come with me if he promises to behave, Becky. I don't go out with men who don't behave.'

Dottie smiled indulgently at Ben who suddenly was very determined to go with her, no matter what Becky said. He knew instinctively that Dottie liked him and he didn't meet many people who did.

Before Becky could engage his mind and put him off going, Ben was out of the door eager to carry the bag Dottie was collecting the envelopes in. Becky hastily grabbed her coat saying, 'I'm coming too.'

It took longer collecting with Ben than Dottie had anticipated because he loved talking to all the people she knew and to whom she introduced Becky and Ben. Eventually they headed for home, and Ben went eagerly with them, still clutching the bag to his chest.

'Come in, Dottie. Please,' Becky said knowing full well what was going on in Ben's head and dreading the inevitable confrontation. 'Now, Ben, put the kettle on and you can make us each a cup of tea.' He loved being responsible for making a cup of tea and with strict supervision he managed quite well. 'We'll have those new biscuits. I'll open the packet and then you can put them on a plate. Dottie will like these, won't you, Dottie?' She showed Ben and Dottie the packet of biscuits, desperate to get the money bag from him without too much upset. But his immediate objective was the money in the envelopes despite longing to try the new biscuits.

Becky flashed a desperate glance at Dottie and fortunately she understood immediately what the problem was. Ben had already begun struggling to open a fat envelope and there was no doubt in Dottie's mind because of past experience that it would be full of pennies.

'Ben!' said Dottie quietly, 'I'm not allowed to open the envelopes. I just collect. Someone else really important counts the money. You and me, we're not clever enough to count it, there's so much of it.' She held out her hand inviting him to give the bag to her. 'I don't want that important person to be angry with me. She's very, very important, you see, and everyone does as she says.'

Some of the determination in Ben began to melt away. He ruminated on his problem; after all, it was a lot of money and he would have liked it. A very important person? 'You mean the Queen? She's very important.'

Rapidly grabbing at this fanciful idea even though it was a lie Dottie agreed. 'Yes, it is indeed the Queen.'

Becky also agreed. 'You'll tell the Queen that Ben helped collect the money won't you Dottie?'

'Of course, she'll be pleased to hear about him.'

But Ben had lost interest when the money wasn't forthcoming and went in the living room to switch the TV on and search for a programme that he fancied, the money forgotten.

Dottie, standing on the pavement outside Becky's flat before she left said, 'Look, on Saturday morning why don't you and Ben come to my house for a coffee? Mmm? Or, or … I know! I wouldn't mind having him for an hour or so if you want to clothes shop or get your hair done. Must be difficult to get a few hours to yourself when you work all the time he's at the College. Think about it.'

Becky was filled with gratitude by this idea but was too embarrassed to agree to Saturday immediately – it looked so grateful to do that, and she hated being grateful where Ben was concerned.

'Well, he does seem to like you. And I'd pay you something.'

Dottie gave her half a smile. 'I wouldn't want money. If you need a reference I work at the Rectory four mornings a week.'

'Oh, I didn't mean I wanted a reference and I wouldn't expect it every Saturday. I've learned to accept his … Anyway, I would be glad to have a break this Saturday. What time shall I bring him down? If he's willing, that is.'

'Change of plan. I tell you what, I'll collect him at half past nine and we can go to the coffee morning in the Church Hall and he can meet everyone, then we'll wander off down home and you can collect him from there. I live in that little cottage, Rose Cottage, at the bottom of Shepherd's Hill, the one with the red rose climbing up the front, 'cept it's not flowering at the moment, of course!'

Dottie smiled energetically, pleased with her idea of Becky having time to herself and making Ben welcome in her cottage. 'Ben,' she called, 'do you play cards?'

Ben answered her from inside the flat. 'Yes, I like cards. Snap, I like.'

'That's settled then, Snap it is. I'll be here at half nine. Bye!'

When it came to it Ben didn't know if he wanted to go all the way down Shepherd's Hill to Dottie's house. He'd enjoyed having coffee with everyone at the coffee morning and talking, but walking all that way? And where was Becky?

'Becky's gone shopping for a new dress and she'll be back soon. Let's be off.' Dottie tried her best to persuade him to walk down to her cottage. 'It's not far.' But he wouldn't agree to go.

'I'm going home,' he said. '3a Culworth Road. My name's Ben Braithwaite. 3a Culworth Road. My name's Ben Braithwaite. 3a C—'

Peter, seeing the dilemma Dottie was in, intervened. 'I'm going that way in my car, Ben, would you like a ride down there with Dottie?'

'In your great big car?'

'Yes. My new one.'

'Yes!' Ben was out of the Church Hall in a moment, heading straight for Peter's car which was parked outside the Rectory and struggling to open the driver's door.

'This other side, Ben.'

Peter's car purred down Shepherd's Hill much to the delight of

Ben who sat, tense with excitement, all the way down to Rose Cottage.

'I like this car,' he said time after time as he smoothed his hand over the leather upholstery.

In order to make sure Ben got out without a confrontation Dottie casually mentioned to Peter about her new dog. 'I got him from the dog's home; he was a cruelty case, and I've called him Sykes because he's a Jack Russell and white with black patches very like that old dog of Craddock Fitch's called Sykes. I've had him two weeks and he's settled in lovely, and does he love his food? Yes, he does! Come on then, Ben. Out you get.'

Although it would be two or more hours before Becky came to collect him, Dottie had no problems with Ben because he kept himself busy the whole time with Sykes-dog as he called him.

It was a cold, clear day and they ran round the garden together, played ball with Sykes-dog bringing the ball back to Ben countless times. Finally Ben flopped down on a kitchen chair, out of breath.

'Would you like a drink Ben? Orange or Coke?' Dottie asked.

She came back with Coke for Ben and Sykes-dog's water bowl and the two of them drank urgently. When he'd had enough Sykes-dog flung himself down on the floor, panting, looking as though he wouldn't move another step for hours and Ben said, 'He's all right, Dottie. He's breathing. Not dead.' He leaned against the back of the chair contemplating Sykes-dog's exhaustion. '*Chris* isn't breathing. *He's* dead. That's what they said. They said, "He isn't breathing, this chap's dead." '

Dottie, petrified, managed to ask, 'Who said Chris was dead? Who, Chris? Mmm?'

Two questions at once were too muddling for Ben to deal with so he ignored Dottie and just sat there staring at Sykes-dog. 'Sykes-dog isn't dead, though, he's breathing.' Dottie thought Ben couldn't possibly be talking about Chris Templeton. Could he? Or could he?

'Where did you find Chris, then?' But a question thrown at him so abruptly completely foxed Ben.

To avoid any more puzzling questions he declared he needed the lavatory. Dottie had a downstairs one so she showed him where it was but didn't mention locking the door in case she couldn't get him back out again. However, he arrived back in the living room properly zipped up and ready to play cards.

They played snap for almost an hour before the doorbell rang and when Dottie answered it there was Becky on the doorstep asking, 'Have you been all right? I mean, no problems?'

'Ben, tell Becky who brought us home.'

'Peter, in his new car. Can you buy a car like his?'

Becky laughed. 'No, my little car's just fine for us. Come on, then, let's be off.'

'I want to stay here.'

Dottie answered him firmly, saying, 'Not today, but you can come another day and we'll take Sykes-dog for a walk and you can hold his leash. OK? Had a good time, Becky?'

'Have I had a good time? Yes, I have. Brilliant! I've bought a skirt and top for Christmas and some new underwear and I'm really pleased with it. Thank you so much for having him. It's been great. Say thank you to Dottie, Ben.'

As she turned away to leave, Ben said, 'Thank you, Dottie. I'll walk Sykes-dog when I come.'

As Becky stepped out into the road to get into her car, to Dottie's alarm Ben placed a finger on his lips saying very softly as he did so 'Shush!' and managing to shut one eye in a long, slow wink.

Was there an awful lot more to Ben than she had at first imagined? she wondered. Was he not the simple-minded teenager she'd first thought he was? She laughed at herself for her suspicions and decided it was a load of rubbish she was thinking. But why on earth would he, who had nothing to do with Chris socially, mention him because he saw a dog lying down looking as though he might be dead?

Dottie worried about it the rest of the weekend and by Monday morning had decided that if the reverend wasn't too busy she'd mention it to him. When they were alone, Dottie knocked on the study door and asked for a word. 'I've brought your coffee, Reverend, knew you'd be wanting to be off to the market. But before you go can I have a word?'

Peter nodded. 'Thanks for the coffee. Sit down, Dottie.'

Dottie didn't plunge down onto the big soft sofa but settled for an upright chair; after all, she was here on business, not for an outburst about her spiritual problems.

'You remember you kindly gave Ben and me a lift home on Saturday? Well, while he was at my house he said something rather odd and I thought I'd sound you out about it. I know he's not quite all there,' she tapped her temple to illustrate her meaning, 'and that he says strange things sometimes, completely unconnected to what's going on, but he'd been playing with my new dog till the poor little thing was exhausted so I gave him a drink and then he laid down on the kitchen floor getting his breath back so to speak. The dog did, that is. Ben was sitting on a chair watching him and drinking his Coke, and suddenly he said, "Sykes-dog isn't dead. They said Chris is dead. He's not breathing they said. This chap's dead. Chris is dead they said." When I'd got over the shock I asked him how he knew about it and such but he'd lost the thread and said nothing else.'

Peter shook his head. 'It's certainly very strange. Ben's very obviously seen something no one else has, hasn't he? But he's never out on his own – well, only very, very occasionally if he manages to escape Becky's eagle eye. Will you keep it to yourself, Dottie, because I can't think how to proceed with this just now. I must either talk to Becky or try and talk to Ben, but we don't want ridiculous unfounded rumours going round the village. Thank you for telling me, though.'

Dottie nodded. 'I'm going to have him now and again to give Becky a break, so perhaps you could have a go then?'

'I'd have to ask Becky's permission, wouldn't I?'

'Yes, of course. It *is* worrying though, isn't it, Reverend? You see, he couldn't possibly mention some men and what they'd said nor the fact that they were saying Chris was dead unless he was really dead, could he? Unless he'd seen it happen or touched Chris and somehow realised he was dead. It doesn't bear thinking about, does it? Ben's not clever enough to invent it because he doesn't seem to have an imagination. Well, I don't think he has. But he *is* clever enough to tell me to keep quiet about what he told me, because behind Becky's back, where she couldn't see him, he put his finger to his mouth said "shush" and gave me a very deliberate wink, so he's keeping whatever it was secret from Becky.'

Dottie and Peter left it all hanging in the air for the moment and in the end neither Dottie nor Peter told Becky what Ben had said because he unwittingly told her himself. He went with her to the Store one Saturday afternoon to buy sweets while Becky shopped for a few things for Sunday lunch. She wasn't paying any attention to Ben, purposely leaving him alone to enjoy choosing whatever he'd made his mind up to buy.

There was just Fran serving that afternoon and the only other customer in the shop was someone unknown to Becky, being a newcomer. Nor was she really known by Fran, though she knew the woman came from Penny Fawcett.

Out of the blue the Penny Fawcett woman asked Fran had anything been heard of that flashy chap, the brother of the man who'd bought the Big House for him and his family? 'You'll know if anyone does, because he was a friend of yours, wasn't he, for a while? Chris! Yes, Chris, that was his name. Lovely looking chap and so rich they say. Has he been in touch since he left?'

Fran, taken aback by the question because no one who came in to shop regularly ever deliberately upset her by asking after Chris. As the weeks had gone by his name had dropped almost entirely out of the general chit-chat. 'No! Not since he left.'

As Ben approached the till to pay for his sweets, the woman

from Penny Fawcett pressed on with her investigation. 'I quite fancied that Chris. He always had a lovely word for everyone. It was Chris this and Chris that in Penny Fawcett and it wasn't just me who fancied him. I wonder where he is now?'

Just as Fran decided to change the subject of their conversation, Ben, patiently queuing behind the woman from Penny Fawcett who was digging in her bag to find her purse said, 'Chris is dead.'

The woman swung round to face him, both horrified and delighted by this statement: this really was something to tell them back in Penny Fawcett! 'Dead? What makes you say that?'

'He is. He's dead. They said so.'

'Dead? Who said so?' she asked.

Ben, remembering Becky could hear every word he spoke, shut his mouth. Tight.

'Well? Who said so?' the customer demanded.

Becky stepped forward saying, 'Take no notice of him, he's just teasing. Have you paid yet? I'm in a hurry.'

'Keep your hair on! I won't be a minute.' But the woman was more than a minute. She complained about the price of the bacon she'd bought and handed it back which meant the till receipt had to be altered, insisted on changing two of the oranges she'd chosen and asked to have the cheese weighed again, leaving Ben, as Becky guessed he would be, almost at boiling point with temper by the delay.

'I want to pay,' he said angrily.

'In a minute, in a minute. Keep your hair on.'

Becky said, 'Give me your sweets and I'll pay for them. Just go and wait outside, Ben, please.'

But Ben already had saliva in his mouth in anticipation of eating his jelly babies and he wasn't going to be put off. He banged all his money down on the counter and stalked off.

'Eh! You! Who do you think you are?' the customer shouted.

Fran, determined this woman was not going to bully Ben, said quietly, 'Here's your change, there's your shopping. Thank you for shopping with us and see you again soon.'

Fran's smile did little to calm the woman down. She was very annoyed, not just a bit annoyed. 'This is disgusting! Talk about bad manners, saying that Chris is dead. Of all things. Judging by the God-awful look on his face *he* could have killed him. Maybe he did and we've just witnessed a confession! I think I'll go to the police and tell them what he said. It should be looked into.' She snapped her handbag shut and stormed off at such a speed they really did begin to wonder if she was off to tell the police immediately.

Fran was horrified. 'I am so sorry, Becky. Go and make sure Ben's OK. We don't want him missing. I'll sort your shopping.'

Fortunately Ben was hiding behind the post box waiting for Becky so she didn't have far to go and, knowing him as she did, she never mentioned what he'd said because she knew by now he'd be so upset he wouldn't give her a truthful reply.

She persuaded him to head for home but 3a Culworth Road had never seemed so far to walk before. She gave him his jelly babies to eat on the way in order to soothe him and by the time he got ensconced on the sofa and the TV was switched on he appeared to have forgotten the incident in the Store. So when the commercials came on she chose her moment.

'Why did you say Chris was dead?' Fran asked.

No reply.

'I said, why did you say Chris was dead? You don't know someone called Chris.'

'No, I don't.'

'So, why did you say it, Ben?'

'*They* said it.'

'They? Who's they?' She helped herself to one of his jelly babies. This annoyed him. 'They're Ben's. Not Becky's.'

'I asked a question. I said "Who's they?" Who said Chris was dead?'

'He was. He wasn't breathing. Sykes-dog, he was breathing, you could see. He wasn't dead.'

'No, he wasn't, he was running about when I saw him, but you say Chris wasn't running about?'

Ben shook his head. 'No. Shut up and watch this programme with me. I like it.'

Becky tried another question. 'Where did you see Chris dead?'

Ben got angry. 'I don't know. Shut up, you silly Becky, this is my favourite programme!' He continued stuffing jelly babies into his mouth until there was none left. He screwed up the paper bag and flung it with a wild aim onto the electric fire where it began to burn up then fell on the hearth, still in flames. Becky leapt up and stamped on the flaring bag until it was a smouldering, blackened mess.

'Ben! Of all things. You know not to do that, the flat could have been on fire, then where would we have been? No flat – and we both love this flat, so much better than that old pigsty of a place we lived in all our lives. You've got to be more careful.'

'Becky's a naughty girl,' he said sullenly. 'A very naughty girl, shouting at Ben, burning the flat up.'

'*I* didn't do it!' Becky protested.

'You threw it on the fire.'

'No, I didn't. It was you!'

Becky knew that they were heading for one of those stupidly pointless arguments which neither of them won but which left them both excessively cross with each other and took several days for Ben to recover from, and she didn't want him cross, she wanted him to think straight. Well, as straight as he could, so she could sort out this idea that he'd seen Chris dead. Then she smiled with relief at the thought she'd just had: this Chris person was a character in a TV drama Ben had watched and not a real person at all and him being dead had for some reason seized Ben's attention. That was it, of course! She remembered now, there had been a Chris who got murdered in that police series that she'd barely understood, and it was pure coincidence that the dreadful woman in the Store had used the name Chris and it had struck a chord in Ben's memory. Thank God! That was one problem solved and she sighed with relief at the thought. Her life was difficult enough without inventing things to worry about.

The woman from Penny Fawcett, however, informed every soul she spoke to that she'd been told by the idiot who killed him that Chris was dead, that the murderer was still at liberty and could kill again without compunction at any moment. She embroidered the story about meeting the murderer in the Store so vividly that they were inundated by people coming in just to ask the eyewitnesses all about it, but buying things too in order to make their presence in the Store appear genuine.

The tale went rapidly around the three villages, but due to the impossibility of there being a single atom of truth in it, the story died a natural death after about three days. However, the stigma attached itself to Ben and those who didn't know who Ben was believed the murderer was still at large.

Still, takings were up with this amazing influx of curious people so Jimbo, Tom, Bel and Fran rubbed their hands with glee and Becky and Ben carried on their lives without realising that for three days they'd been the talk of the villages.

Chapter 14

All the hoo-ha about Chris and him being dead did nothing to lessen the terrible fear in which Greta was living. She was losing weight by the day and Vince decided she must visit the doctor.

'And I don't mean our usual GP, I mean Dr Harris, because she'll listen and understand and she knows you very well. You'd feel able to talk to her, wouldn't you?'

'That is ridiculous. She isn't a GP as well you know, and I'm not going. I shall be glad to arrive in Canada looking slim and younger because I don't want those boys of ours thinking I've slipped into old age all of a sudden. I've been saving up for new clothes for our trip to Canada next year so I'll buy them for this new slim figure that I've got and not that saggy bottomed person I've been for years. Just leave it to me.'

'But Greta ...'

'No buts, Vince, thank you. I'm all right. I'm eating plenty so there can't be that much wrong with me.'

Greta went off into the kitchen to avoid Vince nagging her, but before she managed to get the door shut she heard him shout, 'If you looked in the mirror you'd see what I mean.'

Greta didn't have a mirror in the kitchen so she dug into her handbag lying on the kitchen table and grimaced into her compact mirror. She pulled her face together and smiled and then turned sideways and saw that her double chin had all but disappeared, that there were wrinkles where there didn't used to be and her neck looked kind of stringy.

She knew full well that Vince was right and that it was the

worry of the poison pen letters. Now they said some terrible things about her ... well about her and her mother and how they knew about the whole situation of her birth she had no idea, but know they certainly did. The whole picture of what was in the trunk in the Rectory loft and what she herself had kept secret since she'd first been told about it by her mother at just fourteen years old suddenly crept over her, from her toes right the way to the untidy parting in her hair and before she knew it she was vomiting in the sink, something she did almost, but not quite, every day now. It tasted foul and she had to get a drink of water to clear her throat and mouth. Always before she'd managed to keep the vomiting from Vince but tonight he heard her and appeared in the kitchen before she could rinse the sink down.

'Greta! I heard you. Whatever's the matter, love? It's not the first time, is it? So this is why you're getting thinner: you eat but then you sick it up. Bulimia, it's called and it's serious. You'll have to go to see the doctor and I'm going with you.'

Greta sank down onto the nearest kitchen chair and wept with great sobbing, searing cries of pain, so loud Vince was convinced the neighbours would be round any minute, knocking on the door to see what was wrong.

'Hush, love. Hush. What's making you like this? Is it worrying about going to Canada? Or me not going with you? Well, I'm coming with you, I really am, I've decided, so if it's that, don't worry any more. I'll take care of you, Greta, there's no need to be frightened no more. Vince is here and he'll take care of you. Promise.'

But his words of comfort did nothing to assuage her tears. She wasn't accustomed to this kind of gentle treatment from Vince – he was much more likely to be bracing and not supportive, more a 'pull yourself together' attitude and this kindly consideration made matters worse.

'Greta! It's not Canada is it? I'm wrong.' Vince sat down on the nearest chair to hers, put an arm round her shoulders and begged her to tell him what the matter was. 'There's no one else 'ere, just me, and you can tell me anything, absolutely anything, that's troubling you. We've been together that many years I can't count and I know I've not always been the most considerate of husbands but I know consideration is what you need right now. So tell me and I'll listen.'

Vince found a clean tissue on the table that Greta had intended wiping her mouth with when she'd finished vomiting and he dabbed her tears with it, wiped the sweat from her forehead and then threw it in the kitchen bin and found a fresh one for her to use if she needed it. She had no memory of consideration on this level from Vince, never, ever, before and it made her weep even more.

Vince got her a drink of water, with ice in it, and it tasted so fresh, so cleansing, especially being handed to her by Vince and him being so cherishing that she decided she couldn't carry the burden of the poison pen letters by herself any longer.

'I'll have to tell you, I can't keep it to myself any longer,' she sobbed, and so the whole story of the letters came rushing out, the words tumbling over each other as she tried to explain about her fear.

'What have you done with them? Burned 'em?'

'They're upstairs in a drawer under my summer tights. I'll go and get them.'

She sat watching him as he began to read the first ones and she saw his face go pale then blanch with anguish and his first words were, 'You should have said! You see ... Greta ... you see ... I've ... I've always known your secret. Right since before we got married.'

Greta almost passed out with the horror of what he'd said. When she could finally speak she said just one word. 'How?'

'To be honest, your mother told me.'

'My mother told you? Never!'

'She did,' he said and she believed him.

And at last Greta told him how she'd felt all the past years. 'I couldn't tell you because it hurt me so much, it did, knowing what I knew. I was only fourteen when she told me and it was as if she wanted to hurt me on purpose, real bad, you know?'

Vince squeezed her shoulders tighter. 'Remember when we were courting and we had a tiff and we decided not to see each other any more? Well, she was delighted we'd broken up ...'

'Was she? Come to think of it, yes, she would be, she had plans for me to look after her in her old age, didn't want me getting married and having a life of my own. I am so sorry about that tiff we had. I just wanted to see how it felt without you, to prove to myself if I really loved you.' Vince's arm round her shoulders felt so comforting she shuffled closer to make sure he didn't take it away.

Vince said softly, 'She was a bitter, bitter woman. She blamed anyone but herself for it happening. When in fact she could have put a stop to it. All she had to do was tell someone what he was doing to her, that was all, just tell, and she could have saved you from all this.'

Greta appeared to grow smaller, thinner, more frail as she remembered the shock of what she'd been told.

'Your mother gloried in the telling of it and that's what was shaming to me. Said you needed to know when in fact she could have kept that big gob of hers tight shut and never let on. It was as if she wanted to ruin your life because her life had been ruined and she couldn't see why you shouldn't suffer too.'

'Vince?'

'Mmm.'

'Vince? I've often thought, over the years, maybe I should never have married you and had the boys, seeing as my granddad was also my father. The nasty old man doing that to my mother ... Oh, I never liked him even before I was fourteen and my mother – no, my grandmother confessed to me about him. And what he did to her own daughter, Mary Ann, my real mother, time after time apparently.'

Greta stirred in his arms and looked directly into his face, a question bubbling over inside her. She had to ask him. She had to say it out loud because she desperately needed to know. 'Vince? Tell me. When my mo ... no, my grandmother told you about me and my ... origins what did you think? Did you shudder? Did you feel disgusted? Did you loathe me? Because *I* did. Still do ...' The tears rolled down her face and it broke his heart all over again to see her so distressed.

'Stop crying, Greta, right now. Then you can listen to what I say. I shan't speak till you've stopped. I mean it. Stop crying, Greta.'

Greta had to work hard to stem the tide pouring down her cheeks.

'Right. Now. This is the truth and I should have said it years ago but there was always a barrier because you didn't want to be reminded and I didn't want to remember either. Well, we had our three boys, all born right in body and mind which considering ... anyway, that seemed to me to make things right somehow, 'cos they could so easily, because of your granddad being your dad, have been mentally crippled or physically crippled, but they're not. And, what's more we shall never *ever* tell them. No need for their lives to be spoiled as well as yours and your poor mother's. How your grandmother could have let Silas do what he did to Mary Ann is beyond me – because she did nothing to stop it and what sort of life did that poor child have? Nothing but misery and dead at fourteen. You and I shall never talk about it again unless you want to. We've said all there is to be said and talking about it won't make it not have happened. It did – and there's no talk about them two grandaughters of ours in Canada being not all right so there's no need. Now I'm getting the whisky out, I need it and so do you. Right?'

'Oh Vince, thank you for risking marrying me. There aren't many would have. I don't drink whisky as you know but tonight I will.'

'Good! It'll warm you right through.'

'Vince? You love me then?'

'Of course.'

'Like in the films when we went to the pictures in Culworth all those years ago?'

'Just like in the films. And leave this problem to me. I'll find out who's writing them letters – and they'll be lucky to be alive when I've finished with 'em.'

'Peter knows the whole truth about me. He came to tell me because of him opening that trunk and finding out all the details that were in there. You know, I think I shall ask him to burn the contents of that trunk. I don't want to keep black magic things as mementoes and he's done nothing with it since he opened it, apart from reading about the black magic and that. That, apparently, is how my granddad justified what he did. Blamed it on black magic. He practised it, you see.'

'There's your whisky, Greta. Now, let's stop thinking about it and let's drink to you and me and to Canada. Here we come!'

'Oh Vince, I can't not think about it. The poison pen letters are written on a writing pad we sell in the Store – course they could buy it anywhere, not necessarily in the Store, but you've only read the first few: the others get worse and worse.'

'Don't you fret, I shall read the lot. See if they've given anything away. And we have a lot to look forward to you know. Can't wait to begin selling the meat for Jimbo. We'll certainly be in the money with the two of us earning, won't we, what with our wages and our pensions? I shall be like a dog with two tails, busy, busy every day and money to spend. Our lives will be like a new beginning. Let's drink a toast to Jimbo.'

She nodded. 'And tomorrow I shall go see the reverend and together we'll burn that trunk and then perhaps I shall be able to put it all behind me.'

'No perhaps about it,' said Vince. 'You will. And I shall have solved the mystery before long, too. The toast is to us. You and me! Vince and Greta Jones, starting a new chapter!'

Greta went to call on Peter the very next day and there was a brightness in her face and a briskness in her stride but inside she felt really peculiar, as though nothing would be properly mended until that blessed trunk was burned to a crisp. Visiting a member of the clergy, lovely though he was, didn't feel like an event Greta Jones would have anything to do with but here she was, knocking on the Rectory door.

Dottie opened the door and welcomed her in. 'Hello, Greta. Come to see the reverend? There's someone with him at the moment so come in the kitchen. I'm just about to make his coffee – and mine for that matter, so would you like one too?'

'Well, I would but I'm working and I can't be long. However, this is important and Jimbo's been very kind, specially when he knew I was coming to see him.' She nodded her head in the direction of the study.

'Come in the kitchen, the kettle's boiled and I won't be a minute. I always make proper coffee; he likes it best and what he wants he gets.'

'I bet it's lovely working here, all kindly sort of. If ever you want to leave let me know, and I'll gladly step into your shoes.' Greta grinned.

'And you leave a job like you've got with Jimbo? I don't think so. You'll wait a long time believe me, I love it here. Sugar? You certainly keep your figure, Greta, how do you do it?' Greta didn't answer immediately, after last night with Vince and his kindness and that ...

'That's them just going. I'll just take his coffee through and tell him you're here.'

Dottie was back in the kitchen in no time at all and Greta was being ushered in to the inner sanctum, needing to face the truth all over again.

'It's about the trunk.' She said it softly, just in case Dottie might hear. 'I've told Vince and we had a right sort out last night, because I thought he didn't know about me and that granddad of mine being my father but he did! All these years he knew but never said. My mo ... No, my *grand*mother told him because she didn't want us to get married ... just in case, she said, if we had children but really it was because she wanted me to look after her. Anyway, I decided during the night I'd help you to burn the trunk, every last bit of it. Nothing useful will come of keeping those kind of memories, will there? What happened doesn't matter any more, so if we burn it, smash it up and really burn it, that will be that. It won't put anything right, will it but ...'

'I'm sure you're right, Greta, it's the best thing to do. I would have suggested that myself but it had to come from you – after all, it's your history not mine, and it's only right you should decide. You'll feel better for making the decision yourself. So, no time like the present! Finished your coffee? Let's go then, right this minute.'

'No, no, not now, Zack is sure to see us.'

'No, he's out for the day with Marie; she has a relative ill and they've both gone to see him, eighty mile round trip so they won't be back for a while. Don't worry.'

'Oh! Right. Where is it?'

'In the cupboard under the stairs.'

'Where shall we burn it, sir?'

'Remember the plague pit everyone is terrified of? Just outside the churchyard wall? Right there, best place for it, don't you think? All that pain and distress kept in one place.' He smiled down at her and waited for her to agree.

'I guess that's the right place. Yes. Like you say all that pain kept in one place. What shall we start the fire with?'

'I have a can of petrol in my shed in the back garden.'

Greta didn't want to touch the trunk at all; never as long as she lived did she want to touch that blasted thing. Evil was the right word for it, more than pain. She followed him out of the Rectory, she carrying the petrol can, Peter heaving the trunk. Head down, she kept sliding her eyes back and forth as they went up the church path, checking there was no one watching them because what on earth could they use for an excuse to be setting fire to a harmless old trunk? Harmless? She didn't think so!

She followed Peter to the back of the Church, through the little wicket gate in the back wall and there, in the place where nothing ever grew and which Zack had re-turfed twice but the grass had always died despite him watering it, Peter dumped the trunk down well away from the overhanging trees.

'Before I do the necessary, is there anything you would like to rescue, like the jewellery, or the carved cross or—'

Greta interrupted him. 'Nothing at all, no matter how valuable, absolutely nothing. It's all got to go.' She hadn't thought about needing matches but Peter had and he dug them out of his trouser pocket, opened up the trunk lid, threw petrol all over the contents and saying, 'Ready? Stand back!' he flicked a lighted match onto the inside of the trunk and everything in it flared up immediately.

The two of them stood side by side watching the flames greedily consuming the artefacts. The carved wooden cross took a while to disappear, being solid and strong, but eventually the intense heat won the battle. While she watched it burning she did begin to wonder if it should have been saved: it was a cross after all. Then she remembered it had belonged to a man who was evil, a man who practised evil, a hypocrite of the first order for she remembered the prayers he used to ask her to say with him when she was young and she relished the blackened, twisted remains perishing in front of her and rejoiced.

Greta shook hands with Peter and thanked him for helping her to get rid of that terrible trunk and turned to leave. Then she stopped, turned back to face him and ask if he thought they'd done the right thing. 'Burning it and that, sir?'

'I'm sure we have, Greta. Completely certain. We had no other choice. And no one will find out, will they, now we've destroyed all the evidence?'

But Greta was not convinced, not with those blessed letters coming with such regularity. She smiled weakly at Peter, leaving him wondering why she didn't appear confident he was right.

Chapter 15

Fran could never quite rid her mind of the incident with the woman from Penny Fawcett and Ben and it left her puzzled and afraid. Then one morning a few days later what she dreaded happened; the police called and asked to speak to her. She was in the back of the Store taking a quiet ten minutes to drink a coffee and read the morning paper. Having opened up at six-thirty that morning, being on early turn, she was ready for her break at ten o'clock, so when Bel summoned her to the front counter she arrived there disgruntled, coffee mug in her hand.

'Yes. I'm Frances Charter-Plackett, and you are ...?

The man held up his identification. 'Inspector Fraser from Culworth CID in connection with the disappearance of Christopher Templeton. I understand you were a friend of his for a while. Have you heard from him recently?'

Fran's heart jerked and she found it difficult to breathe. 'Shall we go into my dad's office in the back where it's private?' Once in the office, with the door closed, Fran took charge of the conversation.

'No. I haven't heard from Chris. As far as we are all concerned he's gone back to Brazil, and I have heard nothing from him at all. No letter, no phone call, no email. Nothing. So I'm afraid I can't help you.'

'I see. Do you know of anyone who *has* heard from him?'

'No, except perhaps his brother. Has he heard from him? That's Sir Johnny Templeton up at the Big House. Other than him ...' Fran shrugged her shoulders.

'It's Sir Johnny who asked us to investigate his disappearance. He hasn't heard from him either.'

'The last anyone here saw of him was when he almost knocked two little boys down outside the Store. He didn't stop to see they were all right but the boys came in here and with the lady who witnessed the incident we looked after them and then someone took them home. He drove off, not even getting out of his car to see if they were all right, and that was the last we saw of him. Sorry.'

'Could you give me the name of anyone at all in the village that he had any connection to – women he knew or friends of his brothers or people he went drinking with in the pub here.'

'I'm sorry, no.' Fran wished him to melt away and ask his questions somewhere else quick sharp. But he was persistent.

'You were having an affair, were you?'

Fran hesitated for a moment while she composed her reply. 'For a short while, but then I put a stop to it.'

'Why?'

Inspector Fraser's question infuriated her. 'I cannot see why the on/off relationship we had has anything at all to do with his disappearance. I'd told him off good and proper the night before he disappeared, said I didn't want to see him any more and that was that, as far as I was concerned.'

The inspector smiled at her, leaned a little closer to her and asked, 'Why didn't you want to see him any more? Could you tell me? It would help me no end if you could.'

'This is the last question I am willing to answer about him.' She drew in a great breath before saying, 'I realised he was not the kind of man whom I wished to continue seeing. Not any more. Full stop. Good morning.'

'One very last question. Was it because he was ... too demanding for a lovely genteel young lady like yourself? Difficult to phrase that right, but you understand what I am asking? I need to know what kind of a shall we say "lover" was he? Fickle perhaps, had more than one woman in tow which you resented?'

'Something like that.'

'Someone in the village, perhaps?' There was an element of gentlemanly charm in the tone of his voice and Fran found herself replying again when she'd already said she wouldn't.

'No one I knew, but I guessed there might be. Now I really must say good morning, I have work to do.'

He held out his card, intending her to accept it. 'If anything occurs to you? My number's on the card or an email if you remember something, anything that might help me. Thank you.'

He offered to shake her hand and reluctantly she shook it and found his grip strong and almost crushing. But his ginger brown eyes were fixed in a kindly manner on her face and she knew for a fact he would be back sometime to check her out again because he appeared to have further questions hovering on his lips.

She knew nothing of where Chris was but she did know she wished she was in Brazil with him in his flat enjoying his company. This not knowing was crippling to both body and soul. She put up a good front of appearing to be glad he had disappeared, but every now and again the pain deep inside surfaced and she wished, oh how she wished, he was holding her in his arms and they were making love as only he could. Then common sense would prevail and she quickly recognised that that was the very last thing she wished for. Chris was far too demanding, far too self-centred, far too aware of his charm, and let's face it, he loved himself no end. God's gift to women, he imagined himself to be, when no woman of sound mind would want him permanently. It was the mystery of where he'd gone, though, that teased her every day. She was sure Ben had got it wrong – he definitely wouldn't be dead. Not a man like Chris. If he could survive all those weeks in the Amazon jungle and then that tropical disease he could certainly manage leaving good old Turnham Malpas without any problem.

Later that same day there was a phone call for her that brought her sharply down to earth. It was the vet she'd contacted weeks ago. Was she still on the look out for two donkeys in need of a field and a loving home? Fran had forgotten all about the scheme she'd thought up for the Fitch children, but before she had pulled herself together he was inviting her to a farm on the far side of Penny Fawcett. All she had to do was go, introduce herself, and take a look. No money required: the owners would be delighted to know the donkeys were being well cared for. She should have said no immediately, but somehow she found herself saying yes, she'd visit the farm in the next day or two.

'Dad, will you go with me to see these donkeys? Please? I shall never be able to say no and then where will we be? Especially when I haven't even spoken to Graham and Anita, to say nothing of the children.'

'On no account ask the children before you've got the permission of Graham and Anita! After all, they'll be responsible for them in the long run, not the children. I don't know if I'd be any too pleased to finish up with two donkeys. Would you?'

Fran pondered on this for two seconds and said very definitely, 'No. Bonnie is enough for me; two big donkeys? Definitely not, never. I do wish I didn't get so enthusiastic about things before I've really thought them through.'

Thinking he was making a hugely inspired joke Jimbo replied, 'You did just the same with Chris, and look where *that* got you.' He could have bitten his tongue out as soon as he'd spoken, but it was too late, he'd said it. Fran literally exploded into tempestuous tears and fled the Store in such a panic she was outside and fleeing down Shepherd's Hill in a split second with Jimbo miserably failing in catching up with her. He shouted, 'Sorry, Fran, sorry.' But she was already far too far down the Hill to hear him.

She realised she was heading unwittingly for Dottie's cottage and her feeling of relief was tremendous; she would understand, would Dottie, even if she wasn't a special friend of hers like she was to Beth Harris. She hammered on the door but there was no reply. Of course there wouldn't be; she'd be working at the Rectory. Damn and blast! Fran crept round the corner of Dottie's cottage and leaned against the wall out of sight while her panic slowed. Once she'd managed to dry her tears and pull herself together she knew her mindset was such that she could have laughed at her dad's joke because, in fact, she didn't want to burst into tears about Chris; in fact, this morning, she felt more like kicking his backside for his flagrant disregard for her feelings.

There would be no more being miserable about him, she told herself. If he *had* disappeared then basically it had all turned out for the best for her because there'd be no more moaning and despairing, she'd learned a lesson from knowing him and him disappearing had done her a good turn. When she got her breath back she dried her face, straightened her shoulders and set off at a good pace to walk home, putting her mind to wondering, like the police officer, if there was anyone in the village whom Chris had left in despair.

Fran bounded back into the Store full of energy, daring herself to look her dad straight in the face to let him know she'd cured herself, but he was too busy. In the thirty minutes she'd been out the Store had filled up, Tom had a queue at the Post Office cage, and her dad had the till pinging almost faster than he could cope with, so she'd no need to worry about him because she knew the till pinging was music for his very soul. She spotted that the coffee machine needed refreshing and that several of the special tiny cream pots had missed the waste bin. She put them where they belonged, unhitched the coffee pot and went in the back to sort it out.

She'd go round to Graham's tonight, she decided, and talk to them about the donkey question. Her dad had a meeting to attend so he couldn't go to Nightingale Farm with her but so full of confidence was she now she'd cast Chris to the winds she set off by herself, remembering as she drove all the points of advantage having donkeys would have for the children. What were their names again? The little boy was called Ross, Judd and Max were the other two and the girls, Gemma and Sarah, no Sarah and Gemma in that order.

The donkeys' names were ... heavens above, the vet had told her but it was only while checking the crossroads where she needed to turn left up the farm lane that she remembered – Jenny and Jack, that was it, and they were both too old for Jenny to get pregnant, which no doubt would be a plus.

The farmhouse was really beginning to look perfectly splendid now and had obviously had lots of money spent on it. Some of the lights were on and it was clear that every single room in the house had been redecorated. Fran neatly parked her car beside Graham's huge Range Rover and went to the front door which shone a bright immaculate yellow in the porch light.

It was Anita who answered her knock.

'Yes? Oh! It's Fran isn't it from the Store? Do come in, is there a problem?'

'No problem: I've come with an idea. Are the children in bed? I don't want them to hear, just in case.'

'Sounds very exciting, I love secrets,' Anita smiled. 'Come inside. We'll go into Graham's study and shut the door.'

The two of them sat down in front of a roaring log burning stove which Fran loved immediately. The warmth of it was so comforting and somehow it encouraged her to start on her scheme for the children. 'I've got this idea. First, have the children settled better now?'

Anita sighed. 'Not really. There are times when Graham and I wonder if we should return to Leeds, then we realise we've burned our boats there and we've got to stick it out. His job, my job ... neither of us want to go back now we've settled. Do you have some bright idea that would help the children settle?'

'You've hit the nail on the head as my grandmama would say. The children are bored – well, I think so anyway – and what they need are country pursuits to keep them busy. I've come up with an idea for the two fields you've kept. A few sheep in one, then they'd have lambs to look forward to in the spring, and in the other field, a couple of donkeys. I know someone who would be a great help with the sheep – he has two hundred of his own to keep him busy in his early retirement and he used to be our milkman but he isn't now.' Fran paused to assess how her news was being received and got a surprise when she noticed Anita's expression. 'If it's the money for the donkeys, they come for nothing because the present owners would be only too glad for them to have a happy home and be well looked after. And perhaps the children could ride them ...' Her voice trailed away as she saw the horror growing more evident on Anita's face. 'I'm sorry! Obviously, I've gone completely off map as far as you are concerned. Please, don't worry, I've made no promises about the donkeys. Only I did think the children needed something countrified now that's where they're living.' Fran picked her handbag up off the carpet and made to leave, saying as she headed for the door, 'Please, Just consider me an interfering old busybody and forget all about me calling!'

At the moment she put her hand on the door knob in order to make her humiliating exit, Anita said, 'Just a minute, Fran! Look never in all my life have I ever had any connection with animals of any kind, not even a single goldfish in a bowl on the sideboard let alone a dog or a cat and definitely nothing as big as a donkey! But I do think you may have a point. The children have nothing to do, that's why they're so naughty. We could have a cat which would make sure the mice we were plagued with a few weeks ago will stay away and possibly a dog to guard the house. They need something and live animals need caring for and animals they could play with ... of course that could be the answer.' Anita leapt to her feet. 'You brilliant person! Leave it with me. Graham and I will talk about it and I'm sure he'd agree. Why have we never thought of it ourselves?'

Almost breathless at the prospect that she might just might have hit on a good idea to alleviate the children's boredom and relieve both the village and the school from their bad behaviour, Fran hugged Anita saying, 'I'll give you my phone number and you can let me know. I'm so excited, I thought at first you were appalled.'

'I was! Then I saw how right you were. I'm getting sick of the people in the village not liking us and even more so the fact that Craddock Dad gives us some really foul looks when he informs us how naughty they all are at school. "A constant thorn in the flesh," he declares, and they're not like that really, or at least they weren't. Thank you so much for calling with this brilliant idea. Graham and I will talk and I'll let you know. I'm certain the children will be delighted with the whole idea. Thank you!' Fran got a kiss for effort and disappeared off into the night, thoroughly pleased with her evening.

At the weekend Fran was invited to accompany Anita and Graham and the children to the farm on the other side of Penny Fawcett to see the donkeys. She didn't know who was the most excited, the children or herself. There wasn't enough room in the Range Rover for her as well as the Fitch family so she led the way in her own car.

The elderly couple with the donkeys were delighted to welcome them all and it was obvious from the way they greeted the children that they were well accustomed to having children around.

'Come in, come in or shall we see the donkeys first?'

The children all nodded silently, too excited to speak, so the elderly couple took everyone round to the back of the old stone farmhouse and there, in all their glory, were the two donkeys frisking about in the field nearest the house. The two of them immediately trotted across to the fence to inspect the new arrivals. Their coats were brown, their kindly, interested eyes dark brown, and their first contact with the children was to search their pockets for food. The damp warmth of their mouths, the smell of their breath, the snuffling noise they made as they endeavoured to find some treats to eat, the whiskery bits that tickled as they searched and the interest the donkeys showed in the children and their pockets excited and intrigued every one of them.

Judd shouted out his disappointment at not having anything in their pockets they could give Jack and Jenny to eat, but the old farmer sprang into action and disappeared into a barn attached to the house, emerging with a big tin bowl filled to the brim with an assortment of fresh vegetables already cut up.

The next few minutes were hectic. There was a lot of stroking and patting going on and only Ross decided he was too afraid to touch them. But Graham lifted him up and eventually persuaded Ross to pat Jenny. Jenny loved it and braced her neck for more stroking. 'There! See, Jenny, or is it Jack, loves you stroking her. Do it again That's it! Here, hold this carrot for him.'

Gemma asked quietly, hardly daring to in case the answer was no, if she was too big to ride the donkeys?

The old lady heard her whisper and said, 'If you want them, they come with their very own saddles and reins. Bright red they are, very fancy, and I swear they know they look smart, I'm sure they do. My granddaughters used to ride them when they were little.'

'Want them?' said Sarah. 'You don't want to keep them then?' She turned to face her dad, her shining eyes telling him more than words ever could how much she wanted to take the donkeys home.

Graham took the old man to one side where the children couldn't hear what he was saying, and said, 'We have two fields, one with two big stables and one with a barn in it. We'd love to have the donkeys, but we've no experience of keeping animals so we've a lot to learn from you, and I'm definitely not comfortable with not paying for them. There must be something we could do to recompense you in some way.'

'See here, young man. These two donkeys have been part of our family for fifteen years. It's as though they are our children and would you sell your children to any Tom, Dick or Harry? Or would you prefer to give them to someone you feel confident will care for them? Mmm? We've sold the farm, we're too old to work the land now, and seeing as there's no money in it unless you go all commercial, our girls don't want to farm so we're going to a small cottage we've bought in Little Derehams in four weeks' time. So ... we can't take the donkeys but we would be glad, so very glad, if you will take them. Never mind about paying for them; what you can do is not mind if we call occasionally, only occasionally, mind, just to see Jack and Jenny are doing all right. My wife would love that. Where do you live?'

'We've bought a farmhouse the other side of Turnham Malpas with just two of the fields. The rest of the land we've sold to a neighbouring farmer. It's where the crossroads meet up and it's called Nightingale Farm. Do you know it?'

'Do I know it?' The old man's face lit up with pleasure. 'What a coincidence! My name's Ted Nightingale so no need to explain where it is. I was born there and bought this farm for myself after working for my dad for years. My big brother and I didn't get on so he inherited Nightingale Farm and I struck out on my own with the money I got from my parents when they died.

'It'll be wonderful calling to see you and my old home, watching the children enjoying Jack and Jenny. Go home and have a serious think about it and ring me if you decide to have them both. I honestly hope you will have them because it'll be grand for them up on those hills. I know exactly which fields you're talking about, I can see them in my mind's eye, and they are inseparable so they need to share a stable, if that's all right by you. Wonderful!'

Fran had stood to one side all the time they'd been there, knowing that this was the moment the children would bond or not bond and that it was important that they had the whole wonderful experience to themselves. She was thrilled to bits that the idea had worked just as she wanted it to – she didn't need a man like Chris to give her a purpose for living, she'd done that all by herself. And now she'd spend her rare Saturday off doing exactly as she liked, which in fact turned into spending the rest of the day with Alex Harris who was home for a few days and had called into the Store while she was out on the off chance she might not be working that day. Jimbo rang to tell her and Fran rang Alex at the Rectory and she couldn't help but notice the delight in his voice when he found out she was free for the rest of the day. Alexander Peter Harris really was a very gracious man and they had a wonderful day.

Chapter 16

It hadn't gone unnoticed that Fran and Alex had spent the day together, because Dottie had gone on the lunchtime bus to Culworth, had shopped for hours, decided to have afternoon tea in the little café by the bus station and saw that the film she'd been waiting to see for weeks was advertised on the hoarding at the cinema round the back of the market square and was joining the queue at the box office when she spotted Alex and Fran coming out of the cinema as it was emptying for the next session. She couldn't help but wave and Fran saw her and waved back and Dottie thought how very happy the two of them looked together. Oh, he was much more suited to Fran than that pain in the neck Chris Templeton! Much, much more, she thought and her heart rejoiced.

Fran shouted, 'You'll enjoy it, Dottie! It's good. Got plenty of hankies? You'll need 'em!'

Dottie laughed and shouted cheerfully, 'Thanks for the warning!'

Alex smiled and waved and Dottie decided he was so like his dad. Just what Fran needed, he was.

Dottie was out of the cinema by half past six, just in time to catch the last bus back to Turnham Malpas. She'd finish off the day by going to the pub on the off chance there'd be someone to sit with at that favourite table of hers. Now that the bus route had been extended the bus took her right to the bottom of Shepherd's Hill so she stepped off the bus and had her key in the door in seconds. Sykes-dog got popped out into the garden to stretch his legs and while he was out there Dottie decided to make a cup of tea and eat a nice thick slice of that date and walnut loaf she'd made the other day. Besides pouring her own cup of tea she poured some into Sykes-dog's bowl and beside it placed a small square of date and walnut loaf. After all, he'd been a long time on his own today.

So they sat together in front of the stove, each enjoying their treat. When he'd finished his tea and cake Sykes-dog looked up at her with a pleading expression on his face but she refused him any more. 'No, sorry, you've been indulged enough. We'll go for a quick walk in a while and then, sorry, but I'm going out again, it's Saturday you see.' Dottie knew she was being soft in the head apologising to a dog that hadn't the faintest idea what she was saying, but then his ears drooped and the saddest expression crossed his face and Dottie felt loaded with guilt. She recollected how old Jimmy Glover's little Jack Russell had always gone into the pub with him and knew to keep quiet under the settle and was rewarded for his good behaviour with a long drink from Jimmy's last glass of ale before they left for home. Could she do the same? Was this Sykes-dog clever enough to understand what to do?

He'd get some exercise that way too, walking up the hill and back. As the idea mellowed in her mind she decided she'd try it. If it didn't work then she'd leave, but it was worth a try, better than him being left all alone again. It could become her Saturday night ritual. She gave Sykes-dog a penetrating stare as she contemplated her new idea and he returned her look with a twinkle in his eyes and her heart jumped.

Surely he didn't understand … did he? Now she really was soft in the head! Thinking outrageous thoughts like that about a dog she'd only had four weeks.

'We'll give it a try shall we then, Sykes?'

Sykes was on his feet and heading for the door before she'd even got out of her chair.

When they went into the bar there was not a single person sitting on the settle so Dottie was able to pop him under there without saying a word to anyone about him. After his brisk uphill walk he was ready for a sit down, and when Dottie told him to lie down, he curled up willingly. He was smaller than the old Sykes had been, not yet being fully grown, so there wasn't a single inch of him, not even his tail, showing from under the settle.

Georgie was serving at the bar tonight and Dottie did wonder if she should apologise for bringing Sykes-dog in when she knew that for years, after a major fight between two big dogs that had taken a dislike to each other and the clientele had scattered far and wide to avoid getting bitten, dogs other than Jimmy Glovers hadn't been encouraged. Thinking Georgie hadn't noticed him she decided to say nothing, but Georgie's first words were, 'Quite like old times.' She grinned and nodded towards the settle. 'What's his name?'

Dottie cleared her throat before she spoke. 'His name's Sykes.'

'It's OK so long as he behaves, Dottie. Got to think of my other customers, you know. He's the spitting image of Jimmy's old dog though, isn't he, my word?'

'Yes, he is. Of course. Thanks. My usual please.'

Within half an hour everyone she'd expected would be wishing to sit at her table had arrived, even Sylvia had come having left Willie at home as he didn't feel he wanted to sit in the pub. 'Lovely this is, someone to talk to at last!' she said. '*He's* sat there all day watching TV sport without a word for the cat. He gets worse.'

'I didn't know you'd got a cat,' said Dottie.

'I haven't. It's just a saying. How's that dog of yours. What did you call him in the end?'

'What else could I call him but Sykes now Craddock Fitch's dog's got run over? Poor thing. They say he was quite cut up about it, not the dog, I mean Mr Fitch, and the children at the school have been upset too. He'd started taking the dog in to school at Storytime a couple of times a week so they got friendly with him as you can imagine. Awful, when your pet dies.'

'How's things with you, Dottie? Busy as usual?'

'Well, apart from four mornings at the Rectory and doing an afternoon for Harriet, and the embroidery group every Monday afternoon, next Saturday I'm having Ben Braithwaite for the morning while Becky gets some clothes shopping done in Culworth.'

Sylvia was nonplussed. She knew what she wanted to say but knew she mustn't. 'Oh! Right. How will you manage him without Becky?'

'He likes to play with Sykes-dog as he calls him, so that occupies an hour because Ben's inexhaustible and can keep going longer than my Sykes can. Then we play—'

'You've had him before, then?'

'Oh yes! Next Saturday'll be the third time I've looked after him. He's no problem just so long as you don't ply him with questions. One at a time he can answer but two questions in one sentence ... he can't manage that.'

'I can't tell what he says.' Sylvia took a couple of sips of her drink while she waited for Dottie to answer.

'It can be hard; you have to be in charge of the conversation, then you're all right. But he did say a funny thing the first time I had him. He talked about Chris, Chris Templeton, being dead. He'd seen him he said.'

Sylvia gave a quick intake of breath.

'Now that did make me uncomfortable, that did. But he didn't mention that the second time he came, thank goodness. Other than that he's fine, no problem.' Dottie smiled at Sylvia, feeling confident that she would approve.

'But he couldn't have seen him, how could he? He's never out on his own. Except in the taxi, though why they get that paid for I do not know. Think of that expense, five days a week, all year round. No wonder the government has no money, Dottie. I bet if *we* fancied a taxi to take us for vital food shopping in Culworth, I bet we wouldn't get *that* paid for despite how old we are. And I bet he doesn't appreciate it either; he'll think he has a right to it.'

'Sylvia! What a thing to say! That's not like you.' Dottie was disgusted by Sylvia's statement and almost wished she hadn't come in for a drink now. So unlike Sylvia.

Dottie glanced at Sylvia and saw her eyes were filling up with tears.

'Don't worry, Sylvia, I expect you're not feeling well.'

Marie and Zack agreed with Dottie. 'You are looking a bit peaky, Sylvia, perhaps Dottie may be right.'

The entire conversation came to an abrupt halt when they all looked at Sylvia's face and saw she was looking completely horror-stricken. 'There's ... I've got a feeling of something warm on my leg! Do you think it's a stroke starting? I can feel it all hot on my leg. Oh my God! It's moving up my leg. I must be going mad.'

Not yet used to having a dog, Dottie had completely forgotten about Sykes-dog hiding under the settle and was as horrified as Sylvia about the hot patch on her leg. 'Stand up! Shake your leg about, it might just be cramp,' she said.

Sylvia said scathingly, 'Cramp isn't a hot patch on your leg that gets hotter!' Even so, she stood up and as she did so an agonising yelping could be heard.

Dottie shouted, 'It's my Sykes! He's under the settle and you're treading on his foot or his tail or something. Sit down and lift your feet up. Quick!'

'Any more orders? Stand up! Sit down! Shake this! What next?' said Sylvia.

There could no longer be any pretence about no dog being allowed in the bar because the yelping grew louder and louder until Sylvia responded to Dottie's shouting and lifted up her feet in turn.

Out from under the settle struggled Sykes-dog, limping and whimpering. If he'd been on the stage at the London Palladium in the presence of royalty he couldn't have given a better performance. He stumbled towards what he knew were Dottie's legs and leaned against them, yelping.

Sylvia, still indignant and not much inclined to feel sorry for the one who'd caused her fright asked, 'And what about me? Don't I deserve something for the shock I've had? Why didn't you tell me he was there? Frightened me to death, he did.' She sat, trembling from head to foot just as Georgie appeared at the table with a small brandy for her. 'Brandy for shock. No arguing. Down with it.'

Then Georgie crouched in front of Sykes and stroked his back while Dottie hugged him and kissed the top of his head.

'Something for shock, I think, Dottie.' Georgie went to the bar and returned with another glass of brandy. Dottie, thinking it was for her, raised the glass to her mouth but Georgie snatched it from her.

'Not for you! That's for Sykes!'

So, not yet old enough to be consuming alcohol, little Sykes downed the brandy before anyone could stop him and then retired under the settle again, hurt feelings put to rights.

Then they had to laugh. It began with Dottie who recovered quicker than Sylvia, then Vera then Marie and before they knew it the men had joined in and then every single person in the bar was laughing. Gradually the laughing died down, someone speculated on how much Willie would have enjoyed the whole incident, and then Sylvia became sober again. 'Sorry for being so miserable all the time. It's Willie, he's getting me so depressed and I can't think what's matter with him.'

'Get him to the doctor, see if they can give him a boost. I miss his miserable old face.' said Zack. 'There's no face more miserable than his at the moment so like I said, he needs a boost of some sort, Sylvia.'

'Perhaps I will; he usually grumbles when he reads the news-paper, you know, "what's the government thinking of? Why don't they ...?" But he says nothing now. In fact, I think he just sits with it in front of his face because he can't think of anything else to do instead, because there's no gardening to be done, this time of year.'

Vera suggested he had something on his mind. 'Worrying him

like, and doesn't want to say what it is. Frightened, perhaps.'

'Frightened? What of?' Sylvia demanded.

Vera wished she'd never said that word. 'Well, I don't know, if I could see inside his head I'd tell you. Health worries, perhaps.'

Sylvia leapt to her feet, squeezed out past Vera's chair, hastily remembered to say goodnight to everyone, remembered to thank Georgie for her brandy, and left.

'You should never have said that, Vera,' Marie remarked.

'Said what? About health worries? See here!' Vera tapped the table with her forefinger to emphasise her point. 'You hear of people who do nothing when they've got something wrong with 'em because they're too frightened to say, and they keep it secret and finish up doing something about it far too late and nothing can be done to help 'em. I've done them two a good turn. Believe me.'

'Well,' said Zack 'you've got a point, but there's nothing … you shouldn't have interfered, Vera.'

'Are you saying there's nothing wrong with him? We know he's changed, not the man he was even a week ago, isn't Willie. Lost all his edge, he has.'

Dottie, finding the turn of the conversation too grim to say the least, decided to change the subject. 'Saw someone we all know coming out of the cinema this afternoon. Looking very happy together, they were.'

The atmosphere changed instantly. 'Tell us, then,' someone said.

'You'll never guess.' Dottie smiled teasingly.

'Go on. Tell us. We know you're bursting to say.' This from Marie, who'd heard no interesting news of any merit all week.

'Fran …'

'Fran? By herself?'

'With?'

Dottie had to tell them, she couldn't wait any longer. 'With Alex.'

A satisfied, indulgent smile went round the table.

'Well, that's lovely. They make a terrific couple don't they? So much better for Fran than that Chris. I do wonder sometimes though where he is,' said Vera.

'Never mind about him, he's well able to take care of himself with all that money. They are loaded that lot. Believe me, the South American Templetons have so much money they don't know what to spend it on next. Much more interesting is Alex and Fran getting together. Although apparently the Templetons are buying hotels in the UK now and Johnny'll will be keeping an eye on them. I tell you, they are *loaded*.' Zack emphasised his point by giving a vigorous thumbs up sign.

Vince, thinking Zack had some inside information he wouldn't want to divulge, said sarcastically, 'Been in the library reading the financial pages, have you then?'

'Yes, if you want to know. I have. It's interesting.'

They all burst into laughter.

'You didn't expect that now, did you, Vince?'

Before the laughter had died away the outside door opened and in walked Alex and Fran.

Apart from some kindly 'Good evenings' from just about every-one in the bar as they all knew them in one way or another, silence fell. The ones at the table with the ancient settle down one side wished they could offer them seats but they were already squeezed in as it was, so Fran went to sit at the small table by the inglenook fireplace, which was the only empty one, while Alex went to the bar to get their drinks.

None of them wanted to be caught staring at the two young people but on the other hand none of them wanted to miss what they were saying to each other. It was a dilemma for everyone. They looked so ... what was the right word? So compatible. That was it! So happy. So in tune. So absorbed in each other.

Everyone in the bar tried hard not to listen out of the respect they had for the two of them but it was so difficult. In the end their natural courtesy won out and they returned to their own conversations, leaving Alex and Fran to enjoy each other's company.

On everyone's mind was the question, 'Would Alex win fair lady?'

Chapter 17

That night when Fran went to bed she was so tired and so joyously happy she thought she'd fall asleep the moment her head touched the pillow but she was wrong. She was still turning restlessly a whole hour later. Fleeting cameos filled her head. Alex laughing wholeheartedly in the cinema at a joke apparently none but the two of them had noticed. Alex smiling at her when she caught him looking at her over the top edge of his menu in the restaurant at the George Hotel. She'd suggested a small Italian café she'd grown to like round the back of the library but no, for Alex only the George would suffice. However, he didn't make his point in that same arrogant way that Chris would have done, it was all reasoned so gently she really couldn't take offence.

That was the thing about Alex, he was always so ... gentle with his persuasion. Briefly, right at the back of her mind, when they were in the George she did wonder if he would ever get round to suggesting making love at some stage. Or even just a kiss. Did she want to? No. Well. Yes. Not really. Suddenly she'd lost the thread of what he was saying to her.

'I'm sorry, Alex. What did you say?'

'I said we've never discussed it, you and I, but I do know all about what happened with Chris, and I want you to know I found his attitude unbearable. It must have been very painful for you and I am ashamed that a man in his position treated you with such disdain. You are far too precious and far too lovely for him to treat you as he did.' Alex saw her eyes begin to fill with tears. 'Please, don't let him hurt you any more. Right? He's not worth it.' Alex reached across the table and gripped her hand just as the waiter came to take their orders.

'Are you ready to order, sir?'

'Have you chosen, Fran?'

She shook her head.

Alex glanced up at the waiter and said, 'Not yet, thanks. Sorry.'

He said this so gently that the waiter smiled benignly and trotted away without a single inch of annoyance in his gait. That was how it was with Alex, he was so like his dad.

Fran decided on fish and Alex chose steak.

'Alex, it's terribly expensive in here and you're not earning yet – would you let me use some money Grandmama gave me when she knew we were going out for the day? She popped in with some message or other for Dad and when she found out I was all dressed up to go out with you that was what she did. Gave me fifty pounds to put to whatever you wanted to do today. "That dear boy," she said.'

Alex couldn't believe anyone could be so kind. 'Fifty pounds? Is that true? Such generosity!'

'Yes, she's been in love with your dad ever since she came to live here, you know, though she does find his clerical collar a bit of a hindrance, she says.' Fran had to smile. 'Now you're grown up she loves you too. So I've got to use at least some of it because she'll ask me what we spent it on.'

'I intended paying for everything.'

'I know you did. But I shall pay at least half with this money she's given me.'

'Will you thank her on my behalf, for her kindness?'

'Of course.'

Rather hesitantly Alex asked, 'I'm not going back until the evening tomorrow, so I'm going to early service and I wondered if you would want to spend the rest of Sunday with me? If you're too busy I quite understand.'

He looked so stressed at the thought she might have other things she would prefer to do that she almost laughed. Impetuously she reached across the table, took his hand in hers and briefly held it tightly. 'There's nothing I'd like to do better than spend tomorrow with you.'

The waiter came back, took their order and disappeared again.

'Alex?'

'Yes?'

'I have to ask this question. Are you intending when you've got this master's degree to follow in your father's footsteps and go to theological college afterwards? You know, work for the church? As a rector like he does?'

'No. I'm quite simply not good enough, neither morally nor spiritually. I'm not like Dad. I'm too judgemental and I'm a scientist, not a religious man. I go to church purely and simply for his sake, not my own.'

'Right.' Fran felt relieved that she'd got that idea out of the way.

Alex looked her straight in the eye. 'You appear ... relieved.'

They looked deeply into each other's souls for a long moment and then Fran said, 'I'm like your Beth, and apparently like you: I go because I can't not go, but not because I have a deep faith or anything.'

'We've got that out of the way, then, the two of us.' Alex cheered up at this juncture and boldly went for it. 'We've never kissed properly either, have we?'

'Er, no.'

'Big mistake, that.' Alex replied. 'Time we did.'

'Is it?'

'Yes.'

'Oh! Right.' Fran recognised that intense, penetrating look she thought only his father possessed. 'You look just like your dad!'

'Everyone says that. Spitting image they say.' Alex took a deep breath. 'You do know, don't you, that my mother isn't my real mother? She is in absolutely every way, but she didn't give birth to me.'

'Yes, I've known for years. Have you ever met her? Your real mother.' When Fran saw the change in his expression at the mere mention of his real mother she wished to goodness sake she'd never mentioned her. 'I'm so sorry, Alex. It's none of my business. I do beg your pardon for being so outspoken. There's no need to explain.'

He still looked devastated. In a moment or two he regained his composure but his voice sounded oddly strained.

'My real mother thought that my dad loved her and that he would leave Mum and go to live with her and bring the two of us with him. But he didn't, obviously. He and Mum have the deepest love I have ever witnessed and there is absolutely no question of them being parted whatever has happened between them, because without each other they are nothing. Imagine, just imagine, my mother being willing to adopt us both, despite my father's unfaithfulness? What unbelievable courage! But she did it because they are bound by ties so powerful nothing can break them apart. Nothing at all. My biological mother has three daughters and yet she wanted Dad and the two of us too. No way! Beth and I both said no way. She lives in America, now, with her own two sisters, running a school, so there's scarcely any chance of ever meeting her and I'm glad and so is Beth.'

Fran, intuitively, heard the unspoken words behind what he had said. 'What you are explaining to me is that you want your parents' kind of love in your relationship with your wife whoever she is, and nothing less ... nothing less will do. That's a huge expectation, Alex, and I reckon it's almost impossible.'

'It is, but there we are. I've seen the deep joy such a relationship brings and I'm not willing to settle for less.' Alex laid his knife and fork neatly on his empty plate and grinned at Fran. 'End of marriage counsellor's consultation!'

His smiling, apologetic face, the handsome features he'd inherited from his dad, the colour of his hair (a slightly darker shade of strawberry blond than his dad's), the shape of his elegant ears –

could ears be elegant, she wondered? She didn't know, but his were – everything about him made her heart spin. Suddenly truth became extremely important to Fran. That was something she had never enjoyed with Chris. For a brief moment she experienced the strangest of happenings. She was no longer with Alex but somehow was sitting opposite Chris and she thought about the other women he'd been seeing besides herself. She didn't know who they were, except for Annunciata, but she was sure she was right, and this upstanding, honest-to-goodness man sitting opposite her now, namely Alex Harris, with his staunch views of truthfulness and love, towered, literally towered, above Chris Templeton. Chris shrank into a non-existent person, a man of no consequence, a male nothingness, a faded person more like an old photograph of a long-gone man. Was he indeed dead now?

Alex broke her contemplation by asking if she wanted to order pudding.

'Yes, please, I *always* want pudding. In fact, I love puddings. I'll have the crème brûlée, please.'

'OK. Pudding it shall be, I'll catch the waiter's eye.' The waiter came over immediately Alex caught his attention. 'Two crème brûlées and then coffee, please. Is that all right with you, Fran? Coffee?'

'Yes, please.'

While they waited for their puddings she told him the story of the donkeys and the Fitch grandchildren, and the possibility of them having some sheep with the promise of lambs next spring.

'You *are* surprising! I never connect you and farm animals, Fran, and the countryside. What a lovely thing to have engineered for the children.'

'Possibly, we'll have to see how it works out. The children are thrilled about the donkeys but they don't know about the sheep and lambs yet. The ewes will go to Nightingale Farm when they've been … is it mated or been with the …' She blushed.

'Tup.'

'That's right. Yes, tup. How do you know that?'

'I know someone who is a vet student.'

'Oh! Right.' Fran felt so uncomfortable and when she dared to give Alex a quick glance she saw he was smiling at her. 'I'm not usually so embarrassed about the facts of life, Alex, and it's not even a rude word. Sorry. I've suddenly come over all foolish, when I'm not really.' Fran fidgeted with her pudding spoon and longed for the crème brûlée to arrive to distract Alex from her crass stupidity.

'Change of subject. Do you know where Chris Templeton is at this moment in time?'

Fran was surprised by the abruptness and directness of his question, and for a moment had no answer for him. Eventually she said firmly, 'No, I do not, and when a police officer asked me that same question I gave him the same reply. I never saw or heard from him again after I made my big declaration in The Wise Man the previous night, when we were supposed to be having dinner together. All I know is that he almost knocked down two of the Fitch grandchildren the following morning outside the Store, but I never actually saw him because he didn't stop to find out if they were OK.'

Alex fell silent while he absorbed the implications of her answer. So too did Fran. They avoided looking at each other until finally they both said together, 'The crème brûlée is a long time coming.'

Then they burst out laughing and it cleared the air.

'It's still early,' Alex said. 'Shall we go in the Royal Oak for half an hour after we leave here?'

Fran checked her watch. 'It is early. Yes, I'd like that.'

When they finally pulled up outside Fran's, Alex said, 'Don't forget to thank your grandmama for her contribution, it really was exceptionally kind of her, and thanks for being such lovely company tonight, Fran. See you tomorrow morning at eight o'clock in church, OK? Goodnight.'

The kiss he gave her before she went in the house was the sweetest, most beautiful, most sincere kiss she had ever received.

Chapter 18

Vince Jones, in his pursuit of the writer of the poison pen letters Greta was receiving, had thought long and hard about them and arrived at the conclusion that they were being written by someone old enough to have been in the village when it all happened, but where were there people old enough to be remembering?

It hit him in a flash one morning when he was sitting in Zack's shed in the churchyard enjoying a midmorning break drinking Zack's tea out of Zack's pint pot while replacing him in the verger department seeing that Zack was on holiday. He'd replaced him before when Zack was ill once and he did everything except wear the verger's outfit in church. That he quite fancied doing because he enjoyed the idea of the verger's cassock swishing about his ankles as he strode round the Church, but apparently it was not allowed. He shrugged.

It was exceptionally cold outside but with Zack's little two bar electric fire working non-stop inside he was comfortable. His massive pint pot of tea with two spoons of sugar in it was warming the cockles of his heart. Thinking that reminded him of his mother because it was one of her favourite sayings and in doing so he remembered the name of an old friend of hers, Mrs Oldroyd. That was her name! Martha Oldroyd. He'd heard she was living in the nursing home in Penny Fawcett where Vera used to work.

She wasn't his mother's kind of person really, but somehow they got on well with each other. His mother used to say of her, 'That woman knows more about people and what they get up to than anyone I know. It's disgusting, most of it.'

His dad would say, 'Well, then don't encourage her if you don't like what she says.'

But he always got the same answer: 'She's lonely, been a widow for years and years she has, someone has to talk to her and no one else will but me.'

Now that same old lady was living in the nursing home, Vince thought as he slurped down another mouthful of his hot sweet tea but how on earth could he get access to her without it looking suspicious? There was no way on this earth that he would be visiting her out of the goodness of his heart but he could bet his bottom dollar that she was the most likely source of the poison pen letters. Not, of course, that she was writing them herself; at her age she'd not be capable of holding a pen, never mind writing sense, but she might be gossiping about the situation to someone working in the home and they were the ones making his Greta's life a misery. He guessed the very next move would be blackmail, promising to tell no one a single thing about Greta's birth if she paid up ... regularly.

To his delighted amazement the whole problem of how to make contact with the old girl was solved for him, without the slightest effort on his part and it was Jimbo he had to thank for that.

The afternoon of the day he'd been thinking in Zack's shed Jimbo rang him and asked him to come up to the Store immediately. His voice sounded full of enthusiasm and Vince arrived in the Store eager to find out what was afoot.

He found Jimbo in his private office, obviously bursting with an idea. The few wisps of hair above his ears, now rapidly greying, were in disarray, his face was flushed, his straw hat had slipped sideways, and he was drinking whisky in the middle of the afternoon which he never usually did. 'I've had an idea, Vince. Sit down and listen. Before we launch our meat range on the internet, I've realised that we need to arrive on the internet meat scene with a great bang. So we have to do something that will get us in the paper, get us known, put us on the map, so to speak.'

Vince nodded vigorously, immediately seeing the wisdom of whatever Jimbo was planning.

'So ... how about if we – well you – have the van and take, as a gift mind you, meat from our supplier to places like the golf club, the nursing home and that college where young Ben Braithwaite goes, and the children's orphanage the other side of Culworth? I know they don't call it that nowadays, but you know where I mean. Anyway, give them some to try. It's an expensive way of spreading the good news about our meat project but at least we'd be getting our name known. We'd get a piece in the *Culworth Gazette* about our generosity etc., etc., because they're always very generous with me about publicity, and perhaps a photo of you beside the van delivering the meat. We'll get you an outfit making you look like a butcher with – I don't know what yet – but something emblazoned across your chest to tell everyone who you are.'

Jimbo sat back to await his reaction. He needn't have worried; Vince was already as excited as Jimbo about the whole idea. 'That'll make a start, Jimbo, and not half. Talk about starting with a big bang! Marvellous. It'll be costly but well worth the publicity. You can count me in. When's the van due?'

'Next week. They're painting the name on it as we speak. I did have the idea that Harriet would cook a meal for everyone at the nursing home and the College and that, using our meat, and that would make more of a "do" of it but she's got two weddings to cater for, several wedding cakes to do and a twenty-first birthday bonanza to contend with, so she can't fit it all in that week. Bit of a disappointment, really, but there we are.'

'We can do the rest though, like you said, Jimbo. Nothing stopping us doing that, is there? Better that than the cooking meals and the whole idea not being done right because of the lack of time. Best do what we can as well as we can.'

'Exactly! Here I've written a letter to everyone about to be given the meat, what do you think?'

Jimbo passed a copy of the letter to Vince, and he was delighted.

In the letter Jimbo made it sound a terrific idea and Vince was sure it was, even before he'd finished reading it. Every word in the letter positively bounced with enthusiasm and anticipation.

'This coming week, then?'

'That's right. This coming week. You and I are going to make a real job of this, you know. Money! Money! Money!'

Jimbo pretended to be counting money and had a glorious greedy look on his face and the two of them laughed like a couple of evil conspirators. Finally, when at last they'd stopped laughing so heartily, Vince asked, 'Be like that, will it?'

'Absolutely! Why not? Everything we touch will turn to gold. Who's that chap in Greek mythology? I know! Midas! Everything he touched turned to gold. That'll be us!'

'Ah! Right.'

'Letter this week. Delivery next week. Be ready for your photo call. You, not me, in the publicity. Right!'

Vince walked back home filled to the brim with excitement. That Jimbo! He'd be coming up with bright ideas with his dying breath, he thought. As fast as he gets one idea out of the way he's on with the next and wasn't he, Vince Jones, lucky to be part of his enthusiasm? He then came up with a bright idea of his own. Of course! This was his opportunity! He'd go to the nursing home with the meat, get talking, engineer a place at the table at the lunchtime when they ate the meat and get talking to Martha Oldroyd. If she was living in the past it wouldn't be too difficult to get her talking about Silas Wilderspoon. She might even tell him the name of the person to whom she was telling the stories about him. As he put his foot on his own front doorstep it did occur to him that if he found out who was writing those cursed letters what would he do about it? Confront her? He was sure it was a woman writing them, though he didn't know why he did. Frighten her by sending her some poison pen letters in return? No, he mustn't do that. Wouldn't be right, that wouldn't.

'Greta!' he shouted. 'Are you in?'

There was no reply and disappointed, he remembered she would be at work, of course. But perhaps it was for the best because he mustn't tell her his plan in case nothing came of it. Then, like a flash of light, he knew what he had to do when he found the evil writer; he'd tell her that she had to stop writing them and if she didn't he'd report her to the management of the nursing home and she'd lose her job. That would sort her out! Given all the unemployment they'd soon find someone to replace her and what's more they'd be unwilling to give the poison pen writer a good reference.

Plan of action sorted out, Vince put the telly on and fell asleep, glorying in the busy week he'd have driving that brand new van and wearing his brand new uniform and manoeuvring an invite to the nursing home meal.

Life was full of surprises, except Vince got a bigger surprise than he had ever expected when, without any effort on his part, the invitation from the nursing home was offered for him to join them all at the special meal. The manager invited Vince to sit beside her and on his other side the oldest resident in the nursing home was seated. And, yes, it was Martha Oldroyd in her best dress with a shawl around her shoulders because she always felt the cold she said.

The manager introduced the two of them and Martha Oldroyd asked in a high, piping voice, 'I know you, don't I? What's your name, tell me again?'

'I'm Vince Jones. I work for Jimbo Charter-Plackett who gave you the meat you're going to eat.'

Her bright brown eyes looked straight at him. 'I don't know anyone with a daft name like that, but Jones rings a bell. Ida, that was her name. Ida Jones. Any relation? I knew her well, always ready to listen to me talking, she was.'

'Ida Jones was my mother. She often talked about you. You

must have been good friends.' A bit of buttering up wouldn't go amiss, thought Vince. 'Always seemed to me you were great friends, she mentioned you often.'

The manager was called away for an emergency phone call so Vince took his opportunity. He leaned towards Mrs Oldroyd and asked as loudly as he dared, if she remembered Silas Wilderspoon and his granddaughter Greta. That did it! She remembered! The horror in the village, what was said, who said it ... how on earth was he going to shut her up when the manager returned? How Silas was not Greta's grandfather but her father. Out of the corner of his eye Vince saw the manager on her way back. She threaded her way through the packed dining room and sat down beside him – and to his huge relief old Mrs Oldroyd gave Vince a wink and concentrated on her food.

'Lovely meat, Mr Jones. I shall have to change my supplier!' the manager said.

'Always the best if it's supplied by Turnham Malpas Village Store,' he said, proudly.

The manager shook her head regretfully. 'Unfortunately we can't afford their prices.'

'I don't know why,' said Mrs Oldroyd very loudly. 'I don't know why. You charge enough. Too much, some would say.'

'Now, Mrs Oldroyd, you're letting your tongue run away with you. You're all well looked after, don't you think so, Mr Jones? En suite rooms, immaculately clean, lovely caring staff, what more could you ask? Isn't that so, Mr Jones?'

'Not for me to say, I've never been here before, you see. This meal's certainly nicely cooked and I'm looking forward to the pudding.'

Unwittingly he'd chosen to mention one of Mrs Oldroyd's major complaints. 'Them's too small is the puddings,' she said. 'Today it'll be different, the puddings'll be more than adequate because we have a guest, but tomorrow they'll be half the size, believe me. And I love puddings.'

The manager looked to be biting back a withering comment. The charming persona she'd displayed to begin with had disappeared and in its place was a bitter, angry woman and Vince decided that he definitely wouldn't like to live in a home with her in charge. He was on the verge of apologising and asking their permission to leave but he recalled his mission. Well, two missions, one for Jimbo and one for his Greta, and he decided not to leave just yet. He couldn't.

Jokingly he said, 'Better make the best of it then today, Mrs Oldroyd, while we can.' Vince smiled and winked at the manager meaning to imply he bore no grudge against her for small puddings, but she didn't take kindly to his humour.

The manager slapped down her knife and fork, adjusted them so they lay neatly side by side, and then, looking him straight in the face, said, 'As an invited guest, out of the kindness of my heart I might add, I think that remark was completely unnecessary.'

The thin, piping voice of Mrs Oldroyd suddenly gained strength. 'So even the truth is banned now, is it? Anything else banned while you're at it?'

For someone so old, Mrs Oldroyd appeared to be remarkably on the ball, thought Vince. Worried he might be asked to leave before he'd achieved his objectives, Vince decided to take action. He whispered in the manager's ear that he thought it might be best if Mrs Oldroyd ate her pudding in her room and he'd be the one to take her there. 'Keep the peace you know, rather than upset all the others. Eh?'

'Very well. Good idea,' said the manager, slightly mollified and relieved that Mrs Oldroyd would be out of the way. So Vince found himself seated in Mrs Oldroyd's sitting room where their two puddings and coffee to follow were brought in and nicely laid on a side table for them. With the door shut, Vince had Mrs Oldroyd to himself.

The moment the door was firmly closed she reverted to her distant past and Silas Wilderspoon and Greta's mother. There was a whole lot of rambling coming out of her mouth, so it was only snatches of it that Vince was able to understand, but it was enough for him to comprehend and he shuddered at the prospect of what Greta's mother and, indeed, her grandmother, had tolerated.

Martha Oldroyd finished her pudding, drank down the last of her coffee, and said to Vince, 'That manager who looks after us all, she's a wrong 'un. Believe me, she is. She thinks I'm daft but I'm not.' She knowingly tapped the side of her nose with her forefinger saying, 'Who is it who's taking money out of my bank account? It's not me, I never go out, so I can't. One day I'll catch her at it, though.'

Her eyes snapped shut and she was asleep before Vince had thought of a reply to that surprising statement.

He'd have to go. He cleared the dishes onto the tray and took them into the kitchen.

One of the kitchen hands seemed suspiciously over-eager to know what Mrs Oldroyd had been talking about. She said, laughing, 'Kept you talking, has she? Never stops. Don't believe her, though. It's all rubbish. She makes it up as she goes along.'

'Not today she hasn't, she told me all the story about something that I know is true because I know the people involved, so I'd be a bit careful if I were you.' Vince wagged a warning finger at her. 'She might know things about you that you don't know she knows. Like what you get up to in your spare time. She'll know because she's much more alert than you imagine.'

The kitchen hand found that hilarious. 'No, that's rubbish, that is! She isn't alert! She's away with the fairies most of the time.'

Vince drew closer and whispered very confidentially, 'I'd watch it if I were you – she knows who's stealing money for one thing.' He started back from her, clapping his hands to his pockets as though he thought it might indeed be she who was thieving, and in a strange, sepulchral voice said. 'So beware, I mean it. There's more to Martha Oldroyd than you might think. I reckon every-one thinks she's fast asleep most of the time, but she isn't, she's listening to what's going on.' His voice returned to normal as he said, 'Thanks for the lovely lunch; the meat was cooked to a turn! But mind what I said about ... you know.' He shut the door with a loud bang and a great wide smile on his face.

Vince climbed into his van, certain that he'd put the wind up someone, though he wasn't sure who it might be, but at least he was absolutely certain the story he'd told would be spread around the staff ... who were not so clever as they had imagined themselves to be, for Mrs Oldroyd was sharper than they ever dreamed.

Chapter 19

Fran's mobile rang but she was serving a customer and couldn't respond. After the customer had left she took her chance and without even looking at the screen to see who was calling she simply pressed the button to make the connection and couldn't believe what she heard.

'Hi! It's me.'

'Me? Who is me?'

'Fran! It's not that long since I left, is it? It's Chris.'

Fran had trembled at the mere sound of his voice when she heard those first words, 'Hi! It's me,' but she wasn't going to give him the satisfaction of knowing that her first reaction had been not Chris! Please God, not Chris? But it was.

'Yes?' she said.

'Don't sound so surprised. I'm here for a few weeks.'

Fran assembled her commonsense. 'Where are you?'

'Not at the Big House, believe me. I appear to have burned my boats there. Guess? Go on guess!'

Fully expecting he was probably right outside the Store she rushed to the window to look out. No. Not there. 'Stop playing silly games with me. Tell me exactly where you are.' She was praying he was in London or somewhere equally remote. Rio would be even better.

'You're not trying very hard, my sweet.'

Where'd he got 'my sweet' from? That wasn't one of his expressions.

'You completely disappear and expect me, after all these weeks, to know exactly where you are? If you can't be bothered to tell me then I'll switch off.' With her index finger poised over the off button she waited about two seconds and when all she could hear was Chris chuckling at the other end of the phone, that was what she did, she switched off. He rang her four times after that and each time she immediately rejected his call. Thoroughly rattled by his idiocy she continued sorting the greetings card shelves but with shaking hands. How dare he play silly games with her? Was he honestly expecting her to fall gratefully into his arms? Yes! he was! If so, he'd made a huge mistake. Since her major speech in The Wise Man that night she was much more astute and even more determined than previously. Added to which she felt as though she could see right through him and was no longer soft in the head, bending to his every whim. Not likely. After all, there was Alex now ...

A customer came in, one Fran didn't recognise. 'Good evening, how can I help?' she asked in her brightest and most welcoming voice.

'Lovely shop,' said the customer, 'so well stocked! For such a small village it's amazing.'

The customer looked almost foreign in appearance yet her English was first-rate.

'We actually serve three villages so we need to be well stocked,' Fran said. 'Can I get anything for you?' She smiled her best-ever smile to encourage a purchase.

'I'll just choose some chocolate bars – I'm visiting people who have children. And I'd appreciate directions. I'm looking for the Big House? I've been twice round the village and can't find it.'

'Turn right out of here into Culworth Road pass Glebe House and the gates to the Big House are just beyond it. Have you got a car? Because the drive is one mile long.'

'Oh yes, I've driven from Heathrow, you see. It's the Templetons I want to see. Johnny and Alice and those two darling boys of theirs.'

'Ah! Right. I'll just put those bars in a bag for you.'

The customer smiled her thanks, paid her money and left.

Fran's phone rang again. And again. And again. 'Yes!'

It was Mum. 'You sound cross, darling.'

'Sorry. I'm not, just had an irritating customer in. Anyway she's gone now. What do you want, Mum? I'm just about to close up.'

'That's what I was ringing about, to remind you we close at six on Saturdays. You don't often do Saturday afternoons on your own so I thought you might need a reminder. Food's just about ready. Dad and I are going out so we're eating early. See you!'

Fran was in a temper, she didn't know why, but she was. Nothing worked. The complicated locking-up system designed by her dad irritated her more than ever before but it had to be done or the insurance wouldn't pay out if they got burgled. Finally it was done to her satisfaction and she wandered off home with her phone in her bag, still ringing furiously. Chris must be an idiot. Well, no, he wasn't, not really, but all he was achieving was raising her temper levels even higher. Fran paused before opening the front door; she'd switch off her phone, then he couldn't make it ring, that would sort it. So she did, even though Alex had promised to ring her tonight, but he'd be sensible and blame not being able to communicate with her on the terribly bad reception they had here in the village. Honestly, the twenty-first century and they still hadn't sorted that problem out.

So she'd sit by herself all Saturday evening, watching TV or reading that dratted book she'd bought and couldn't for some reason enjoy though according to the reviews she should not be able to put it down. She could ring Alex she supposed, just in order to stop herself falling for Chris's charming apology, because there was no doubt in her mind that was what it would be. Although it might, in fact, be an invitation. No, he wouldn't, would he? Yes, he would, she knew that. He had that kind of brazen cheek, had Chris, because he imagined no woman alive could resist his charms. But those days were long gone as far as Frances Charter-Plackett was concerned.

Fran almost jumped out of her skin when the doorbell rang. That would be Grandmama. She had an uncanny sixth sense when it came to guessing if either one of them was on their own.

Fran opened the door and there stood Chris. Her blood hammered in her brain and rushed through her body at a powerful rate of knots, leaving her flushing like a giddy, inexperienced teenager. For ten seconds she couldn't speak and when she did all she said was, 'Yes?'

'Right. I will.' He stepped over the threshold as he spoke. With his arms outstretched as though waiting to embrace her, he took one further step towards her and she backed away.

All the anguish he'd caused her, all the heartache she'd suffered suddenly made her incredibly angry. 'I wasn't asking you in, Chris! I was asking what it was you wanted, because there's nothing for you here. I am no longer interested.'

His face showed extreme disappointment. 'You know you don't mean that. I can still feel the vibes. You love me, really.'

'Love you?' She was furious. 'Huh! Not any more. Just disappear and never ever ring that doorbell again, because you make my flesh ...' She searched in her bursting head for the right word and it shot out of her mouth before she could stop it '... creep!'

Fran stood glaring at him, only a couple of feet away from an embrace which she would not allow herself to invite. But he stepped nearer to her, a bright inviting smile on his face. How dare he assume she would welcome him, how dare he assume she wanted all the painful heartache and the fierce passion he would arouse, it simply wasn't fair! Confidently, Chris, eager to renew all that had gone before, stepped closer, his arms reaching out to pull her to him, forcing his lips onto hers as he kicked the heavy front door shut with his shoe heel, knowing from the power of her response that he was back where he'd been longing to be all the time he was away.

What was it about her that kept him coming back? Whatever it was it felt good right now. He opened one eye and pushed her in the direction of the staircase.

But his voice saying commandingly, 'Go on up, up you go, you know you want me ...' broke the spell. Fran, despite being clutched so tightly, managed to bring her left stiletto heel into contact with the top of his right foot and she ground the heel heavily down.

The pain made Chris release his grip on her instantly and Fran, now without his support, sat sharply down on the third step up. Furious, Fran kicked out, shouting and screaming at him to leave.

'Still the same Chris! Your way, always what *you* want. Get out! Go on. Get out!'

To her amazement, Grandmama, ever the one for well-timed entrances, was surprisingly standing in the hall white to the gills with temper. 'Yes, get out, because this time it really is the police if you don't do as I say. Out, and never darken this door again.' She was using that powerful, dramatic voice that she could call up at any time, standing haughty and forbidding, pointing a well-manicured finger at the front door.

Fran began to laugh, from hysteria not amusement, and between her gusts of laughter she kept saying, 'Do as she says. Go on! She really means it.'

Chris stood close to Grandmama and snarled, 'Time you got put down, you miserable old bitch, you.' Then he turned to Fran to say softly, 'I still love you, Fran, you haunt me night and day. I'll be back. You know where I am.' He bunched his fingers and kissed them. 'Love you!'

He left the front door wide open so Grandmama slammed it shut and locked it then turned towards Fran, holding out her arms, inviting Fran to have a hug. She was always good at hugging and that was exactly what Fran needed. A mighty great big hug from someone who loved her selflessly, not selfishly like Chris did.

They stood hugging for a long minute and then Grandmama said, 'I want a drink and I don't mean hot chocolate. What shall we have? Mmm?' She let go of Fran, took off her coat and headed for Jimbo's drinks cabinet.

While Grandmama browsed through the bottles making up her mind, Fran, still in a state of emotional turmoil, asked her why she'd come?

'I knew your mum and dad were out and for some reason, right in the middle of a very exciting chapter in the book I'm reading, I heard you calling my name.'

Fran protested, 'But I didn't.'

'You may not consciously know you did, but you did. So I came straight round. Good thing I did! He is a ruthless, dangerous man, is that Chris and not right for you. But Alex is ...'

In a strange, wobbly voice Fran replied, 'Oh! I see. I have to marry Alex because my grandmama has fallen in love with him and not only that but also, to add to the fun, with his father too. Not a very good reason for marriage, is it?'

Indignantly her grandmama replied, 'I would have thought it was an excellent reason! I'm having whisky, neat. What do you fancy?'

But Fran, torn by emotions she simply could not comprehend, burst into wild tears so the two of them finished up on the sofa hugging again. 'Oh! Granny!' Grandmama forbade herself to make her usual complaint at that dreadful name; this was not the moment. Fran dabbed her eyes and tried to speak rationally. 'I'm so confused. I know he's dangerous, I know he thinks of nothing but what he wants, I know he likes having things all his own way, but he is so attractive! So unbelievably attractive. He only has to touch me and ...'

'I know. I know.'

Fran sat up and wiped the tears from her face. 'He is, isn't he? Very attractive?'

'I'm not too old to see that for myself, thank you very much. He is indeed very, all-consumingly, attractive. But ... he is also totally selfish, my darling, self-centred and self-assured. He admires himself above all else, which is a nasty trait in a man as glamorous as he is, a very nasty trait. He has to be avoided at all costs. Do you hear me? Avoided at all costs because he will bring nothing but heartbreak to you. Right? And ... I can't forgive him for saying I should be put down!'

Fran sat up and, looking her grandmama straight in the face, said, 'That was nasty – and believe me, *I* don't think like that. Honestly, I don't.'

'I know you don't. We may have had our differences when you were younger but we're friends now, aren't we? Now you're older and with more sense. You see, I married the wrong man and suffered for it while ever he was alive, and I'm not going to stand by and see it happen to you.'

'But I've always thought you loved him!'

Grandmama paused for a moment and then said, 'I did and I was heartbroken when he died, but I still should never have married him. That's why I only had Jimbo, because every day of our marriage I expected it would be the last and that he'd leave me for ever.'

'But he didn't! You were there when he died, you've said so.'

'Has your dad never told you?'

'Told me? What?' Fran scrubbed the last of her tears with Grandmama's tissue and waited for her reply.

'That he had another family? Bigamously and had three boys with her?'

'You mean Dad has three brothers? Really!'

'Half-brothers.'

'He's never mentioned them!'

'Of course not, because your father is a gentleman – unlike Chris Templeton who wouldn't know how to be honourable if honour jumped up and hit him in the mouth.'

Fran shook her head. 'I think I'll have a whisky too. Neat.'

'Is that wise?'

'No, but I'm having one just the same.'

'You shouldn't really, Fran. Look! Off you go to bed and I'll bring you the whisky upstairs before I go, shall I?'

The whisky when it came was watered down but not being a regular whisky drinker Fran didn't realise. 'Thanks, Grandmama. Don't take any notice of Chris saying what he did. I want you to live for ever!'

'Thank you, darling Fran, I intend to. Goodnight, dear.'

Chapter 20

At half past seven the following morning Jimbo's mobile phone rang. Being Sunday, he was still in bed. Fumbling to find his phone on his bedside table, he desperately hoped it wouldn't be trouble with a capital T. It was Mother. Harriet had already gone downstairs so he was alone when he heard the news about the events of the previous evening. 'What!' 'Here in this house? Why did you come?'

'You don't know why?' 'Mother, are you exaggerating?' 'Thank God you came!' 'I thought the sod had gone for good.' 'He said *what* to you?' At this point Jimbo leapt out of bed. 'Come round for breakfast. Right now. I mean, when you've got ready, of course, not in your dressing gown.' 'No, I haven't spoken to her, she's still in bed I expect.' 'Just come, Mother, and we'll play it by ear. Right. OK. Half an hour. Yes. See you.'

Thirty minutes later Harriet, Jimbo and Grandmama held a conference around the breakfast table.

'Presumably he's staying at the Big House, then?' Harriet asked.

Grandmama shook her head. 'I've no idea, but Johnny did throw him out. Well, not literally, but told him to go.'

'I wonder if Fran knows where he's staying?' Jimbo cocked an ear and whispered, 'That's her coming downstairs now. Morning, Fran, as you can see your gran has come for breakfast. All right, darling?'

'You can't fool me,' Fran said. 'I know exactly why she's here.'

'Good, that means I don't have to explain how close you came to being raped last night.'

'Dad! What a dreadful thing to say! He wouldn't do that, of course he wouldn't.' Fran was appalled at first, believing implicitly that what she had just said was right and then having immediate second thoughts. He was, after all, forcing her up the stairs when Grandmama walked in. She glanced at her and saw her eyebrows arched in disbelief. Fran declared to herself she wouldn't have let him anyway. Then she remembered he'd apparently regained his strength while he'd gone walkabout, so possibly she wouldn't have been able to stop him. Fran shuddered and remained silent.

'It's Sunday and Johnny will be in church this morning, so-o-o, round about noon I shall march up to the Big House and have it out with them. Mother, you stay here and keep us all in order, then we'll have lunch and go for a drive if you like, if there's anywhere special you'd like to go ...'

'What a wonderful idea! Thank you, dear. Harriet, I'll give you a hand in the kitchen. Fran, you are the only one not organised, off you go and get dressed, get cracking!'

While stacking the dishwasher Harriet and Grandmama talked. 'You see, Harriet, I saw what he was up to. Forcing her up the stairs, he was, and he had her well and truly in his control. She only got a respite because she stabbed his foot with her stiletto. I hate those high heels she wears but for once I was glad she had them on. He is an abominable, loathsome creature despite his good looks and his charm, which he has in spades as we all know.'

'Jimbo told me what he said to you; I'm so sorry you had to hear that.'

'It was worth it if it means Fran is safe and sound. She's a dear girl and I love her to bits. Here's another knife and I think that's it. I never say much in praise of anyone but I'm glad Jimbo married you. I wasn't sure at first, because I'm not used to career-type women, but here we are, happily stacking the dishwasher and not a cross word between us. That's worth a lot. The older I get the more appreciative I am of my family.' Grandmama clasped Harriet in her arms saying, 'Thank you, dear. Your children are a credit to you, and what's best is the fact that Jimbo loves you very dearly. Now, that's enough praise to last for the next ten years! I didn't sleep a wink last night so I'd better go and sit down for a while to recover.'

It was twelve noon and Jimbo was confronting the Templetons as he had promised. Johnny was replying as best he could.

'I'm sorry, but I don't know where he is. He's certainly not living here and we haven't heard from him since the day he nearly ran the Fitch grandchildren over.'

'So, where the blazes is he living, then?'

Johnny shook his head. 'I simply don't know.'

'I can tell you this, I *will not tolerate him entering my home and attempting to drag my daughter upstairs to bed.* Only my mother coming to visit, quite by chance, saved her.'

Johnny was appalled by Jimbo's frankness. 'Surely that's an exaggeration, Jimbo, he's not that kind of man. I know he has his faults but—'

Jimbo held up his hand to stop Johnny saying any more. 'Sorry, but what I am saying is the truth. Ask Fran if you like – she, after all, is the victim in this.'

Alice intervened at this point. 'I believe you, there's a ruthlessness about Chris that maybe his brothers and certainly his mother cannot see. But I can. If he wants something enough he'll do anything to get it. Jimbo, I'm very, very sorry it has come to this. And I do have an idea where he might be.'

Jimbo took a step closer to Alice and asked, 'Where? If you know where he is tell me and I'll tear him to pieces. Scum like Chris deserve all they get. Well? Where is he?'

But Alice stood her ground and refused to tell him. 'No, definitely not. Will you leave him to us to sort out? Please?'

Jimbo looked very gravely at Alice while he sought for an answer. Finally he said, 'I don't want this incident to be all over the village, for Fran's sake, not mine, she's put up with enough notoriety because of Chris. I just want it to stop. I'll leave it with you, then. But the very next incident with that damned brother of yours, Johnny, and it will be a police job. I know enough top-level policemen to get a very good hearing and something done about it without ever going to court. I'm going now. I'm not saying sorry to you, because I'm not sorry, I'm damned angry and at the end of my tether!'

'There's a lot more to that Alice than meets the eye, you know, Harriet. She point blank refused to tell me where Chris is. She might look all sweetness and light but there's steel inside that woman, believe me.'

'She doesn't look as though she's made of steel. Now your mother . . .'

Jimbo had to laugh. 'I know. I know!'

'No, you don't. She and I are closer than we have ever been, Jimbo. She told me so after breakfast when we were stacking the dishwasher together. The secret-sharing of the tea towel and the bowl of hot soapy water has been replaced by stacking the dish-washer but it's just as effective. We had a really intimate chat.'

Jimbo, longing to know what had been said about him, because he assumed, quite wrongly, that the intimacy had been all about him, suddenly remarked, 'I reckon Fran will know where he is. I'll find out before the sun goes down, believe me.'

He tried very subtlety to persuade Fran to tell him when they went out for a drive after lunch, but every hint he dropped was ignored and he had to go to bed not knowing if Fran knew where Chris was.

As she left the sitting room on her way to bed, Jimbo said, 'Whatever you do, you won't go and see him, will you? He is becoming dangerous where you are concerned, and I love you too much for you to be taking risks. Right?'

Fran paused at the sitting-room door and, without looking at her dad, she said very seriously, 'After what happened last night I know for certain that, attractive as he might be to me, he is bad news, just like your dad was to Grandmama. She told me all about him last night. Dad, have you ever met your brothers?'

Jimbo shook his head. 'Never, my mother saw to that.'

'Don't you want to?'

'No. There's no point in opening up old wounds. What good would it do? None. Neither to me nor them. The whole situation is loaded with emotional baggage and getting to know them would be too complicated ...'

'And it would hurt Grandmama.'

Jimbo nodded his agreement. 'And also my brothers, well, half-brothers.'

'Do you know their names?'

Jimbo shook his head. 'Don't want to.'

'I see. You know, if my baby had been a boy I would have called him James, after you.'

'Fran, darling, don't hanker after he or she. All water under the bridge, you know. Just wasn't meant to be, and what's more you didn't do anything harmful to cause it, so you are not to blame, remember that.'

'I know. But it's so hard. You're thinking perhaps I shouldn't have had that drink; maybe it was going out and about too often – but I didn't know you see, just didn't know I was pregnant.'

From the sound of her voice, tears were not far away, so Jimbo hastily changed the subject. 'Heard from Alex lately?'

'This morning.'

'Is he OK?'

She knew he wasn't referring to Alex's health. 'Yes, I think he is.'

'Pure gold through and through, is Alex.'

'I know. When did you know that Mum was the love of your life, Dad?'

'One night she'd driven herself back to her rooms and when I rang to check she'd got there safely there was no reply. I rang every hour, right through the night, and I knew then I must be serious about her. James Charter-Plackett staying awake all night worrying about a girl? Never!

'Eventually she rang me at half past eight the following morning to say her car had broken down and she'd spent the night at an old schoolfriend's house and they hadn't got a phone. This was in the old days before mobile phones, you see. Goodness, I'm breaking out in a sweat just thinking about how I felt! That was when I knew. I'd had loads of girls of one kind and another but there wasn't any one of them that I would have stayed up all night for, worrying about them being safe and it took me a year to persuade her I was the one for her. Remember her mother, your Granny Sadie?'

'Vaguely.'

'Wonderful woman, on my side right from the start.' Fran turned to look at him, and, seeing the mixture of happiness and sadness on his face, she guessed he was miles away, thinking about the past. How would she feel if Alex was 'missing'? She really didn't know, not yet anyway. 'Good night, Dad. Say goodnight to Mum for me.'

Just as Harriet was falling asleep she muttered, 'I wonder if he's at The Wise Man?'

'Who d'you mean?'

'That Chris . . .'

Of course thought Jimbo.

Chapter 21

The very next morning as soon as the rush of the mothers dropping their children off for school had subsided, Jimbo asked Tom if he would mind holding the fort. 'Got an important job to do, shan't be long and Fran's doing a quick run round for supplies for Greta so she won't be long. OK then?'

Before Tom could reply, Jimbo had left, his car keys rattling in his hand.

The Wise Man was just waking up. A barman was busy filling up shelves with cans of lager, a cleaner was putting the finishing touches to polishing the bar and the owner was at a table counting last night's takings.

'Morning, Billy. Looks like it was a big night last night.' Jimbo nodded at the piles of notes stacked neatly to one side.

'No days off for a publican, you know, James old chap. Not serving yet, sorry.'

'Don't want a drink, Billy, thanks. Just an answer to a question.'

Billy looked up smiling, 'Fire away.'

'Is Templeton in residence today?'

Billy stacked a pile of two-pound coins and then glanced up at Jimbo.

'I don't know who you mean.' A sly smile slid across Billy's face.

'You mean you don't know your partner's staying in your pub? Tut! Tut!'

Billy, stacking another pile of two-pound coins, looked up, startled. 'Partner?'

'You can't fool me, Billy. When you had that bad time and thought you'd have to close, Chris Templeton helped you out and I know he wouldn't do it for fun; that's where the money came from to convert some rooms into B&Bs. Knowing him he'd want something in exchange, like a stake in this place?'

Billy sneered. 'Friend of yours is he?' The look on Billy's face angered Jimbo. He guessed from that look that Billy knew all about Fran and Chris. Jimbo felt his temper rising to new heights and he needed self-control as he'd never needed it before. 'Room number?'

'He's not here,' replied Billy still counting his money. He'd got as far as one-pound coins now and they were trickier to stack than the two pounds coins so he needed to concentrate more.

Jimbo leaned across the table and whispered something into Billy's ear but Billy ignored him and somehow Jimbo's foot kicked against a table leg and many of the stacks of coins tumbled.

'Aye! Watch it.' Billy got to his feet. 'You know too much for your own good, you do.'

Behind Jimbo, the barman, still filling up the shelves, said just loud enough for Jimbo to hear, 'Room four, you want.' And then disappeared hurriedly into the cellar, supposedly for further supplies.

Jimbo, before Billy knew what was happening, raced up the stairs to the first floor. The door of number four was locked but Jimbo put his substantial shoulder to the door, twice, and it burst open.

And there was the man of the moment, lounging naked and half asleep in bed, alone. Alone!

That was a surprise. Chris must be losing his grip, thought Jimbo. But at that exact moment the en-suite door opened and there, in all her naked glory, was Billy's wife.

Despite his seething anger about Chris's behaviour towards Fran, even Jimbo couldn't linger to witness Billy's reaction when he found out and he wasn't going to be the one to tell him either, but Billy, unknown to Jimbo, had followed him silently up the stairs, so, looking over Jimbo's shoulder, Billy also could see his wife.

When Jimbo realised Billy had followed him up he hesitated, saw Chris had been woken by him smashing the door open and decided to leave immediately, because he couldn't face watching a six-foot-six heavily built ex-boxer like Billy giving Chris what he deserved, much as he might relish it.

Jimbo did, however, ring the police and suggested an ambulance might also be useful.

Jimbo never said a word when he got to the Store as to where he'd been, didn't even apologise for missing an appointment with someone asking about the cost of using the Old Barn for an exhibition for two days in the spring. In fact, Tom, Bel and Fran didn't see him for the rest of the morning; he was shut in his office, working he said, and hadn't time to be dealing with the day-to-day running of the Store.

The story, being such a great piece of gossip, couldn't possibly have remained within the enclaves of The Wise Man public house. A rep from a company that supplied special herbal drinks to the Store and also to The Wise Man called in, eager for a chat. 'Jimbo around?' he asked the moment he walked in.

'In his office and not to be disturbed.' Bel replied.

The rep paused for a moment and then said, 'He'll be more than disturbed when he hears what I've got to tell him. I'm going in.'

It was the rep's determination that persuaded Bel to let him knock on Jimbo's office door. After all, it might even be interesting to her.

With half his mind on the new advertising scheme he was thinking of initiating and the other half-heartedly hoping that Chris was still alive, Jimbo absent-mindedly shouted, 'Come in!'

'Jimbo!' said the rep. 'Sorry to disturb, but there's been a real fracas at The Wise Man – police, ambulance, the lot, and Billy's been arrested for beating up that Chris your Fran went out with for a bit.'

Jimbo slowly half turned to listen, his face non-committal. 'Really? Why?' he asked, apparently without much enthusiasm. In his eagerness to spread his juicy gossip, the rep settled down in the spare chair and Jimbo closed his laptop and waited.

'Seems he, Billy that is, caught his wife and that Chris Templeton you all love to hate, at it in one of those new B&B bedrooms he has. He all but murdered him! Apparently she hadn't a stitch on. She tried to intervene but couldn't stop him and was screaming her head off, trying to pull him off Chris.

'Apparently that Chris went to hospital on a stretcher, strapped from head to foot with barely a limb intact and his face is smashed to smithereens. Blood everywhere. Be some time, it seems, before he'll be able to leave hospital. It's not just a "you'll be home in a couple of days" job, it's intensive surgery he needs, they say. You wouldn't believe it, would you? Poor chap. Anyway Billy's been arrested. Chris ought to have had more sense than trying it on with Billy's wife, him being the size he is.'

The rep felt quite let down by Jimbo's response. He hadn't even turned round to listen properly to this heaven sent piece of gossip. 'Anyway, I'll be off. Bel can give me the order, right?'

Puzzled by Jimbo's lack of interest, the rep wandered off to find Bel and that nice cup of tea she always had ready for him when he called. Now *she* would be interested, he could be certain of *that*.

When Fran got back from a hasty dash round in the Land Rover collecting jams and chutney and things from their outworkers, she found Bel and Tom industriously occupied. They helped her unload the supplies she'd collected but they avoided her eye, spoke about nothing else other than the matter in hand, and quickly returned to their allotted tasks, not even offering to make her a cup of tea which they always did when she got back from her round. What was up?

'Dad?'

'In his office,' said Tom.

Fran walked straight in without knocking. 'Dad, have you all had a row or something? Neither Tom nor Bel appear to be speaking to me. Are you? Speaking to me?'

'Sit down,' her father sighed.

'Right.' She perched on her dad's thinking chair and waited.

'Have you heard the news about Chris?' When Fran shook her head he swallowed hard and told her he was in hospital.

'Why? Has he been taken ill?'

'No, not exactly. Well, yes, he's been beaten up, you see, quite severely.'

Fran shot to her feet in horror. 'Dad! You haven't, not you? You wouldn't, would you?'

Indignant, Jimbo replied, 'I didn't do it. Of course not!'

'Who did?'

'Billy, the landlord at—'

'Not Billy? You mean *Big* Billy?'

Jimbo nodded and Fran sat down again. 'Heaven's above! But why? Couldn't be for not paying his bill, surely?' She smiled slightly at her joke.

Jimbo still had to tell her, if he didn't someone else would. 'His wife, well, she was sleeping with Chris.'

Fran leapt to her feet. 'Sleeping with Chris? Billy's wife? Myrtle? I don't believe it! That is simply not true, it's someone else making up rubbish just to have nasty tittle-tattle to spread, and you're helping to spread it! You should be ashamed, Dad. He wouldn't, not Chris.'

'Trouble is, Fran, it *is* true. Because it was me who found them.'

The blood drained from Fran's face and she sat down rapidly in the thinking chair. '*You?*'

'Me. Unfortunately. So no matter how much you protest, it's true.'

Fran remained silent trying hard to absorb this tale about Chris.

Surely it couldn't be true? Myrtle? Fran still couldn't believe it.

'It must have been someone else. Couldn't have been Myrtle.'

'Stark naked but still recognisable. It was her, Fran. I saw her. It must have been her, otherwise why would Billy beat up Chris?'

'Oh Dad!'

'Yes?'

'Oh Dad!' Fran was trembling and now speechless. Myrtle ... was so ... well, *common*. 'How could he? Honestly. How could he?' Never ever again would she allow him within a yard of her. And under the same roof as her husband! But then again, Fran did know how captivating he was, how amazingly attractive, how he pulled at one's heart strings, how irresistible he was. Those beautiful, splendidly sensitive hands of his ... she shuddered and reached out for the comfort of her father's arms and wept as he hugged her.

Chapter 22

Later that day, just before closing time, Johnny Templeton arrived asking to see Jimbo. The two part timers who kept the Store open until seven on a weekday told him that Jimbo was at home, so Johnny walked round Stocks Row to find him.

'Good evening, Jimbo. There's no doubt you will have heard about my brother.'

'One of the reps told me when he called at the Store for his order. I'm sorry, but it was inevitable someone would get their own back on him. How is he? The rep made it sound life-threatening.'

'He's been badly beaten up, no doubt about that, broken collar-bone, five ribs broken, right wrist broken. Badly bruised face, two teeth missing. It can all be put right but at the same time—'

'Time you saw him as he is, like your dear Alice does. There's no fooling her. It was bound to happen one day, Johnny, you know.'

'I thought perhaps it might have been you who did it; after all you have hit him once before.'

'See here, Johnny Templeton, I did not lay a *finger* on him. Believe me.'

'You were there, though.'

'Briefly, but when I saw trouble was brewing I departed in haste; didn't want to get embroiled.'

Johnny stood in the hall looking thoroughly defeated. 'I suppose I have to be glad he's still alive. A friend for whom he has the greatest respect has come to see him – not because of the fight, she arrived a day or two before that and is staying with us. She's there with him now, though he's so stoked up with morphine I can't imagine she is getting much out of him.'

Jimbo showed some interest. 'Not the Annunciata woman?'

'No, someone he's known since school. Deborah, she's called. Lovely, lovely woman.'

'Oh! Right.'

'But you were *there* then?'

Jimbo nodded. 'I was. Went to see Chris thinking he might be living at the pub seeing as he'd helped Billy out financially when he was in a great big hole some time ago. I shouldered open his bedroom door and he was in bed, with Myrtle just coming out of the en suite in her birthday suit. I left. Full stop. That's all I know except for the over-dramatised story I heard from a rep.'

'I see. Well, I'm going back to the hospital to see him because he had an operation lunchtime to set his wrist. He's one hell of a mess. Believe me. I am so ashamed of him. Maybe at last he'll see the error of his ways.' Johnny smiled wryly.

Jimbo, for Johnny's sake, said he hoped so too, but didn't for one minute believe he would.

'Johnny, I can't be a witness to anything because Billy hadn't touched him when I left. He was still standing on the landing and had to move to one side to allow me to go down the stairs. So there's no question, *no question* of Jimbo Charter-Plackett being a witness. Right? Sorry.'

'Pity.'

Over dinner that evening Fran asked him why he refused to be a witness.

'Because I wasn't. I did not see a single blow struck.'

'You saw Billy on the landing,' she protested.

'Just because a man stands on a landing it does not follow he is going to beat someone up.'

'Chris needs *someone* on his side,' she said.

'Well, I'm sorry, Fran, but it's not going to be me. I do not want my name tainted with such a sordid event, I have a reputation to protect.'

'But—'

'But nothing. It wasn't me in bed with Myrtle, it was Chris, and just you remember that if anyone says anything to you about it, which they will, believe me. I know Billy shouldn't have done what he did, but it is Chris who brought it on himself.'

The prospect of being confronted by a customer wanting to get first-hand information rather alarmed Fran and she remained silent while she worked out what she could say should any tricky questions arise during the day. They'd all be full of it and they all knew she'd been involved with Chris.

'Could I work in the back tomorrow? Keep out of it, so to speak. Or, I know! I'll ring round the rest of the outworkers I didn't call on and say I'm doing the round early this week.'

Harriet cleared her mouth of food and said, 'You've faced worse, best face it immediately or it will cause even more speculation. And don't let them think your dad witnessed it all, because he didn't. He's right about his reputation: before we know where we are they'll have him down as attending an orgy. OK?'

Fran was silenced by her mother's advice. No escape that way, then. She made up her mind that she wouldn't visit Chris in hospital because no doubt there'd be a queue of female admirers hoping to leave a tender impression of their love for this handsome male patient. Or maybe he was handsome no longer with teeth missing and the bruising and the pain of it all. She winced. Poor Chris! Then she giggled at the thought of his missing teeth and felt better for it.

With dinner just finished, Jimbo in his study, and Fran stacking the dishwasher, the doorbell rang. It sounded like Grandmama's demanding ring but it couldn't be; she was on a day outing with the WI.

It was, though. 'Someone rang home on our way back and told us all about what happened at The Wise Man this morning.

Is my darling Jimbo all right? Shouldn't you be at the hospital, seeing how ill he is? I've been worried sick ever since we all got the dammed news, it went round that coach in a flash and before I knew it they were all saying to me, to *me*, how sorry they were about Jimbo. I had a shock, I can tell you.'

Harriet stood looking at her without replying.

'Well?' said Grandmama, stepping over the threshold, anxious for news.

'Jimbo is in his study, not in hospital,' Harriet said. 'He's perfectly fit. He'd left before it all happened.'

Grandmama went from excitement to disappointment in a moment. 'He wasn't in a fight with Chris? Didn't even see it, then?'

Harriet shook her head.

'He had already left before the fight started. In any case, it wasn't a fight. Billy thumped Chris while he lay on the bed and Chris never got a chance to retaliate. It was all over in a moment, according to Johnny.'

Eagerly Grandmama asked, 'How badly hurt is Chris?'

'Come in, find a pew and we'll have a drink and I'll tell you. What's your choice?'

'A whisky, please. Is he badly hurt?'

Harriet told her the list of Chris's injuries as imparted by Johnny.

'I say! Some thumping, then. Just what he deserved.' She stepped closer to Harriet and asked quietly, 'How's Fran about all this?'

'Not too bad.'

'Good. Glad to hear it. Fran! Come and have a drink with your grandmama. That's a good girl. I've had an excellent day with the WI. Their outings are always filled to the brim with things to do and things to buy and things to talk about. I've really enjoyed myself, and good food to eat too. Well a good day apart from worrying about Jimbo when the news burst forth round the coach on our way home! They were all fascinated believe me. By the time the story got to me Jimbo was on a life support machine and there wasn't much hope. They do exaggerate, don't they? They said he helped with the beating up, too, which was apparently a downright invention.' She gave a shifty glance to Fran and to Harriet, thinking that maybe they were covering up something she jolly well ought to know but realised from their demeanour they were telling the truth. 'Can I just put my head round his door and prove beyond doubt that he is sound in wind and limb?'

It took less then a minute to assure herself he was in good health. Back in the sitting room she told Harriet that she was glad he'd left before Big Billy allowed his rage to get the better of him.

'Doesn't do for someone in Jimbo's position to be tainted by unpleasant gossip.'

At that moment Fran's phone rang. She dug it out of her jeans' pocket and escaped into the privacy of the kitchen in case it was Alex ringing. But it was a woman, a woman the sound of whose voice seemed to ring bells but Fran couldn't recollect who she was.

'Yes, this is Fran Charter-Plackett speaking. How may I help?'

'I believe I met you the other evening in the Store in the village. My name is Deborah Charlesworth. I'm a friend of Chris Templeton.'

'Oh! Right. You bought chocolate bars for the Templeton boys.'

'Yes! That's me. Have you heard about Chris's ... ah, shall we say ... accident?'

Warily, Fran answered 'Yes', concerned that he might have died. No, not Chris! Dying would be the last thing on his mind being the kind of man he was.

'Fran, would it be possible for you to call to see him in hospital? He's asking for you. He has something to say to you, you know.'

Fran refused to make it look as though she was in a hurry to see him. 'I could, but I'm not sure when. I'm in the Store very early tomorrow and all day till five. But I could slip out for an hour I suppose.'

'If you would. I'll be there all day and he'll be glad to see you and so will I. Looking forward to seeing you, Fran. He's in intensive care at the moment, room nine.'

'Room nine, right.'

'See you there then, and thank you very much indeed for being so kind.'

Room nine. The silence in this part of the hospital was unnerving. Hushed voices, quiet, unhurried feet, the continuous soft background whirr of a multitude of machines, that clean disinfectant smell, a ward that was too busy for chatter, too serious for bursts of laughter.

Fran knocked on the door gently and stepped inside. Chris appeared to have tubes coming at him from every angle. He looked haggard, his face covered in purple bruises and so swollen around his eyes she doubted he'd be able to see even if he managed to open them. And fast asleep. Perhaps doped to the eyeballs might be a more correct description, she thought.

The woman she'd met in the Store the other day confronted her. 'Fran, isn't it?' and offered to shake her hand. It was the very positive handshake of a woman thoroughly in charge of herself.

Fran nodded. So this was Deborah, dressed with distinction in a classic, beautifully tailored navy-blue suit complimented by a splendidly fashioned ivory silk shirt. Her naturally blonde hair gently curled around her sweetly composed face. Late thirties, Fran rather imagined.

'How is he today?' Fran whispered.

'No need to whisper – he's wide awake, though you wouldn't think so.' In a commanding voice Deborah summoned Chris to life. 'Fran's here, Chris, I know you're awake.'

He immediately stirred and opened his eyes. He greeted Fran in a funny spluttery voice, slightly difficult to understand but quite reasonable considering his swollen face and the missing teeth.

Deborah ignored him completely and said, 'I need a break; be about half an hour and I'll be back. OK, Fran?'

'That's fine. Where's the bell if things gets serious and I need help?'

'Chris has it by his right hand. Haven't you, Chris?'

Chris nodded painfully.

Fran waited until Deborah had gone before she bent over the bed and gently kissed him on the only bit close to his mouth which wasn't bruised.

'Sorry about all this, Chris. You really will have to be more circumspect in your relationships.'

'Myrtle insisted, Fran, it wasn't me, honestly. I mean ...'

'What rubbish! For once take responsibility for what has happened, Chris. Please. Just be an adult, you know.'

'You sound like Deborah,' he said petulantly. 'And you're not like her, Fran, you're sweet and loving.'

'So is she, I think. Who is she?'

He opened his mouth to speak, changed his mind and asked her to help him get his glass so he could have a drink of water. Fran helped him to take a drink and he guzzled it down as though he hadn't had one for at least a week. 'Refill it, please.' Chris drinking water? He *must* be ill. She couldn't remember ever seeing him with a glass of water in his hand, never mind actually drinking it.

She did as he asked and then sat quietly waiting. She'd been told he needed to speak to her so she'd wait to see what he had to say. But he closed his eyes and said nothing. And there she sat beside his bed for over twenty minutes while he apparently slept. But she had a sneaking idea that he was only pretending to sleep, because twice she caught him looking at her for a brief moment. They were still sitting there when Deborah came back, right on the dot of half an hour.

Without any kind of polite preamble she asked Fran if he'd had a word with her.

'Only to ask for a drink of water which I gave him.'

'I see. In that case you might as well go home.'

212

Having said that, Deborah very tenderly traced the line of his lips with her finger, taking care not to touch the bruising.

'Chris! I thought you and I had agreed you had something to say to Fran. She's come to see you when she should be working so you've not to make her visit a waste of time. That's not fair, is it? Saying sorry is what gentlemen manage to do, even in their dying moments and you're not dying, are you?'

Chris appeared to be making a decision about dying. 'No, I'm not.'

'Good. Fire away. We're waiting for your big moment.' Deborah gently took hold of his uninjured right wrist and stroked it and then kissed it.

Chris said, 'I owe you the biggest apology ever and even then it will not be enough. I'm so sorry I didn't care for you, Fran, when ...'

'Yes ...?' she asked him, determined to make him say it even if Deborah was listening. She needed that apology, always supposing that was what he intended.

'When you lost the baby – *our* baby, I should say – I was mean and I'm sorry. So sorry.' Tears slid down his cheeks and Deborah placed his right hand in Fran's and sat back without a word.

Fran gripped his wrist and didn't reply because she couldn't find the right words. It all seemed so long ago and it was an apology that had come far too late, when the crushing pain had almost left her. But he *had* apologised and that was important, and she sensed the effort it had taken him, especially as apologising wasn't in his nature and he was so ill.

Fran spotted a pack of tissues beside his bed, pulled one out and gently dried the tears as they ran down his cheeks. 'Thank you for saying that. I was heartbroken, it being your baby. I didn't try to get rid of it, you know, it just happened.'

'I know you wouldn't have, being the Fran I know. Thank you for letting me say it. I shan't be laid up like this for long. I shall pull myself together like Alice told me to do yesterday.' He smiled slightly. 'She's tough, is Alice, you can't pull the wool over her eyes. In fact, I treated you like rubbish and that simply was not fair. I'd no right to do that. That was my trouble, thinking I could do whatever I liked with people so long as I was getting what I wanted ... you were too lovely for me to behave like that ... too lovely ...' He patted her hand and closed his eyes, weary to death.

Fran refused to cry in front of Deborah and held on to her tears until she was sitting in the hospital car park, waiting for the car to warm up. That Deborah! She was super and just the kind of person Chris needed; beautiful, well mannered, in command of herself and, she rather suspected, in command of Chris when she chose to be. She'd be quite glad to hand him over to someone like her.

Chapter 23

The bad weather had been a big factor in preventing people getting to the pub as regularly as they would have liked. Dicky and Georgie had been worried sick by the drop in takings but there was nothing they could do about the weather and had to suffer their lack of takings as best they could. Snow, then relentless rain and freezing temperatures had all succeeded in making people stay indoors rather than venture out.

The weather, though, had been, relatively speaking, quite mild for the last three days and by eight o'clock on this particular Saturday night it would appear that their regular punters had been tempted to stray beyond their front doors at last. Dicky did a ten minute stint of getting them rolling in the aisles with his jokes which cheered everyone up enormously.

'Cheers, everybody!' Dicky said as he returned to his duties as bartender.

'Now, Sylvia,' said Greta as she and Vince settled themselves into their favourite chairs, 'how's Willie? Feeling better is he now?'

'He is. They've got the tablets just right and he's feeling on top of the world. Says he'll be going out tomorrow – just to church and back, but it'll be a challenge for him and not half. They've done wonders for him at the hospital, you know. No messing. He needed a stent and before he knew it he was whisked off and had the operation immediately. Amazing!'

'He'll be back in here then before long.'

'Fingers crossed. We're going to have a little holiday in another week or two. Just a few days of luxury in an hotel by the sea.'

'That'll be lovely, so long as you keep well wrapped up when you go out.'

'Exactly. Willie won't be able to walk far but I did wonder about hiring a taxi and going somewhere nearby for a change one day.'

'Good idea, that.'

'I'm so glad Vera said what she said that night. It made me overrule Willie and get an appointment for him at the doctors'. He was mad and almost refused to keep the appointment but I told him straight and made him go.'

'You did?' said Greta surprised, knowing how stubborn Willie could be.

Sylvia nodded. 'I told him straight. "No keeping the appointment … result, no meals got ready for you, and I mean it". It did the trick. He hates cooking, you see, and I knew he knew I meant it. So, I've got Vera to thank for him getting cured. They don't hang about at that hospital, you know. Decision made, operation takes place, and the way they've looked after him! Spoiled to death he was. Well, not death, you know what I mean. It's a lesson to us all. All that worrying he did, too scared to take action. Foolish old man that he is!'

'Being out of action, kind of, Sylvia, you'll have missed the story of the century.'

'Story of the century? Which was that?'

'Big Billy up in court.'

'No, I got the whole story from Fran. She told me. Has he been charged, then?'

Greta nodded. She took a long drink of her lager, put the glass down and began to relate the story for the umpteenth time. 'That Chris Templeton was determined he'd be present as a witness at the hearing. Apparently he struggled in, using a crutch. Only one because he couldn't use two because of his broken wrist but apparently he needed two. He leaned on it and it looked very necessary; claimed he'd come out of hospital for the day in order to give evidence, which was true. I wasn't there but a friend of mine went on purpose, terrible Nosey Parker she is, and he gave his evidence in a really weak voice and she said you could see he'd still got no teeth where Big Billy had knocked 'em out. His right, no, his *left* arm was in plaster still as you'd expect, and he had to ask for a chair while he gave evidence because of the pain from his broken ribs. Like something out of a film it was, apparently.'

'No! Really?'

Greta nodded. 'Anyway Billy's out on bail and the proper court case will be in January. Grievous bodily harm, and it is: Chris's face was still black and blue and bruised and swollen all round his eyes! You wouldn't believe how bad it is. He hadn't half taken a beating. That Billy meant business, no doubt about it. He blamed it all on the fact that he loved his wife Myrtle more than anything in the whole wide world and it was a case of passion getting the better of him.'

'So Chris is no longer the most handsome man in Turnham Malpas then?' Sylvia grinned.

Greta giggled. 'Apparently not. They called Myrtle as a witness. Fully dressed, of course, she was. She gave a great performance, said they couldn't help themselves, love at first sight she said. My neighbour said she swore she could hear muffled laughter all over the court when she came out with that.' Greta paused to take another drink of her lager and then added, 'Apparently he's taken her back.'

Disbelief flooded Sylvia's face. 'Chris has taken her back? Myrtle? Never!'

'No, not *Chris*. That would be ridiculous! *Billy*.'

Vince, who'd been listening in with deep interest, said, 'She's too useful for him in the pub for him to lose her, works like a slave she does. Bakes them cupcakes that's all the rage now, decorates 'em, and they sell faster than she can get round to baking 'em. Right money-spinner they've become. Ever tried one? They're delicious, downright delicious. Some people call in for a bagful of 'em to take home.'

Sylvia couldn't resist being facetious. 'Well, Vince, don't you take a fancy to Myrtle when you pop across for a bagful of cupcakes, *you* wouldn't be able to survive the kicking that Chris has had.'

'What a thing to suggest to a happily married man like me! I wouldn't dream of looking at another woman. My Greta's all I want.'

Greta realised after a moment that he'd just been very complimentary to her. 'Thank you, Vince love, for that.' She leaned over to kiss his cheek.

'They say he's got another woman in tow,' Vince announced with a kind of grim satisfaction.

Sylvia nodded. 'He has. I saw her in the Store this morning. I must say she looks a bit of class. Different, from Myrtle, different as chalk and cheese. Very distinguished, I thought, and she spoke to Fran as though they already knew each other, which seemed a bit odd.'

'I hear from that friend of mine who's a nurse at the hospital that Fran's been up to see Chris, at the invitation of that other woman what's turned up. Deborah something or another? She told my friend, the nurse, that she's known Chris for years.'

'Right ...'

There was a silence after this while they contemplated whether or not they should hope that Deborah would marry Chris and settle the whole question of Chris running freely after any woman he fancied in the village. Who would be next on his list after he finally recovered from Big Billy's beating, they asked themselves?

Vince offered to get another drink in for anyone who wanted one but Sylvia declared she was going home and Dottie, who'd been very quiet ever since she first sat down at their table, said, 'Not for me, I'm going.'

'No, don't go, it's too early for you, Dottie. But I've noticed you've been very quiet this evening. Has something unpleasant happened? Someone upset you?'

'No, no, Vince, not at all. But I've ... well, I may as well tell you ... I was going to tell you nearer the time but maybe I'll tell you now.'

A silence fell as though, intuitively, they all knew something sensational was about to be divulged.

Dottie drew in a loud nervous breath and then said very positively, 'I'm getting married.'

Everyone within hearing of this very public statement was astounded.

'You? Getting married? Who to? I can't imagine you married,' said Greta almost lost for words with shock.

'Well, I am getting married. No need to sound so surprised.'

'Who to?' Vince inquired.

Suddenly Dottie blushed bright red. 'No one, and I mean no one, has ever suggested I might be marrying material, so his proposal came as something of a surprise. It's one of my cousins.'

Each person sitting round their favourite table said in unison, 'A cousin of yours?'

'I thought you couldn't marry a cousin,' Greta protested.

'You can, I've checked, and that's what I'm going to do. We've known each other all our lives. He's six weeks older than me and we've decided that's what's going to happen. Oh, say you're pleased for us?'

'But you've always seemed so happy on your own, I mean ...'

'When did you last ask me if I was happy, Sylvia?'

Sylvia hesitated while she had a think. 'I ... well ... do you know, I don't think I ever have, I just assumed you were. You always *seemed* all right.'

'Well, I haven't been happy for years, not really happy, Sylvia. Always conscious of my past, I suppose, and I always wanted to get married.'

'I'm real sorry you've felt like that, Dottie,' said Vince, 'just never realised. You should have said.'

'And what would you have done about it then, Vince? When I said how unhappy I was. Married me?'

Vince shuffled uncomfortably, saying, 'Well, of course not, I'm already married.'

'Exactly! His name's Maurice and he can't make ends meet, I can't make ends meet, money gets worth less and less it seems to me, so we've decided if we shared a house ...'

'Well, I think that's a very brave thing to be doing. Mind you, I think it's a bit dodgy ...' Greta shook her head despondently. 'He'll be more like a brother.'

Dottie said sharply, 'Well it's nothing to do with what *you* think, it's between Maurice and me and we've always been keen on each other and that's how it's going to be. Peter's marrying us next month.'

'Next month!' Greta was astonished. 'Well, it won't be a shot-gun wedding at your age, will it?'

'No point in hanging about, is there? I can't afford a big affair so I haven't organised anything yet, can't decide what to do. Oh, I'm so pleased, you've no idea. Thrilled to bits, I am. Are you pleased for me?'

Greta said, 'Of course we are. *Really* pleased. If you suit each other then why not? No point in being lonely all the rest of your life 'cos you're too frightened to take hold of what life has to offer. Get on with it, I say.'

'Maurice what? Is he perhaps someone we know?' Vince inquired.

'Deede. Maurice Deede.'

'Oh! You'll be Dottie Deede then?'

Dottie studied this idea for a moment as though events had overtaken her and she had never contemplated what her name might be. Dottie Deede, that sounded ridiculous. 'I might stay Dottie Foskett like these modern girls with careers do. I'll ask Maurice what he thinks.'

'You'll have to have a party of some kind, even at your age,' said Vince, regretting those last four words the moment they were out of his mouth.

Dottie gave him a steely glance but made no comment about what he'd said. 'Well, I'll be off. Maurice said he might come tonight to meet you all but it's getting late ...'

Dottie shrugged, got to her feet and made to leave. But Greta thought something more encouraging should be said before she left.

'Look here, Dottie. We're all a bit shoc ... *surprised* as you can expect, but at the same time we are delighted for you. It'll be lovely having someone new sitting round this table and we ought to say Congratulations! And good luck, take your happiness where you can, I say!'

Waving a vigorous goodnight to everyone, Dottie went home.

She left behind her a long silence. Stunned by Dottie's news Vince went off to get refills. He asked Georgie if she knew about Dottie's plans and she was just as amazed as the others were. 'Dottie? She's having you on!'

'She isn't, you know. She means it.'

'Well, I never. What a surprise. Who is she marrying?'

'One of her cousins – he's called Maurice Deede. Short of money they both are, she says, so sharing one house will be better financially if nothing else.'

'Has he been married before?'

'I don't know, she never said. She's getting married here in the Church at the end of the month.'

'She's not letting the grass grow under her feet, is she? There we are, Vince. That's everything.'

'Thanks. We'll have to give a party for her, won't we?'

'I'll have a good think about that,' Georgie said. 'I might be able to help there.'

'Brilliant! Better get some plans laid and quick.'

Dottie getting married was the main subject of their conversation right through to when Georgie called time. Someone said they thought the name Maurice Deede rang a bell: was it something to do with cricket? How sad that Dottie had always wanted to get married, but then who'd want her with her unfortunate early lifestyle behind her, her being a lady of the night to put it politely? But what else could she do, considering her lack of education? Her silly mother was to blame, always keeping her at home on the flimsiest excuse so she got no schooling? Poor Dottie. Just goes to show you never really know people, even those who live on your doorstep for years. Dottie! Married! Would you believe it?

They would have believed it if they'd seen the delight on Maurice's face when Dottie arrived home from the pub with Sykes. He was waiting for her by the fire he'd cultivated into a roaring inferno so the house would warm her through when she got in. Sykes greeted him with abandon, but this new relationship Dottie and Maurice had was still very new even though they'd always known each other, so *their* greeting was more restrained than Sykes's but joyous even so, and they sat down to drink the cup of tea Maurice had got ready for her.

'I've told 'em.'

Maurice asked if they were all right about it.

'Surprised, Maurice, really surprised. I could tell they were amazed anyone would want me after the life I led. You didn't come to walk me home, leg playing up again?'

'No, thought it best to let it sink in before I put in an appearance. I've given notice on my flat so there'll be no rent to pay after the end of next month.' He gazed round the sitting room with a satisfied look in his eyes. 'It's a lovely cottage you've got, Dottie, really lovely. This big inglenook fireplace and the old panelling, lovely, it really is. My modern flat hasn't one bit of character about it, not one bit. We shall be very happy here, you know. Very happy.'

'It needs decorating, though, in here and the bathroom too. Other than that ... the plus with this cottage is it's not a listed building so we can do what we want with it, and I own it.'

'I'm looking forward to moving in. By the way, I've booked a honeymoon for us.'

Dottie leapt from her chair, flung her arms around Maurice's neck and wept with joy. Cheek to cheek, her lips close to his ear she said, 'You are a surprising man. You don't look as though you would be full of lovely surprises, but you are. I was hoping we might. Straight after the wedding?'

Maurice nodded. 'Straight after the wedding. Well, the following day.'

'Where?'

Maurice paused for a moment to get the maximum tension in the atmosphere. 'Paris, by air. You once said years ago you'd never been to Paris so I thought that's the very place we'll go.' He tried hard not to look triumphant but that was how he felt when he saw the joy the idea brought her.

'Paris! Oh, I've never been. And I'll pay my share.'

'You won't.'

'I will.'

'You won't, not your honeymoon. That's my prerogative. Now I'll be off because it's late.'

Maurice left her entranced with delight about Paris. Dottie asked herself if she had finally joined the human race? She must have. That's what real people did, booking a holiday, having a holiday to plan for, getting married – and she'd never really felt like a member of the human race before, except when she was at the Rectory. There, she knew, she was respected by all four of them.

Everyone else, because of what she had been, merely tolerated her. Though she had to admit she'd found her niche in the embroidery group where yes, she was valued just the same as everyone else. My word though, Maurice was special. A honeymoon!

'Thank you, Maurice,' she shouted out loud, an enormous grin on her face.

Chapter 24

Becky Braithwaite had news of her own but she hadn't divulged it to a living soul. Since Ben had started work at the Big House garden now he'd finished his course, he was out of the house for longer hours than when he was at College which gave her more freedom and the chance of other work to fill their coffers. Ben's money also helped. To her utter surprise he'd taken to working regularly like a duck to water and having money to spend thrilled him. He'd worked out how to take the shortcut to the Big House by using the little wicket gate in the back wall of the churchyard and merrily took himself off by seven-thirty each workday morning and didn't return until five o'clock.

The biggest surprise had been him discovering the joys of working in the glasshouses. The very first time he went in there, when Johnny was first showing him round, he drew a great heaving breath of surprise and was immediately fascinated by the vines growing in such abundance that he tenderly trailed his hands along, gently touching the leaves and stroking the stems, muttering to himself. He'd turned to look at Johnny eventually, who recognised the fascination in his eyes.

'They're lovely, aren't they?' Johnny said.

Ben had nodded and asked without any prompting, 'Can I work here? I'll dig like I said but can I work here as well?'

Johnny replied. 'I'll ask Greenwood. He doesn't let anyone work in here, only special people he likes.'

'Greenwood. Who's Greenwood? I don't know Greenwood. Where is he? Where's Greenwood?'

'Well, that's his name. We all call him Greenwood and he's one of my bosses.'

'Well, that's what I'd like to do. All the time with Greenwood. Will he like me?'

'He doesn't actually *work* in these glasshouses, he's too old now, but he comes every day to inspect everything and see nothing has died in the night. First he'll want to see how clever you are at digging and not sitting about doing nothing when you should be working, but I'll recommend you to him.'

'Thank you. Thank you, thank you, thank you. Do you think he'll like me?'

'Let's wait and see.'

Ben repeated, 'Let's wait and see. Let's wait and see. That's what Becky says, "Let's wait and see."'

He ambled out of the glasshouse reluctantly but when Johnny handed him his brand new spade with his name on it and took him to the vegetable garden he set to with a will.

He couldn't remember why Becky kept saying, '*Let's wait and see*' then halfway through digging the potato patch he did. Of course. It was that new man she was cleaning for. He'd been to the flat two times for Sunday lunch but what was his name? Ben straightened up and, leaning on his spade, he tried to remember. That was it, Roger Walking. Yes, of course ... but no, that still didn't sound right. It was Roger but not Walking. His mind wandered off into thinking about his dad. He'd gone walking off but he never come back. Where had he gone? He couldn't remember. Dig! He'd have to dig or that Green Man wouldn't let him into the glasshouses. Dig. Dig. Dig. His fingers itched to touch those vines. *Let's wait and see.* Let's wait and see.

Ben was right about Becky saying that; she had done several times just lately because it was the answer she gave to Ben when he asked her questions about Roger. Inside herself she trembled at the very thought of him. It was quite by chance that she'd got the job cleaning his cottage in Hipkin Gardens.

She'd been in the Store shopping for their evening meal when the man came in to put a card on Jimbo's notice board. It read:

Cleaner required at 4, Hipkin Gardens, Turnham Malpas. Two hours each Friday. Tel:- 497479

It sounded just right for her and when she looked at the man himself he felt just right too. He was comfortably dressed in a checked sports jacket, a checked shirt and a brown woollen tie and everything about him was immaculately clean.

She decided not to mention her plan in the Store or it would be all over the three villages before she'd even cooked the food she was buying, so she made a mental note of the number, paid at the till and swept out, as she thought, unnoticed.

That night Ben went to bed earlier than usual in order, he said, to be fresh as a daisy the next morning hoping, hoping the Green Man might invite him into the glasshouses if he saw him arriving early for work. So, with her household chores done before she set off to her first cleaning job, Becky was free to ring the immaculate man's mobile number.

He'd sounded cheerful and literate and interested that she lived in the village. He answered her query saying, 'I'm busy all this week but I'm free Saturday morning. Come about ten and you can see the house and decide if you fancy working for me. The house is small and because there's only me and the work won't be arduous. Ironing, perhaps, too.'

'Don't mind ironing; in fact, I like ironing. See you at ten as you suggest. Oh, my name is Becky Braithwaite and you are ...?'

'Roger Walker. Ten on Saturday morning, then. Bye.'

'Bye, Mr Walker.'

That same night she went into the pub with Ben for a

much-needed conversation with anyone who was willing to put up with her. She'd had enough of Ben talking endlessly about Green Man, as he called him, allowing him into the glasshouses for the very first time. They'd got on famously, by the sound of it. but there was a limit to the number of times Becky could listen to the story and sound genuinely interested, so she told him they'd have a little celebration of his good luck in the pub, and what drink would he like? This gave him something else to think about and by the time they set off Becky was already feeling less stressed.

She gave Ben the money for their drinks while she found somewhere to sit and he went to the bar and ordered a large Coke for himself and a gin and orange for herself. There was no doubt about it, working at the Big House had certainly improved his speech. It was much clearer and he appeared to actually know what he was talking about when before all he had really been doing was repeating what she had told him to say. They sat together at the old table so favoured by the regular clientele. None of the regulars had arrived yet but Becky didn't mind because Ben was occupied drinking his Coke and enjoying a packet of salted peanuts he'd chosen for himself, so she could relax.

Gradually the settle and the chairs began filling up with Maggie and Sylvia and Willie, now back in circulation, as well as Vera, Vince and Greta and Dottie, accompanied for the first time by Maurice. Maurice's arrival caused a lot of consternation, but not for Becky because she'd met him a week ago when she visited Dottie unexpectedly and found Maurice comfortably occupying a big plush armchair new to the cottage.

They all shook hands with Maurice and gave him a great welcome which did Dottie's heart good.

Ben, to their amazement, said, 'Maurice Deede. I know Maurice Deede. Cricket. He plays cricket. He does. I know Maurice Deede plays cricket.'

Maurice blushingly admitted he used to play cricket. 'Not for a long time, though.'

Vince said, 'Of course! I remember now. Scored one hundred and twenty-three at the Oval though I can't remember the year. Saved England and not half. The year we won the Ashes back. Very pleased to meet you, Maurice, it's an honour!' Vince got to his feet and wholeheartedly shook Maurice's hand. 'Well, I never!' and sat down in astonishment staring at Maurice unable to believe his luck. 'My word. Then ... didn't you have an accident and couldn't play any more?'

'That's right, certainly put paid to my cricketing career. I never played for England ever again.'

'No,' said Vince, 'but you were the man for the moment and not half. My word, what a thrill that was. Your finest hour, eh? I insist on buying you a drink. Name it, right now.'

'Home-brew! I understand the landlord here has a knack for good home-brew.'

'He does.' Vince leapt to his feet immediately and came back with a whole pint and placed it reverently on a new beer mat in front of Maurice. The evening went with a swing and when the news of who Maurice really was spread throughout the bar Maurice got more free drinks.

Dottie, totally unaware of the extent of Maurice's cricket fame until then was thrilled to bits by his reception and enjoyed the bliss of his popularity. It became one of the best nights Dottie had ever experienced in the pub and, as they walked home to Rose Cottage with Sykes, she told Maurice so. 'I never realised how well known you were in the cricket world. I knew you played ... but for England!'

'Well, I moved away when I started playing cricket and didn't get to family events for years but when I retired it seemed a good idea to be somewhere where I could meet my own cousins from time to time.'

'I'm glad you did. I'm so happy, so very happy, Maurice. We're going to make a real go of it, you and I. We might be knocking on but I know we'll enjoy ourselves. We will, won't we?' Dottie squeezed his arm to show how much she appreciated him.

Maurice pulled up and turned towards her, and taking hold of her elbows he said, 'They'll be the best years of our lives, Dottie Foskett. I've led a lonely life for years, very lonely, but you and me, with friends like you've got, well, we'll want for nothing. I could perhaps find myself a part-time job which would keep me busy, but not too busy, and the rest of the time would be ours.'

'Tell you what, Maurice, they are in great need of some cricket talent in the village; our team is rubbish at the moment.'

'Well, it wouldn't bring any money in but it would be wonderful to be back into cricket, even if they are terrible!'

'What a thing to say! The cricket team's not that bad!'

'It was you who said it, not me.'

Dottie gave him a push for his cheek and they had to laugh. Then they couldn't stop laughing.

Finally out of breath, Dottie, in the excitement, almost suggested he stayed the night. But suddenly that was too much out of character for her. They'd both decided they wouldn't until their wedding day because it seemed more dignified. To wait would make the big day richer and to do things properly would put Dottie's life right-side up. So reluctantly, but firmly, she said, 'Goodnight, see you tomorrow.'

'I'll be off, then. See you tomorrow.'

She waited until his little Citroën roared off down the road, put her key in the door, told Sykes to go to bed and climbed the stairs, relieved she had put off suggesting Maurice stayed the night, *knowing* she would feel better for doing things the right way round. But what about Becky? They hadn't had a chance for a private chat all evening there'd been so much going on.

Ben had been in a peculiar mood the Saturday morning Becky had her interview for the two-hour cleaning job on Fridays. In the end she took him with her as she daren't leave him on his own. It all appeared to be because Greenwood had not taken him into the glasshouses the day before. He'd expected to go in there and begin work immediately because that was what he wanted. Becky tried to explain to him that maybe the Green Man wasn't well and couldn't do it, or perhaps he was taking a day off for some special reason. 'Don't worry,' she said, 'he won't have forgotten.' But nothing would pacify him and so here she was at the door of 4 Hipkin Gardens ringing the doorbell with Ben in tow.

When she'd seen Roger Walker in the Store she'd been impressed; she was still impressed by him when he opened the door to them both.

'Mr Walker, it's Becky Braithwaite about the cleaning job. This is my brother. He wouldn't be coming with me because he works every day up at the Big House in the garden, so I'm free to come to clean. What time would you like me to start? That's if you employ me, that is.'

'Please come in. You are ...?' Shaking Ben's hand he waited for his reply.

Ben being Ben and awkward this morning, he didn't answer.

'His name is Ben.'

Roger Walker winked at her. 'Bad day today, then? Come and have a look round the house; it won't take long. I'm a bachelor but even so I do like to live in a clean and tidy house so when you come – if you decide to, that is – the house will be tidy but needing cleaning. These houses are a nice size for one person – rooms nicely square with lofty ceilings. Bathroom upstairs, downstairs loo.'

They dutifully followed him round the house and Becky was impressed. She hadn't expected the two equally-sized bedrooms or the big square kitchen with a huge window letting in the light. As for the living room ... well, she was overwhelmed by it and wished it was hers instead of the squashed, narrow one in their flat.

'I shall leave your money out for you each Friday and a key under the front door mat so you can get in when it's convenient for you and the money would be left out for you on the kitchen table. Ten pounds an hour I pay.' He propped himself against the edge of the kitchen table, folded his arms and asked, 'Well, what do you think?' Becky's head was buzzing and so full of her liking for his attractive, relaxed manner that she almost didn't answer him.

'I'll have to replan my Fridays a bit, but if you want me I'd like to work for you.' Becky felt sure he must know her heart was thumping far faster than it should.

'Well, I don't mind *when* you do the work so long as you've gone by the time I get home, which is usually about five.'

'Right, Mr Walker, that suits me fine because Ben gets home just before five every day so ...'

'Like working at the Big House, Ben, do you?'

Ben, who'd been lounging about the room gazing at Mr Walker's pictures, immediately said, 'Yes. I'm digging then I'm in charge of the glasshouses and growing grapes and peaches and things.'

'That'll be interesting for you. Really enjoy it, do you?'

Ben nodded. 'Enjoy it. Yes. Enjoy it.'

Mr Walker shook hands with Ben and then with Becky and she could feel a lovely kind of warmth in his skin and took pleasure in the grip of his hand, confident and likeable. Pity she wouldn't see him from one week to the next.

As it turned out she did because he was a regular at the Saturday coffee morning in the Church Hall where she was on the helpers' rota and he had joined the new adult choir led by Gilbert Johns which Becky always made a point of attending with Ben, mainly to get her out of the flat and to enjoy a good sing. Singing always lifted her spirits.

When they met socially for the first time he insisted she called him Roger. Becky knew her liking for Roger was totally pointless and the quicker she threw off her fascination with him the better. After all, who in their right mind would want Ben around as a permanent fixture? Not even on his pleasant days. Roger might be a charming, attractive man but even he would draw the line at the idea of Ben as an added responsibility. Then she would despise herself for having such thoughts, pull herself together and make each day 'Ben orientated' for a while to make herself feel better.

She had to admit that Roger did know how to get the best from Ben; there were no long silences and no sulky manners when Roger was around. If only it could be 'goodbye' to the narrow living room and ghastly electric fire and 'hello' to his big square sitting room and the log burner. But when she recollected the thrill and the gratitude she felt when they first moved into the flat she was ashamed of herself. Then, sitting watching TV when Ben had gone to bed, Becky faced reality and knew without doubt that her longed-for dream of Ben and Becky and Roger living in the same house could never happen. And she could manage perfectly well without a man in her life; she'd managed without one for the whole of her forty-one years, hadn't she? So why start now?

Chapter 25

Peter sat at the Rectory one morning, contemplating his life. Caroline, the centre of it, was seriously considering retiring from being a hospital doctor to give herself time for ... well, she didn't know what. She thought about taking up the piano again if she had time to practise, or social work of some kind or ... no, she needed to be more deeply involved with something truly worthwhile, studying perhaps? Sitting on some medical committee or something like that? She went to find Peter to ask his opinion.

She tapped on his door and went in. His desk was so tidy she knew he was thinking, not working, and asked outright for his opinion on her dilemma. 'If I retire, Peter, what would I do? The children are both fully occupied and hardly ever at home and it doesn't take me all day to look after you because you're out of the house so much ...' She placed her hand on his shoulder. 'What do you think? Any ideas?'

'How about if we both retire and I spend time writing these books I talk about but never write?'

Caroline flopped down on the sofa in surprise. 'That's a whole new idea! Where did that come from?'

'You remember the trunk in the loft and what we found in there ...?' Caroline nodded. 'Think of all the incidents that have happened while we've been here! Simone's terrible death, the Senior sisters Thelma and Valda and their fire, Jeremy really being called Sid and her something equally awful that I can't remember, Muriel and Ralph meeting up again after all the years apart – the list is endless! Well, I did think I could possibly write about that.

I've enough material to last a lifetime.'

'Write it from the point of view of a member of the clergy, you mean?'

'No, just as a writer of fiction.'

Caroline studied over this surprising statement in total silence. Very slowly she answered, 'Well, I think you would do a much better job by writing about your huge obsession, religion. Books for young people or older people, perhaps, about religion and how to live in this modern world which is so very different from the one we grew up in. The challenges are so different and Christianity is under threat from all directions in this century, in a way it never has been before. Everyone is searching for answers and I know you could help them with that. Not fiction, Peter, but real issues, you'd be good at that.'

Peter shifted his position so he was looking directly at her. 'You mean it, don't you?'

'Yes, or I wouldn't have said it. Written in words ordinary people could understand, not some intense, highbrow rubbish that has no relationship to normal people. But not talking down to them either; they'd soon pick up on that and shut the book and not read another word. You know how down-to-earth Becky Braithwaite is? Write it for her. She has problems. And not half having poor Ben to look after every day of her life, like it or not. What a commitment! You've had scores of people sitting on this very sofa telling you their horror stories, hundreds of real life problems and, best of all, given them some very good answers to take away. And I don't mean agony aunt stuff either.' Caroline heaved herself up out of the sofa and headed for the door. 'Well, I've given you advice but I'm no wiser for myself, so like a dutiful wife I shall go make lunch in the hope that I might get inspiration in the kitchen! Oh, that's the doorbell, I'll go.'

Standing on the doorstep was Dottie Foskett soon to be Dottie Deede. 'Good morning, Dr Harris, I know it's Saturday and his day off, but I need to speak to the rector. I shouldn't be bothering him today of all days but I'm in such a fix and I know he'll have the answer.'

'Come in, Dottie. Go straight in, he's just sitting thinking so you're not interrupting anything important.' She grinned, making a joke of it, then immediately wished she hadn't because Dottie looked as though she was deadly serious. 'Please, go through, he's in his study.'

Peter smiled compassionately at Dottie, sensing immediately that she was suffering. 'Good morning, Dottie. Please take a seat. How can I help you?'

'I'll sit on this chair, not the sofa, it's too comfortable.' She plumped down on the most rigid, uncomfortable chair in the study. That was usually a sign that this particular parishioner had come about something very uncomfortable.

'Tell me what the matter is, you seem desperate, Dottie.'

Peter just hoped it wasn't Maurice ducking out of the wedding.

Dottie took a huge intake of breath and then said, 'I've decided I mustn't marry Maurice. And I don't know what to do about it.'

'You must have a very good reason,' Peter said, puzzled.

'Can I be truthful, really truthful?'

'Of course. I expect nothing less than truthful when people choose to sit on that chair. If they are sitting on the sofa ... well ... that's different. That chair is designed for truth, for hard facts that cannot be ignored.'

Dottie checked her skirt was pulled down over her knees, looked him in the eye and said, 'I'm not good enough for Maurice. My past life was full of sin and it won't do. I can't stand in your church and get married, I'm too full of sin.'

Peter shook his head. 'Who isn't? I am, most certainly I am full of sin, but I stand in His church and praise Him and He knows me through and through just as He knows you through and through and you can go and get married in the Church if all that is good in you truly loves Maurice.'

'Yes, but *you're* not really sinful, not you, we all know you're not. But I am. I had no choice because there were plenty of days when I didn't know if I had enough money to buy food. I was driven to doing what I shouldn't have just to stay alive.'

'So you did what you did out of necessity, not for fun, not because you chose to because you enjoyed it knowing it wasn't right?'

Dottie blushed bright red. Sometimes he really was just a bit too frank. But he was right. She didn't do it for enjoyment's sake. 'That sums it up. Starvation or ... *that*.'

'I think you should tell Maurice the absolute truth,' Peter said quietly.

'He knows already. A cousin told him in an effort to put him off marrying me. But it hasn't and he won't listen. But I can't. Marry him, that is.'

'How did he take your decision?'

'I've not often seen a man cry but he did. Heartbroken, he was. I've left him in my cottage and run to ask you what you thought. If the rector says I shouldn't then I won't, I thought. But ...'

Dottie's hands were twisting round and round each other in a frantic effort to stop herself from bursting into tears. 'I love him like as if I was twenty! He's so kind, so special and we haven't ... you know, acted as if we're married. I thought I should start this part of my life the right way round to keep it precious, like it should be. What am I going to do?' Tears began to fall as she begged his advice.

'I suggest that I run you home and that you say to him, straight away, the moment you get through the door, that you got it all wrong and that you still want to marry him and you're not going to let happiness pass you by. What you are going to do is to take hold of life and make a success of it. Don't say *the rector told you to*, make it sound like it's completely your decision. Which it is, I am *certain*.'

'But you see what I mean? Almost everyone in this village *and* Little Derehams *and* Penny Fawcett think I'm a waste of space, fit for nothing, someone to look down on and, what's more, tainted by my past life. I can't sweep my life under the carpet, kid on it hasn't happened and ...'

Dottie stopped speaking, too choked to say the rest of what she wanted to say.

'Oh! Dottie! Who can you think of in the whole of the three villages who is entirely free of wrong doing?'

'You!'

'No, not me. I'm just as guilty as everyone else. Well, who?'

'There's Beattie Marsden, she never does wrong things ... no, I'd forgotten she blackened the name of just about everyone in Penny Fawcett a few years ago over that spate of break-ins they had. I suppose you are right, everyone's done something or other they shouldn't have.' Dottie shrugged her shoulders as though giving up the struggle to find someone totally free of wrongdoing. ''Cept some are more wicked than others, aren't they?'

'What matters most is are you sorry for what you did?' Peter said. 'Do you truly wish you hadn't? In your case you had no alternative at the time to being a prostitute; it was that or slowly starving to death. You had no other skills, through no fault of your own.'

Dottie thought there were times when this man sitting in front of her listening to her problems spoke too frankly. She felt a blush coming on; it seemed to start at her feet and was slowly climbing through her body and was just about to reach her face. He mustn't see her blushing. So she looked down at her hands, still twisting and turning with her agony.

'I know you don't go to church regularly, Dottie, but I find just sitting in a pew saying nothing, doing nothing, not praying, not anything, just sitting in the silence and letting it take you over can be very beneficial. You don't have to be a religious person, a committed Christian able to quote from the Bible, knowing the scriptures, praying every day. While you're sitting in silence absorbing the atmosphere, problems get resolved with no effort on your part. I reckon you would know just how much Maurice means to you and how much you mean to him if you tried it. Don't let all that promise of happiness and companionship slip away.'

By the time he'd finished speaking Dottie was convinced he was right because she did love Maurice so very much. Oh, he always brought out the best in her! She dried her tears, shoved her hanky into her coat pocket and getting to her feet she said, 'All right then. It's what I want. He needs someone to look after him, someone who puts him first. He's been a bachelor all his adult life, it's time he had someone who spoils him and I'm good at that. Car keys?'

As they went post haste down Shepherd's Hill and shrieked to a stop outside Rose Cottage, Dottie thought, Bless him for sorting me out. Whatever would we all do if he moved away? And she wasn't thinking of Maurice.

As Peter swung his car round, doing a three-point turn in the very narrow space of Shepherd's Hill, he tooted his car horn loudly in triumph. He knew they'd both hear it and was glad. Two people in need of love and who isn't in need of it? He charged home to Caroline and lunch, grateful he'd been able to talk sense to Dottie. Somehow this place, where he'd lived for what ...? Twenty years? No, longer than that, more like twenty-three years, took a grip on you and before you knew it half a lifetime had passed; people arrived, people died, children were born, next week new neighbours were coming, Seb and Kate Partridge, to work at the veterinary practice in Culworth which might mean new babies being born and so it went on. When he switched off the engine outside the Rectory he paused before getting out and thought how he might feel if he and Caroline ever left Turnham Malpas. Well, he couldn't leave, could he, he loved it too much; loved all of it, not just the thatched cottages, but his beautiful, beautiful Church, the fields, the woods, the inhabitants. Maybe, when he did retire, he could buy a cottage here. He'd ask Caroline what she thought to his plan.

He sprang out of the car and went to find her to see if she liked his new idea.

Epilogue

Three weeks after Peter and Caroline had jointly decided they would buy a Turnham Malpas Cottage to live in when Peter retired, Seb and Kate Partridge moved into their cottage, number three in Stocks Row. They caused something of a sensation because Peter hadn't realised they had two children already and another on the way. Kate Fitch was delighted, as she was always thinking in terms of how many new babies were expected or children coming into the villages from outside, in the hope that there'd be enough to keep the school open, because the council would close it on the thinnest of excuses if the numbers fell, and closing the school was often the death knell for villages.

Seb Partridge (lovely name for a vet they all thought) was taken to their hearts immediately; Kate took a little longer to be accepted because she was so busy with her little children she didn't mix much, but when they did catch a glimpse of her happy face and had the opportunity to speak to her they knew, without a shadow of a doubt, that she belonged to Turnham Malpas.

Greta and Vince had all their plans changed by a telephone call from Canada suggesting that the two of them should come to Canada just before Christmas and go to a ski resort at a fantastic spot where Terry and Kenny had spent the last two Christmases. They knew they would enjoy it, the food and the company and it would be the very best time for all of them. So, as it fell very nicely into their own plans for moving to the Old Barn in the New Year, and Vince starting on the new meat project, yes, they'd come for Christmas instead! Wonderful!! Greta was convinced that burning the trunk had changed her life. She was sure it was because she'd faced life fair and square by getting the trunk burned to ashes and unburdening herself by confessing the secret of her birth to Vince. The air between them had been properly cleared and now she couldn't wait to see her grandchildren. Two girls! What a change from three boys! What an opportunity! Christmas in Canada!

Chris Templeton completed his convalescence at home in Brazil until he could look in the mirror and feel completely satisfied with what he saw. Socialising with two swollen black eyes and his teeth in disarray was not the Christopher Templeton he preferred to portray. Strangely, his prolonged recovery from Big Billy's attack gave him a great deal of time to think about himself and Fran and all the other women he'd experimented with in his adult life, but most especially about Deborah. She had a wonderful way of calming him down when he grew impatient, of caring for him but not making him feel helpless, of laughing at his humour without making him feel he was in possession of unbelievable talent and, above all, he found himself fretting when she chose to disappear for a few days, which she frequently did. She never spoke of where she'd been or what she'd done on those occasions and somehow it made him long even more for her gentleness and her rare sweet kisses, her tenderness when he was low in spirits. Not even his mother's fussing could compensate for Deborah's absence.

She never once asked if he minded her leaving him before she disappeared, and that air of independence on her part, her lack of *clinging* pleased him and he didn't know why. Some women he'd taken a fancy to almost smothered him emotionally, but she never did.

Then, one interminable lonely night when Chris couldn't sleep and Deborah had been away for four days without once getting in touch, he longed for her to give him one of her special kisses, one of the kisses that soothed his irritation at being incapacitated, even though she was only perhaps pressing her lips to his fingers, one by one. He said as loudly as he could, 'Come back, Deborah, come back!'

His mother rushed into his bedroom, calling as she came, 'Darling boy, what's the matter? Mother's here.'

And, smelling as always of that perfume she adored, fussed and asked what she could do to relieve his pain, making so many suggestions as to what he might need that he said, 'For God's sake, Mother, shut up, will you!'

She stroked his bed tidy, patted his arms, adjusted his pillows, poured fresh water into his glass, opened the window a little wider, propped the door open and then sat down on the chair Deborah had bought him and asked, 'Now, what can I get you, my dearest boy?'

'I'm not your dearest boy, Mother,' he said. 'I've been the biggest pain in the backside any son could be and you have not done me a good turn by being so tolerant of me and my behaviour since the day I first stood up and walked. Stop fussing and go back to bed. Please!'

He turned over so all she could see of him was his back, and his skin felt as if it was crawling with despair at the way he'd gloried in her always defending him no matter what he'd done. No mother deserved to do that and he felt ashamed.

The following day Chris was taking a gentle walk in the luscious, beautifully tended communal gardens belonging to the apartments when he heard the oh so sweet sound of Deborah's car engine and he rejoiced.

She was back! She parked right beside him, got out and all she did was smile and his heart went into overdrive. Chris didn't ask her where she'd been, he simply opened his arms wide and she went into them. He clasped her to him sensing the thudding of her heart as she leaned against him.

'So glad you're back, Deborah Maria Charlesworth,' Chris said. 'I've been thinking hard while you've been away. I'm going to ring Johnny, make my peace with him and go home to England, if he'll have me.'

She leaned back and looked hard at his face; somehow there was a different light in his eyes, almost a contentment she hadn't seen before. He held her more firmly. 'I mean it,' he said.

'I'm surprised. "Home to England"? This is your home, surely?'

'But it's not real, is it? It's not got roots, not like they are in Turnham Malpas. I've realised the roots run deep there. Here ... the roots aren't here at all; it's all flashy and money and luxury and false.'

'I thought it bored you to death in England?' Deborah gently stroked his face, relishing every inch of it. She'd returned to a changed man, obviously.

Chris released her. 'It did. But somehow it doesn't now. I wake up waiting to hear the birds singing and they're not, not here in Rio. They've nothing to sing about here. I can try again, can't I? Don't you think? See if I'm right and not just going mad? But I want you with me. Will you come?'

Uncover new secrets
in Turnham Malpas . . .

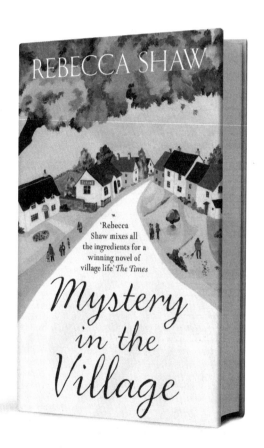

REBECCA SHAW

'Rebecca Shaw mixes all the ingredients for a winning novel of village life' *The Times*

Mystery in the Village

August 2015

www.orionbooks.co.uk